SANJAY SINGH

Some Other Horizon

Matador
9 De Montfort Mews
Leicester LE1 7FW, UK
Tel: 0116 255 9312
Email: matador@troubador.co.uk
Web: www.troubador.co.uk/matador

Sanjay Singh: someotherhorizon@aol.com

ISBN 1 904744 42 7

Cover design: Troubador ©Photos.com

Typeset in 10.5pt Stempel Garamond by Troubador Publishing Ltd, Leicester, UK
Printed and bound by The Cromwell Press Ltd, Trowbridge, Wilts, UK

Matador is an imprint of Troubador Publishing

To Nish & Neha,
who in their childhood innocence
became the first believers of this fiction of mine.

I

It is funny how tempting suicide can sometimes be. Or rather the thought of it. Standing on the edge of the bridge, watching the swirling waters part their lips around the dark pillars in a seductive smile. Looking up at her with open arms, promising to dissolve within all the pain. She bent forward to meet its gaze and held still, her hands trying to muffle the pounding heart. When she could bear no more she turned around and resumed her jogging, down the steps of the Westminster Bridge.

It was the first week of April, officially spring, but winter was still dragging its feet. It had snowed last evening, the proof still perched precariously over the leaves, though the ground had largely cleared. The slight drizzle in bright sunshine sustained the paradox of the British weather.

Puja lifted her face to the sky to catch the few silver drops tingling down her cheeks. It felt cool and soothing and momentarily masked her pain and fear. But then it returned and she began to run, hugging the ground beneath with speed and desperation. To outrun fate. To replace the agony within with physical pain and exhaustion. She ran and ran until she could not. Then stopped, panting and looked behind her. She could still see the building she was running away from. From the distance she could still read the bold letters of 'St Thomas's Hospital' inscribed on the side of the building. It had followed her all along without moving.

Her final year results were due that morning. She knew that she was going to fail. Her fate was sealed in the Medicine orals a week ago. She vividly remembered the expression on the examiner's face. A weird concoction of contempt and laughter subtly disguised in a disfiguring smile that tilted towards one side of the face. Elongating with each short case that she had mis-diagnosed. He physically resembled Saddam Hussein with blonde hair and was no less an evil.

It was the pain of failing despite working so hard for it. What now after she had already given her best?

It was her fault after all. She never had the drive or intellect to become a doctor and should have quit a long time ago. In primary school she had wanted to be a Pop-star. As her maturity ripened with her adolescence, she turned towards fashion designing. Her parents were alarmed by the musings of their only child and as the GCSE's approached she was carefully moulded towards science with gentle coaxing and stern warnings. Her Form tutor confirmed her aptitude in the sciences to her parents which gave wings to their ambitions of making a doctor out of their daughter. By the time her three A's were predicted in the sixth form, the battle was lost and she carefully hid the self designed clothes for her dolls in the attic. The downturn in the fashion industry due to the recession had had a synergistic effect on the emotional blackmail from her parents.

Puja had enjoyed her years at the medical school. She had joined Medicine unsure of her conviction or commitment but as time rolled by her doubts began to wither away. A sense of vocation began to crystallise. Compassion and idealism seeped in. She enjoyed interacting with the patients. Even as a medical student with no powers to heal but just to observe and comment, she would see how often she could kindle a flicker of hope in the patients' eyes. She longed to qualify for the power to heal. She worked hard, sometimes very hard to reach that goal.

And it almost came within reach.

She could see the day unfurl before her in a tortuous fashion. Her father's face draped in shame. Her mother getting her epilepsy back. Auntie Sharma trumpeting her triumph in the envy war over the Chauhans with her daughter, Nisha, graduating in medicine with more Honours than the actual number of subjects.

It was a sheer unfortunate coincidence that Puja, Nisha and Ravi were born in the same year. Though the jealousy war between the Chauhans, Patels and Sharmas was fought out unspokenly on many fronts, the children themselves were at the epicentre of the battlefield. Her earliest recollections from her childhood were that of the dinner parties where the three children would be standing in the middle of the lounge and made to exhibit their academic skills. Backed, cheered and clapped by their respective parents, like horses in the Derby. If Nisha rattled off the multiplication tables for threes, she would be expected to recite the table for fours. The other parents would discreetly try to interrupt the flow by asking something like four into nine, and then when she stumbled, would patronisingly pat her back with concealed satisfaction. She vividly remembered the consequences of falling behind on many such evenings. Savita, her mother, would make her memorise more of the tables over the peeling of the potatoes in the kitchen. Ramesh, her father, burdened with guilt and sense of duty would slip out to WHSmith's and buy some more workbooks for her. They would thereafter settle on the sofa and then with an acquired divergent squint he would make her do the workbooks and watch the BBC news at the same time.

Nitish Sharma, Nisha's father, was a General Practitioner like her own father. He had come to England with hopes of becoming a heart surgeon but after a few years of grinding as a junior doctor, he realised that the glass ceiling was all but shatter-proof. He had despaired and wanted to return to India but by then his wife, Savitri, had become so accustomed to the shopping delights and her automated kitchen that her past life in India appeared to her as an unrecoupable wasted era. They splashed guilt, emotional blackmail and soapy love at each other for the ensuing few months after which as usual Savitri had the last word. They even hosted a celebration party when their British passports had arrived.

Girish Patel came to England after running away from home in India. His father was a prosperous shopkeeper in Gujarat and had wanted his only son to follow his footsteps and take control of the shop after he had retired. He thus took Girish out of the school when he was fourteen, fearing that over education might lure him to higher pursuits of career and employment. He just wanted his son to acquire the basic mathematical skills to manage the till and sign his name instead of resorting to the 'thumb impression' on important documents. Girish was furious at his father's manipulations and was absolutely determined not to become a shopkeeper. He simply hated the notion. He secretly plotted to seek refuge in England amongst his relatives as he was sure to be hounded back by his father if he escaped anywhere within India. So when his father duly married him off as soon as he was eighteen, to avoid being charged under the child marriage act, he persuaded his wife to sell her jewellery and with the money booked the flights. With his meagre educational qualifications and no special skills, he soon stared at his own impotency in getting any decent job. Thankfully he remained potent otherwise and quite unintentionally and unplanned, made his wife pregnant. The erstwhile supportive relatives started tightening their purses and their hints, broadened initially and then turned into full-fledged taunts. Thus cornered by lack of money, relatives and Ravi Kumar in his wife's womb, he saw no other option but to open a corner shop. Even today he would often wake up sweating in the nights, after seeing his father laughing wildly at him in his dreams. The tiny shop meanwhile expanded with the opportunities and now sold everything from grocery, Indian clothes, audio-cassettes to the Daily Telegraph. But he was determined that his son, Ravi, would never follow his footsteps and ensured a private education throughout to facilitate his aim.

Ravi, partly due to atavistic genes and partly as a result of his father's sermons, was currently studying Business Management.

The three families had gelled into a close hub with spokes into the general Southall society since a time that stretched beyond Puja's faintest childhood recollections. Like a large Indian joint family, they defended and praised each other in public and envied each other in private. Not that it affected the closeness or affection between the families but on the contrary ensured an equilibrium, which was necessary to sustain such a relationship. So when Nitish elevated himself to a detached status from a semi-detached one, the rest followed suit within the next few months with the same number of bedrooms.

Puja vividly remembered another such incident.

It was a bright and sunny summer afternoon on a week day when Mr. and Mrs. Sharma turned up at their house to deliver jointly a jar of home-made pickles. Savita was, to say the least, surprised to see Nitish skip surgery to deliver a jar of pickles. The pride and joy on their faces greatly outstripped the quality of the pickles in the jar. Nevertheless she invited them in for tea and thanked them for the pickles. It was whilst sipping the tea noisily, that Mrs Sharma casually mentioned the car.

'We thought we would buy some mud flaps for the Mercedes. They did not come as standard.'

'The Mercedes?'

'We bought it last week,' said Mr. Sharma.

'It is the new E-class,' intervened Mrs Sharma. 'Come, come. It's parked out side.' She dragged Puja with her fat strong hands while Nitish requested Savita to follow.

Outside they were feasted to the sights with a zeal that would have shamed a car salesperson. Mrs Sharma lifted the boot of the car and asked

Puja to climb in to prove how spacious it was. Mr Sharma climbed on to the backseat and waved his legs in the air to emphasise on the leg space. They were shown the exotic cup-holders and briefed upon the merits of electronic protection system. Once they had left after reminding Savita to return the pickle jar, Savita looked at her Honda Accord parked in the driveway with a scorn that was to seal its fate.

Two weeks later Girish Patel drove in to deliver some groceries in his new Mercedes with leather upholstery. It was but a foregone conclusion that the Chauhans would be taking some remedial action soon. The neighbours waited in anticipation.

But oblivious to the outside world, there was a battle being waged in Puja's house. Defying protocol, history and tradition, Ramesh wanted to buy a Jaguar.

'Absolute nonsense,' Savita had retorted angrily. 'In our Asian society there is no parity in the status symbol of a Jaguar and a Mercedes.' She quickly rattled off a long list of known families who owned a Mercedes and challenged her husband to name anyone with a Jaguar. 'Besides, who has heard about the Jaguar in India. You might as well buy a Skoda and no one would tell the difference.'

Ramesh was visibly irritated. 'It is not for the society here or my relatives in India that I am buying this car. I prefer a Jaguar over a Mercedes and that is a good enough reason to buy it.'

'Isn't Mercedes a good car? Is everyone a fool to buy it?'

Ramesh was tired of arguing anymore. He threw in the punch line. 'It is my money which I have earned, it will be me who will drive the car and it will be my decision which car to buy. End of discussion.'

A few weeks later their new car stood on the driveway. A gleaming black Mercedes. Not with leather upholstery, but a S-class.

Ramesh had mumbled apologetically when Puja came back from school. 'Perhaps some other time. I do believe in rebirths.'

Thoughts are diversionary but only temporarily. She surveyed the present around her. As the sun continued its ascent, the sleepy rustling of the spring leaves turned into the wakeful cries of the vehicular traffic. There were more people crisscrossing her path now. No signs of failure on anyone of the faces. Tomorrow was a big day. It was her parent's twenty-fifth marriage anniversary. She would beg Nisha to keep her results a secret till the anniversary party tomorrow evening. She could not run anymore and she slowly dragged herself to her flat.

When she opened her door she found, Carol, her flatmate standing in the hallway. Her face was grim and there was no need to say anything. Carol hugged her and Puja sobbed softly on her best friend's shoulders.

'Despite making my life a virtual hell for the past week,' Carol whispered into her ears, ' you have passed my sweetheart. Congratulations!'

II

Ramesh was wide awake when he heard the rustle and the soft thud of the morning newspaper drop onto the floor. It had been a long time since he had woken up that early, the last time being nearly a year ago when he had to catch a morning flight to India.

He rolled over gently to face Savita who was still deep asleep. Her face partly buried in the pillow as usual. A hint of a smile across her lips as if she was dreaming something pleasant. Twenty-five years, since he first saw her, and it felt as if time had chosen not to leave any imprints on her face. The skin still sallow and satin, the few strands of grey hair over her ears almost an aberration. He smiled at the white ceiling where a silent movie flickered in slow motion. Time shrank to bring the yesteryears into focus like yesterday.

The news of his own marriage had come as a rude surprise to him. He had just turned twenty three and was in the final year of his medical school with no intention of marrying for at least the next four years. He had been aware of the numerous approaches with the incremental dowry offers with each year he passed. He had begged and warned his mother not to succumb to any of these until his career was more consolidated. He had hoped that the message would filter down through to his father with whom he could never summon the courage to talk on such matters.

Coming from a small village, he had initially found it hard to adjust to the urbane climate of the medical campus. The rural-urban divide was apparent from the first day and he was outraged at being relegated to the 'Pyjama-shirt' tribe by the self-professed urbanites. But nevertheless the embarrassment led him to throw away all his pyjamas and get two pairs of trousers stitched cheaply by the village tailor. He hated the Urbanites but resolved secretly to emulate their ways. He persuaded one of his four roommates to try to converse in English when they were alone and changed his gait to a more measured and conscious one. Leather sandals replaced the rubber plimsoles and he started to save for a pair of shoes. He even contemplated shaving off his moustache and only a divine intervention in form of a dream of his father's reaction saved the visible symbol of male pride. The final milestone in this journey of urbanisation would be to get acquainted with a female classmate and he began to plot for this ultimate goal.

However he soon realised that it was much easier said than done. Six months after his revolutionary change of the 'Self', he had not managed having even a single conversation with any girl. Nevertheless he fell in love with at least three of his classmates and undecided, decided to go for the first one that fell to his charms.

Skipping a lecture and then asking for the notes was the commonest way of starting an acquaintance. It was an oft tried and a well-known tactic but nevertheless in the absence of a viable alternative, had thrived over a number of years. If a girl responded by inviting the boy to the 'Ladies hostel', fondly known as LH, to collect the notes then it would signal the start of a tortuous courtship which could lead to holding hands in six months, a kiss in a years time and sex soon after their parents agreed on a wedding date. If, though very unusual, a girl asked a boy for the notes then marriage was highly probable in the following six months and stardom was instant. Refusal to share notes was normal and did not attract any negative criticism. Once one had walked past the tall, rusted iron gates of the Ladies hostel, his social status would have risen far higher than those of the teeming hundreds whose evenings were spent camping outside the gates on the 'FLA' square.

The Frustrated Lover's Association was first founded by Lord Ranjit Singh who was awarded the honourary Lordship after failing for the fifth consecutive time in the Finals. It was an unwritten rule among the professors that such candidates were eventually passed on their sixth attempt as it was felt that the trauma and frustration of re-examining such pupils was far greater than their moral obligation of passing only the deserving. Most qualified automatically for membership of the FLA even if they wished otherwise. The chair of this self-support group rotated between those members whose plight was the worst on that given evening. The square in front of the Ladies hostel was the ideal meeting point of the like-fated for their daily evening congregation. The town hawkers were the first to realise the business potential of this massive commune and within weeks the temporary stalls selling tea, samosas and sweets sprang up trying to provide an alimentary solution to the hungry hearts. At the first hint of dusk with the cool summer evening breeze luring them out of their rooms, the first arrivals would begin to settle on the wooden benches and the orders for the tea would follow. Bashir's tea stall was the most popular as he was the only one to give credit instead of cash if one so desired. He diligently maintained a register on all his customers and the dues were recovered as soon as the 'Money-orders' came from the respective Guardians.

Most of the crowd stayed late until dinner time chatting, gossiping and reciting 'shers' as many hearts would be laid bare and new infatuations put into the public domain. The square gave a good view of the girls wandering in the gardens beyond the walls or on the rooftop. They also viewed with envy the privileged few streaming inside to meet their girlfriends and whistled at them as they walked past the gates. As the evenings slipped into darkness, passions would run high and some of them would even declare their love at the top of their voices, calling names of their desired ones. On their part the girls often strained their ears to identify the culprit and strengthen their collective hate for him. Once positive identification was struck, information would disseminate rapidly and that person's name would be blacklisted for good. The moths risked the flames in desperation, the sane aspirant did not.

As the night deepened, the crowd would thin out for dinner and studies except for the few prospective Lordships who would stay back and sip whiskey under the silver moon, in front of their own Taj-Mahal.

Ramesh soon became a regular at these jaunts. His coterie of close friends had gradually expanded with the acquisition of a transistor radio and leather shoes. He passionately indulged in this new found pleasure of gossiping endlessly on nothing important. The topics were drawn from a wide range, but usually began and ended on either the feminine sex or politics. Politics usually aroused great passions and the debates would frequently degenerate into loud slanging matches not unlike, Ramesh thought, the debates in the Parliament. Nehru and Patel were the most frequent personalities debated and the differences between the debating factions were greater than the personal rivalry between the men themselves. The war of words would usually end once the topic shifted to the feminine sex. Intelligence was shared, every move analysed microscopically. Rumours would be sown. Poems would be recited and couplets exchanged with sighs that would have put Romeo to shame.

After a few months, Ramesh selflessly decided to narrow his infatuation to just one girl from his initial shortlist of three. Being religious, he prayed for the other two girls to get equally good grooms and families. Her name was Pramila and she hailed from a Punjabi Khetri family who had migrated a generation ago to establish a thriving business in textiles away from their home state. He shared this secret with only two of his closest friends. Both offered him moral support and gave him expert advice without having any experience themselves. Ramesh's own love-life climbed perilously up a few notches over the next few months. In the lectures he would always sit in the back rows with his gaze fixed in her direction. When the whole class was taking notes on muscles and bones, he would be drawing a picture of the heart in his notebook. His eyes would scan her dark long hair, flowing over the cotton blouse with the ridge of the bra strap and the milky pale skin underneath it. He would close his eyes and run his fingers over the desk in front of him. His heart became a shrine where he worshipped her with total devotion. Every smile, every gesture embossed on its walls. In the evenings he would often sit alone in his room and dream about them both together. He would write long letters interspersed with poems and 'shers' stolen innocently from novels and movies but would never post them. If she coughed in the class, it was to attract his attention. If she bent to pick up a dropped pen, it was to steal a glance of him. He saw her smile at him and only he could see it. He saw the yearnings in her lost eyes and cursed himself for holding back and making her suffer. She was waiting for him if only he could pick up the courage.

Such were the state of affairs when news of Pramila's marriage to some unknown doctor elsewhere was delivered by one of the canteen lads who worked inside the ladies hostel. The marriage was an arranged one and the groom's family were one of the wealthiest families of Patiala. Ramesh felt completely numbed when he heard the news. Reality ravaged him with such fury that pain and agony itself descended into a state of trance that had no nerve endings.

It was in those vulnerable days that he was introduced to alcohol by his able friends. He had found the transition in taste from sugarcane juice to Coca-cola a difficult one but alcohol was a wholly new proposition. On the very first occasion he had retched and vomited but his friends advised that the bitterness was there to cut the bitterness of his grief.

Suddenly the movies started to make sense and he could more easily relate to Dilip Kumar and Gurudutt in the movies. And thus a girl he never knew and never spoke to became a perfect alibi for his alcoholism against all the sermons and warnings his mother had given to him before joining medical college.

It was on one fine, brightly lit morning, after a drunken stupor the previous evening, that he opened his bleary eyes to a white silhouette obstructing his doorway. It took him a few more seconds to realise that it was his father. He quickly scrambled to his feet and bent low to touch his father's feet. Chaudhary sahib mumbled a quick blessing and after surveying the whole room for any signs of moral sacrilege, settled into a wooden chair. Ramesh rushed out on the pretext of getting some water and breakfast and on his return found his father lying on the bed. It was usually an overnight journey by train and it was often very difficult to get a sleeper berth reservation owing to the rush. Ramesh quietly put the water down and sat on the edge of the bed and began to massage his father's leg. Chaudhary sahib relaxed his muscles, closed his eyes and softened the creases on his forehead. There was silence except the thud of his pounding heart. His father had till now never paid him a visit and in the past if the need be, he was often summoned back home by letters or emissaries who worked on the farm. A feeling of impending doom loomed over his mind.

And then it came. Like a bomb dropped with an inbuilt silencer, creating no sound but only blast waves ripping apart everything in silence. With his eyes partly closed and his lips barely moving, he informed his son that his marriage had been fixed.

Ramesh froze for a second. His hands tightened on his father's calves which he let go after a wince from his father. Pain was the outcome but momentarily he was confused by his own emotions. Anger, despair, sadness, helplessness. Inside his head a volcano had erupted. He was squeezing his eyes and clenching his jaws to prevent it from surfacing. There was his life; checkmate and game. He tried to say something but his tongue felt glued to the floor of his mouth and in the end he gave up. He had never spoken up to his father and even that day he could not better it. A quake came and went without even registering on the Richter scale. He wiped his tears on his shoulders and continued to massage his father's legs. Chaudhary Sahib did not open his eyes to see his son's reaction.

So in the end when his father had finished furnishing the details of the marriage plans and the bride's family and asked him to come home by a certain date, he shut his eyes and nodded slightly. For all the good that his parents had conferred upon him there was this one grievous wrong to keep the balance. He had paid or his parents had extracted a large installment of the debt back.

His pall of gloom lifted steadily over the next few days and by the time he set out for Bishanpur it was in fact replaced by mixed emotions of curiosity and faint excitement. His first love was firmly behind him and his sacrifice for his parents had elevated him in his own eyes. He felt good about himself and the prospect of a real woman in his life began to erase all the doubts he had nurtured so far. His sister wrote to him describing the bride as a piece of moon. She told him that her name was Savita and somehow the link to the moon and the name helped him to conjure a more accurate portrait than he would have otherwise done. He was desperate to match that portrait with the actual photograph.

Reaching Bishanpur in itself was a feat and one had to endure or enjoy every mode of transport except for flying. The train was crowded to start with but a large proportion, mainly peasants, alighted down three stations later where they were assembling for an annual village fair. There was only one other person left on his berth and Ramesh quickly seized the initiative and spread his legs to conquer the space vacated by the departing passengers. He was quickly asleep and luckily was not disturbed till the morning when the train pulled up at Hakimpur station. The bus stand was right across the road opposite the station and he raced his way through the crowd while a coolie lifted his luggage. It was crucial to reach the bus among the firsts as it filled rapidly from the arriving train as a slight delay could mean spilling over to the rooftop.

This indeed was the case this time and he soon found himself huddled with his luggage at the front end of the roof, clasping tightly to a rusting iron railing. The space was shared with other passengers, mainly farmers, all forms of luggage and cattle including goats and hens. The bus conductor would probably get a goat and a few hens as bribe for illegally loading the cattle. He has already selected the goat he would take and had instructed it to be positioned in the centre with passengers in the periphery to prevent it from falling over. Simtara, his next stop, was a just nine miles from Hakimpur but it took little over an hour to finish that journey. Twice everyone except the women and the animals had to alight and push the bus to kick-start it when the engine with reason and without warning decided to stop.

At Simtara, Garvu, his father's most trusted lieutenant, was waiting with the bullock-cart. As Ramesh alighted from the bus Garvu rushed to touch his feet and hastily took charge of the luggage, loading it on the back of the bullock-cart. The oxen snorted on recognising their master. Ramesh ordered him to take the luggage home and himself decided to take a walk through the fields. It was the sowing season for rice and the fields were alive with activity. Farmers in ankle deep water planting the saplings, children splashing the muddy water in sheer joy. The gentle breeze lifted his moods and he hummed as he half-walked, half-ran on the narrow footpaths. He reached the river earlier than Garvu and waited for the boat. Though the monsoon season was over, the river was still swollen at the banks. The silt and sand on the adjacent fields lay as proof of the floods earlier in the year. The river had changed direction as well and the loop that was beginning to shape last year was in full formation now. The currents still were quite strong and he decided against a swim.

Both Garvu and the boatman arrived at the same time. The boat was then dragged onto the banks and the oxen freed from the cart. The hull of the cart was rolled onto the boat so that the wheel rested on either side of the boat. Garvu then gently coaxed the oxen into the river and soon they were making their own way across. The boat was then pushed back into the river and once in knee-deep water they jumped back onto the boat and the boatman started rowing briskly. Once on the other side the same process was repeated in reverse for unloading the cart and then Garvu ran to fetch the oxen that had drifted further downstream due to the strong current.

As he entered the village he was first spotted by a group of village urchins playing the 'Gulli-Danda'. On seeing him they let out a shrill cry and ran towards his house in a race to be the first to announce the groom's arrival and get sweetmeats as reward. Ramesh could hear and feel the small commotion that had stirred up in his house. Stupid though it felt, for the first time he was overcome with shyness and embarrassment on entering his own house. Something had changed irrevocably.

There were around twenty women in the courtyard with his mother leading the group holding a brass plate with the 'Aarti' on it. As he stood up after touching his mother's feet, he saw tears in her eyes. Some of joy, some of pride and a few of sadness. Then without warning the women broke into a chorus singing marriage folklore and Ramesh, red in his face, bent once more to touch as many feet he could in one wide sweep and ran towards his room. The women burst out laughing and his sister and cousins ran after him.

'Would you like to see the photo, Bhaiyya?' teased his sister as soon as he entered the room.

'Maybe later,' replied Ramesh trying to put on an uninterested expression while his heart almost audibly cried 'yes'.

'Well, I am currently charging ten rupees for this privilege but since you must be so desperate, I am tempted to charge you five rupees extra,' she said.

Ramesh lunged forward to grab her but she had anticipated his move and ran for the door. The tide of the cousins meanwhile refused to budge and the only plan that sprang to his mind was to head for the bathroom.

It was not before the next day that he could get hold of the photograph from his sister. He did have to pay his way out. He slid the photograph without looking at it inside his pocket and walked a mile to the mango orchard. He found a dark spot under an overgrown mango tree and looked around to ensure that no human was mimicking the copulating cries of the frogs in the ditches. He then took out the photograph and held it out to a coin of sunlight piercing through the leaves.

His first emotion was that of relief. She was not ugly. He looked more closely again. Into the dark eyes that looked back at him. At the lips that parted slightly like petals of a rose bud, at the dark long hair that drooped on her shoulders like dark careless clouds. Suddenly a beautiful face began to emerge. He began to fill the black and white photograph with colour and gently ran his fingers over it. He tried to decipher some message from the dark eyes which looked back at him with a half-broken smile. Then he broke into a laugh as he concluded that the bosom exceeded his expectations.

The marriage was still three weeks away but the festivities had begun in right earnest. The relatives had begun to stream in slowly. Tents began to spring up in the front fields of the house for the male gentry as they were slowly squeezed out of their rooms to make way for the expanding number of female guests. Special cooks had to be enrolled to supplement the existing servants. The house kitchen was abandoned in favour of a larger temporary kitchen to cater to the hundred odd relatives who had begun filtering in from two weeks before the marriage.

Ramesh's infatuation meanwhile grew in multiples and soon surpassed his previous high with Pramila in the medical college. He resumed writing long letters to his to be bride and stored them neatly under his mattress. He re-befriended a childhood friend, Munna, who lived in the village and had married last year for some expert advice and counselling.

His friends from the Medical College surfaced just a day before the marriage and that evening a special seminar was held amongst them to chalk out a strategy for the 'First night'. None of his friends were married and none of them had had any sexual experience before but even then there was no shortage of expert advice. There were conflicting suggestions from his friendly advisers. To do or not to do, was debated fiercely with arguments and rebuttals galore. The legend had it that consummation on the first night was obligatory but was it true? The married adults could shed some light on it but no had the guts to do that straw poll. Carnal theories were abound but hard facts were missing. Ramesh, flushed and sweated, as the debate progressed but failed to reach a consensus. The only comfort, one of his friends pointed out, was that at his bride would be even more nervous than him. Smaller ignorance shall triumph over greater ignorance.

In the absence of a consensus it was decided that his friends would buy him a pack of condoms just in case the need arose. Since it would be too embarrassing for any individual to go to the shop to buy them, it was also decided that they would have to go in a group so that shopkeeper would not be able to affix his smirk on any one of them.

The marriage itself next day was a lavish ceremony and the bride's family had left no stone unturned in the reception of the '*Baraat*'. Every '*Baraati*' had his own personal masseur looking after their smallest of needs. Dancers were brought in from Varanasi and imported Liquor specially smuggled for the occasion from neighbouring Nepal was flowing in abundance. The house itself was decorated like a bride with coloured bulbs and fluorescent tubes. The military band specially brought in from the capital alternated with the Flute player in creating a continuum of delightful music.

Ramesh was however not destined for these pleasures and soon found himself dragged inside the house and imprisoned by the women folk. Even his own friends were not allowed in initially but were assured that they would be able to witness the actual marriage ceremony. Ramesh had instructed his friends to try bribing the priest to cut the whole ceremony short, but the old Brahmin that night was determined to invoke all the thirty three millions Gods and Goddesses for their blessings and refused to be swayed by any worldly gratifications.

And so the marriage began just before midnight. Most of the male gentry retired to watch the dancers or to help themselves to more alcohol lest it provoked bad memories while the women remained firmly entrenched. They would intermittently break into a chorus singing marriage songs while Ramesh struggled to recite the Sanskrit mantras after the priest. His eyes were red with lack of sleep and the fumes from the sacred pyre. The bride's face was covered throughout with a large '*Ghunghat*' and all his disguised attempts to steal a look met with failure.

It was four in the morning when he was shaken from his half-asleep state and informed that the ceremony was finally over. He was still in a daze when he was pushed into a room and the door bolted behind him. Then as if washed with a sudden tide of adrenaline, he woke up to the reality of being alone with his bride in a locked room.

He felt his heart accelerate rather unsmoothly uncertain of its rhythm like the mind and the body. He saw her sitting, on the edge of the four poster bed, with her chin resting on her knees. The shimmer of silk, the glitter of gold and somewhere from behind it, like her sister said, the radiance of the moon. He stood transfixed and waited for his heart rate to come down to an acceptable level. His hands fumbled inside his *Sherwanis's* pocket to feel for the ring he had bought for her and the pack of condoms. Suddenly all the lines he had carefully rehearsed seemed to desert him. He inched forward towards the bed clearing his throat to signal his arrival. On sensing his approach, Savita became even more nervous and drew her *Ghunghat* further over her head. She closed her eyes and awaited his next move in total suspense.

Ramesh reached inside his pocket for the ring and looking directly at her face said softly, 'It is the custom of our family that the bride receives a gift from the groom on the first night. I bought this ring myself especially for you and I hope you like it.'

To his utter surprise he saw her face convulse in total shock. He looked down and there lying in his palm instead of the ring was the yellow packet of condoms. His jaw dropped and his tongue moved but no words would come out. Savita meanwhile recovered from the initial shock and laughed uncontrollably. Suddenly they were both laughing and the ice melted without trace spontaneously.

The rest of the night was spent exchanging information about the various family members and the pre-marriage events that had taken place at their respective homes. Ramesh, determined to avoid any further fiasco, shelved any plans for physical contact on that night.

The mystery was however solved. The legend was indeed fiction.

Since then time had flown as if with wings on it. As the years had passed by, the predictability of marriage, work and children had puts its mundane stamp on the romance somewhat, but unseen and unfettered the shoots of love had grown and spread deeper than ever.

But still it was difficult to believe that twenty five years had come and gone since he had first seen her. He could almost smell the freshness of that memory.

With his smile breaking into a silent laugh he brushed aside the memories that had flooded him this morning and tiptoed to the chest of drawers at the other end of the room. He carefully drew one of the drawers and took out a small jewel box and slowly opened it. In there lay the anniversary gift for Savita. A Cartier diamond necklace in white gold, which sparkled catching the first sun rays filtering through the window.

III

It was the crush of warm breasts on naked skin that made his hand twitch and the thin red line emerge on his right cheek. Ramesh slowly put the razor down and turned around to embrace Savita. They remain locked in each other arms for a few moments gently swaying to the vibrations within in perfect equilibrium. When he opened his eyes he saw the foam on her hair. He scooped some with his index finger and planted on her nose.

'Happy anniversary,' he smiled into her eyes.

Savita was in no mood to talk. She reached upwards and kissed his lips. The ensuing waves jarred his balance and he leaned against the wall for support. But the waves kept coming, each stronger than the previous one knocking down their resistance, forcing them to lower themselves gently onto the floor.

A few minutes later they looked at each other, panting, in disbelief.

'I had told you before that we should have carpeted this bathroom rather than having it tiled,' said Ramesh.

'You have lost all shame.' Savita disentangled herself and gathered her clothes.

Fully clothed, they hugged each other again. It was a strange desperation to crystallise all those unspoken assumptions that had held them together in this one day which was fast melting into tomorrow. To summate those twenty five dream years and then to continue the same as before. The symbolism of this day was not clear to them but drawing close to each other physically somehow vindicated that symbolism.

'Thank you for the necklace. I did not know you had such exquisite taste. It is simply adorable.' He had left the present by her bedside.

'Well, Puja helped out in choosing the necklace. It was our joint choice.'

'Every thing okay for the evening?'

'I hope so,' said Ramesh. 'Girish had asked me not to bother the least and that precisely what I have done. But that chap is a veteran on organising functions. I am sure everything will be fine.'

' I have something for you as well.'

'Oh! I thought that was it,' Ramesh said pointing to the floor.

Savita thumped him on the chest and slipped into the bedroom to get the present. Ramesh carefully took the wrapping off as Savita looked on.

It was a Rolex watch bought from Harrods.

Savita was unsure of his expression. 'I have the receipt if you don't like this one.'

'It is beautiful. I could not have asked for a better present. It must have cost a fortune.'

'Don't ask. It might just ruin your day.'

'I won't.'

'I had no idea about buying watches. Puja did all the research.'

'Where is this double agent of ours. Or must I say doctor Puja now. That girl was needlessly worried about her results. I never had any doubts about her.'

'She was out celebrating with Carol and a few other friends last night. She did warn that she might be a bit late coming in this morning,' said Savita.

Savita got up to make some tea but at the door change her mind. She went back into the bathroom and hugged Ramesh again who finally gave up on his shaving.

Puja had not spent the evening with Carol and her friends. Once she had stopped crying and laughing and hyperventilating she had picked up the phone and called Lennie. She told him that she would be at his flat within the hour. There was no else she had wanted to be with at that time.

As the front door of his flat cracked open, she lunged forward to embrace him in a tight hug. She locked her lips with his and drew him in. Entwined they staggered to the bed, wordlessly, where astride, she began to strip him down. She made love to him with tenderness and a fury that released all the suffering and the tension she had dammed within herself. There was revenge in her rhythm, victory in her swearing.

'Good God Puja!' Lennie had exclaimed afterwards looking up at her. 'Anymore exams around the corner?'

'Darling,' Puja bent forward to kiss his lips. 'I have passed despite you.'

Puja meant every word of it. Lennie had been a big distraction throughout her finals. They had met only six months ago but love had multiplied like an uncontrolled virus within her body. There was something extraordinary in this ordinary looking bloke which had jangled her wires completely. While Carol had imposed a curfew on her boyfriend, she had to see Lennie every other day even if it was for a few minutes. He came to her between Diabetes and Stroke and stayed there till she literally banged on the books and swore at herself. It was insane yet uncontrollable but this unrealised vulnerability was playing havoc with her revision.

But in the maze and crevices of her inner sanctum there was happiness taking roots everywhere. Even at the prospect of failing in the finals. Even at the risk of her parents discovering about her affair with a white boy. Something indefinable was beginning to define her new life.

And so she let go and resurrected her belief in God.

'Dinner at a nice restaurant?' Lennie was offering.

Puja placed back a strand of hair that had crossed over his eyes. Why would she let anything else come between them tonight.

'Pizza, video and an all night cuddle.'

Lennie smiled signalling his approval.

'Congratulations Puja! I am really proud of you.'

'Thank you. Now you congratulate me, after nearly half an hour?'

'No apologies for lasting that long. '

Puja ordered the Pizza. Making love always made her desperately hungry afterwards. Gluttony satiated, she settled on the sofa with an oversized quilt and her boyfriend wrapped fastidiously around her. Lennie went to sleep halfway through the movie but Puja wept and laughed all night with the triumphs and travails of Scarlet 'O' Hara.

It was the ring of her mobile that woke her up in the morning and then froze her. It was her mother.

'Where are you?' Savita was asking.

'In my flat,' Puja had said without thinking.

'Then why are you not picking up your normal land-line phone?'

Lennie was stirring. She quickly put her hand firmly on his mouth. He was fully awake now.

'I was sleeping mum. That phone is in the lounge and the mobile was by my bedside.'

'You have not forgotten the party this evening?' Savita hinted.

She had indeed for a moment.

'Happy anniversary Mamma! Happy, happy, happy anniversary.' Savita was laughing.

'Come home *Beti*. Your father is dying to see you.'

'On my way Mamma.'

The time printed on the official invitation was half past seven.

Or was it?

'Let me recheck. I still have the card somewhere in the car,' said David Refitt and hastened back to the car, leaving his wife behind with John Hancock.

All three had stood bemused in front of the community hall in Ealing. The building was locked, the lights were off and there were no signs of a party in honour of Ramesh Chauhan's silver wedding anniversary.

David came back from the car park.

'It is the right place and half seven is the time printed on it.'

'This isn't a wind up? There is no trouble between you two?' Elizabeth, his wife took a dig.

'You must be joking.'

Just then a car came screeching to a halt in front of them. Girish emerged from it and presently rushed towards them with an apologetic face and folded hands.

'I am so sorry you had to wait. Please accept my apologies,' he said.

'It's all right Girish,' John said. 'But where is Ramesh?'

'He has been up and ready since half past six. It is Savita who has been in front of her dressing table for the past two hours.'

'She has every right to take her time,' said Elizabeth. 'After all she is the first lady of this evening.'

Girish chuckled. 'I was comfortably sipping tea with Ramesh, waiting for Savita, when suddenly he jumped from his sofa and said that he has invited some English friends who are likely to arrive on time. And then he virtually pushed me out of the house to get here as fast as I could.'

David laughed. 'And I thought I knew all of your customs.'

David was a General Practitioner as well but their friendship had started on the golf course a few years ago. He was fascinated by Indian history and architecture and in him Ramesh had found a captive student who would take all his exaggerations about India at face value. Ramesh also regarded him as a fine conservative Englishman who readily shed his Englishness after a couple of drinks and had remarkable sense of humour thereafter.

And David often paid for those drinks himself. So the friendship had bloomed.

John Hancock was Ramesh's Practice manager.

The guests had slowly started to filter in and the party warmed up as the first few units of alcohol entered the circulation. Ramesh and Savita entered the hall to the applause of the guests and a beat from the band. The pair looked radiant under the spotlight. Ramesh was wearing a cream coloured prince suit. Savita was draped in an embroidered red Benarasi silk sari. Her hair was neatly closed in a bun which exposed her long neck to dazzle in its diamond encirclement. They mingled with the guests under the glare of the video lights which followed their every step.

Typically the sexes segregated on arrival. The male bastion held its fort close to the drinks bar. Every one was either talking or pretending to be listening intently. The traditional party orators like Dr. Alam and Girish Patel had cornered their own audiences. Some serious debates would soon ensue. The ladies had positioned themselves at the other end near the stage where after the preliminary round of exchanging guesses on Savita's diamond necklace, were settling down to more mundane issues. The children had occupied the centre stage converting it into their own playground where they were running amok.

Meanwhile the temperature of discussions had risen in Dr. Alam's corner. Dr. Alam raised his pitch in a valiant attempt to drown the voices of the other two speakers who had started simultaneously. It was impossible to drown whiskey whipped speeches with an orange juice led voice. So he started to gesticulate.

'Let's be honest, let's be honest,' Dr Alam said swinging his hands, gesturing the other two to shut up. 'The reason that we stayed in this country is because we are cowards in our actions and myopic in our goals for life. Cowards, because we did not have the guts to go back to our own country to make a living. We did not have the confidence to succeed in our own country. So we chose the easier way. Myopic, because our sole aim thereafter became just to lead a good materialistic life in a quiet corner of England where no one knows us and no one gives a damn about us. Terms like pride, dignity, fame, and identity ceased to have any meaning for us. We are neither today British at heart nor Indian or Pakistani on paper. We are nobodies who have a spent an entire lifetime running after house and then a bigger house, car and then a bigger car and nothing else.'

It was apparent that the speech had not gone down very well. A few shuffled uneasily while others took rapid sips at their glasses. Ultimately Omshanker broke the silence.

' Yaar Alam, you are depressing.'

'My friend the truth is depressing!' retorted Dr. Alam. 'I have only spoken the truth that every one of you is aware of but refuses to admit.'

'You speak of the subcontinent as if it were a golden fairyland,' said Omshanker. 'We are not here because we fell in love with this country but because conditions are so bad back at home. You do not need courage to go back. You just need to be corrupt to survive there and that is where most of us made our choice. It is the dishonesty, corruption, inefficiency that often requires one to stoop to that level or get swept away in the tide. You are right. No choice is made without making compromises. As long as the pluses stack up more than the minuses, you have made the right choice.'

'But Om,' said Dr. Alam. 'Good or bad that country is yours. It nurtured you, it gave you an identity. You don't abandon your child if he has a deformity. You try even harder to make his life more worthwhile. You have got a British passport. Try telling, you are a proud British on the top of your voice at Trafalgar Square. Try walking into a country village pub without people turning to look at you. The pure fact is that you can never be accepted as part of the larger society and that I feel is big a compromise to make.'

'It is a common baser instinct in quite a few of us human beings.' Dr Prasad interjected. 'Here it is different skin colours so we have racism. In India we have the same skin colour so we have communalism. In areas where numbers do not favour that equation, we have casteism and then sub-casteism. Most of us just need an excuse to hate each other. Why blame the English alone. We are as guilty. At least here we do not slaughter each other over race or religion. We have more whites than blacks in demonstrations against the BNP or the National front. When did you last see the Hindus rallying on behalf of the Muslims in India?'

'Riots do not necessarily reflect the extent of the problem,' another gentleman who was also a GP intervened. 'Other factors like illiteracy and poverty come into a play when it comes to riots. Now let me give you another example. India has approximately ten percent Muslim population and since Independence there have been two Muslim presidents, scores of Cabinet Ministers, Chief-Ministers, top bureaucrats and political party presidents. Britain has approximately the same percentage of the ethnic minority population. How many Prime Ministers, Cabinet Ministers, top bureaucrats, party presidents have come from this section?' he paused for effect, 'That dear Prasad gives a more accurate reflection of the extent of the problem than the headlines of riots etceteras.'

'It is wrong to generalise,' Ramesh intervened. 'Let us talk about our own complexes and inadequacies. If we get turned down for a job we jump to blame it on racial discrimination rather than pause to reflect that we might have been wanting. Don't we turn our heads to that odd English man who walks into a Southall food store to buy some Indian spices? Is that a natural instinct triggered by something which is different and hence rouses interest or are we too racists. How can we put a slur on the vast majority who are perfectly decent human beings, who have welcomed us amongst their midst and abhor racism no less than us. You want Asian Cabinet Ministers without us being interested or indulgent in politics. First sweat for it and then ask for the prize. There are good and bad human beings in blacks and whites alike and it is unfair to pick just one side for all the ills. Let India have a Muslim Prime Minister or a defence chief first and then I shall agree with your argument.'

'If you felt so strongly about going back Alam, than why did you choose to stay in this country?' asked Nitish who had been a silent listener so far.

'Because I am a coward and I am the first to admit that,' said Dr. Alam.

'I don't think that is the only angle to this issue,' said Nitish. 'For most of us if you had a wife who loves you and does not divorce you, children who respect you, have good careers and don't send you to nursing homes in your old age, we would have had more than our fair share of God's blessing and would want no more. These higher conflicts of life philosophy don't bother us and most of us are quite content and happy with that.' He paused and added, 'And tell me what is wrong with that. Isn't that what most people black and white alike are striving to achieve? A happy family and a good standard of living.'

There was a growing rumbling of discontent within the crowd at the direction the debate was going. Sensing the open hostility, Dr. Alam said no more. Some switched loyalty to Girish who in one corner was trying to argue the merits of shop keeping over general practice.

In the women's camp the hot topic of discussion was Dr. Prasad's daughter's marriage to an Englishman. Though this was not the first inter-racial marriage to hit Southall, this particular marriage had attracted much publicity because the Prasads had initially put up a tough resistance. They tried coercion, feigned illness and even threatened to drop her from the will but, Neeta, their daughter was in love and went ahead with a church wedding. It had been only three months since they had married and now there were rumours that the couple's relationship was on the rocks and divorce was imminent. Mrs. Prasad severely embarrassed by this whole episode had stopped coming to all parties and gatherings and had virtually excommunicated herself from the rest of the community. Today at the party Intelligence was being collated to get the latest update on the whole saga.

'I have seen Neeta's car parked at the Prasad's a few times,' said Mrs. Verma who was Prasad's immediate neighbour. 'So one thing is definite that they are still in contact and haven't thrown the poor girl out.'

'Nitish told me that the Prasads were going to India next month,' confided Mrs. Sharma. 'Apparently the plan was made abruptly only a couple of days ago and the rest of his partners were quite unhappy at the short notice because finding a locum would be very difficult.'

'Is it true that the divorce has already taken place?' asked one of the Ladies.

'I am not sure,' replied Mrs. Verma, who by virtue of being Prasad's neighbour was getting the most attention. 'But I just wonder about the purpose of this sudden trip. Could it be that they are planning to give Neeta an arranged marriage in India and thus have a dignified ending to this whole episode. They did in fact have a boy back home who was agreeable before all this happened.'

'And that boy would have no pride and marry a girl who just got divorced from a white boy in three months flat?' asked Mrs. Sharma.

'They don't have to tell the groom's family about this entire affair,' said Mrs. Verma.

'What!' exclaimed Mrs. Sharma. 'You mean tell a lie and base the marriage on that? Do you think the truth will never come out? I can tell you one thing for sure that these things never remain under the carpet for long.'

'Don't be childish Savitri,' said Mrs. Verma. 'It is not lying. It is just not telling them anything. Do you think that any respectable family would marry their daughter after knowing the facts? And even if it is found out after the marriage I agree there might be a storm but that will eventually settle down. It happens all the time. No damage will be done in the long run and at least their daughter would have been married and have a stable family.'

At that moment Savita asked them to hush up as strangely Dr. Prasad was making his way towards them. He was obviously drunk as was evident from his staggering gait. A teetotaller till his troubles began a few months ago; he had embarked upon alcohol with a vengeance since. Every one fixed their eyes on the floor and waited for him to speak.

'My common Namaste to all the assembled beautiful bhabhis,' he said in a slurred speech. 'The band is playing such beautiful music. Aren't you ladies coming to the dance floor?'

'You leave your wife at home to come to flirt with us,' said Savita, relieved that he had not overheard anything.

'Yes, but without much success.'

Everyone laughed, almost as if to give him some moral support in his troubled times.

'There were better days when I was in medical college,' he added. 'Girls used to flock around me.'

'It is a common lie shared by our husbands,' retorted Savita.

Dr. Prasad merely laughed and turned away to make his way to the drinks bar.

Puja received a text message from Lennie whilst at the party.

'Romantic weekend in Paris. Shall I book?'

'No. Too dangerous.' She had replied.

'Terrorism?'

'Worse. My Parents.'

With dinner concluded, the band started to play some enticing tunes to lure the couples on to the dance floor. The second generation, conscious of their superior dancing skills, abstained in favour of their parents in order not to embarrass them. But the oblivious immigrants, on a waft of Indian music, nostalgia and sheer joy, danced late into the night until the police knocked at one pm and requested them to honour the midnight deadline.

IV

Puja received her sex education from her mother on a Friday evening a few months after she had turned twelve, just after her maiden menstrual bleed. Savita was massaging coconut oil on her scalp and informed her image in the mirror that she had no head lice.

'Do you know anything about sex?' Savita then asked.

Puja looked up at her innocently. By the expression on her mother's face, she knew that she had got away with deceiving her.

Savita was pleased with her daughter's ignorance.

'It is how babies are born,' said Savita, uncertain about how to move the conversation forward.

'So it is not by eating plenty of apples?'

'No.'

'But you told me that we all were born when mothers ate lot of apples.'

'Never mind what I have told you in the past. Listen carefully to what I am going to tell you now.'

Sex was something, she was told, grown ups do after marriage. Before marriage sex was an absolute sin. At school her friends might talk about boys and some might even have boyfriends. To have a boyfriend would not only be wrong in the eyes of God but also would bring dishonour to the family. She should never make friends with girls at school who talk about sex or try to do it with their boyfriends. English girls are different. They have to find their own husbands and so they have to go through many boyfriends to find the right one. But for her, her father would find the best husband in the world when the time came. She should not try to emulate her English friends but should try to follow her own culture. Arranged marriages seldom broke up because not only the couples were matched but also the families.

The message on sex education was clear. No sex at all.

An embarrassing silence had followed the discussion. Daughter and mother looked at each other through the mirror. The distracted strokes of the comb made Puja wince in pain and Savita apologised. No words were exchanged, but Savita tugged at her pleats and Puja had nodded in agreement. Relieved at concluding her task, Savita got up and left the room. Only then Puja got up from the stool, jumped on to her bed with the pillow stuffed in her mouth and began to laugh wildly.

She knew more about sex than her mother could ever imagine. Sex and boys had begun to permeate in her life in its non-physical form. They talked about it, they shared knowledge and often smuggled pornographic literature to validate their knowledge. A collective effort was being made amongst her friends to nurture the tree of carnal knowledge.

That tree bore fruits sometime after she turned thirteen when one of her friends' tempted fate to test the hypotheses. They had huddled the next day around her in the lunch break, behind the net-ball court. Puja had listened to the graphic details with an open mouth, choked with curiosity and disbelief.

By the time she was fourteen most of her friends officially had boyfriends. Though sex was uncommon, the urge to quench the other physical desires often took precedence over romance in most relationships. But it was still dignified with the stamp of love. Puja was often tempted by the approaches from the opposite sex but the gravity of her Hindu upbringing and her mother's lectures often pulled her back.

Her first physical encounter happened a few months after fourteenth birthday and was quite awkward and unsettling. It had happened during one of the not so infrequent tripartite picnic jaunts of the three families when they had gone to Leeds castle in Kent. She had drifted apart from the crowd to avoid the boredom and made her way towards the woods. She stopped by a small stream. A peacock was unfurling its bright colours on spotting the clouds above merging in the sky. She sat down on a bench nearby, transfixed and still to avoid any attention from the dancing peacock. Suddenly from nowhere Ravi, Girish's son, appeared. He too had made the run from the elders and the two settled on a bench and started gossiping as usual.

With hindsight she realised that the drift of the conversation towards girls and boyfriends was deliberate on Ravi's part. He asked her whether she was seeing someone and slightly taken aback by the abruptness of the question, had replied an emphatic no. He told her that he had fancied her for a long time but had not been able to gather the courage to disclose it to her. Puja was only partly successful in not blushing and had kept her gaze on the grass below without answering back. And then without warning he was all over her. She struggled initially as his arms tightened around her and then his moist lips came to rest on hers. It somehow had a magical effect on her. Her arms limped to her sides and then slowly crept upwards around his back and neck tightening its grip. Her body turned jelly to arch into him as her mouth responded to his warm Lips. She could remember no more as sheer ecstasy overcame all other senses.

She did not know how long they had been entwined together but when she next opened her eyes, she saw the distraught peacock retreating its steps and Ravi's face buried under her blouse with his right hand between her legs, battling with her stockings.

An incestuous pungency rose through her gullet and almost made her sick.

She jerked away from him and stood up from the bench, trying to catch her breath. Ravi was taken aback by this sudden rebuff and was mumbling incomprehensibly. Puja shouted at him to go away and by the tone of her voice he knew she meant business.

Even after he had gone, the anger and embarrassment was yet to dampen the fire he had lit within. The taste of his tongue was still in her mouth, her nipples were taut, wet with his saliva and she was moist between her legs. She was shaking uncontrollably and dug her nails into the wooden bench to steady herself. A tiny spark had set alight all the nascent explosives she had managed to keep under wraps for so long. In the end she gave up, closed her eyes and waited for her heart and breathing to settle down.

Adolescence etched into her body bewitching curves which were beginning to attract some flattering attention from the opposite sex. She would often stare at herself, naked, in front of the mirror. Most of her friends now had boyfriends and it was almost embarrassing to be beautiful and single.

So at fifteen she invented a boyfriend. He had to be a family friend and an Asian so that there would be no probability of her friends ever seeing this fictional character. She adroitly wove a web of lies to keep her ego inflated in public.

At seventeen she saw the stupidity of the whole exercise and duly dumped him and declared herself single again.

When she moved out of her parent's house to do medicine, she found the fresh smell of her new found freedom exhilarating. Late night parties, clubbing and pubs began to mould her life in a new way that tickled the hitherto suppressed baser instincts and brought them to full bloom. The transition to alcohol was not without its hiccups but after some experimentation and perseverance she overcame her problems of taste and effects.

And a few months ago she had met Lennie.

The occasion had been a party at Carol's boyfriend flat. She had met Carol when she joined medical school and soon enough they had become the best of friends.

Thankfully, not everyone present was a doctor. As Puja waded through the introductions she met lawyers, accountants and budding writers. It was a relief. She had often found a compulsive urge amongst her fraternity to indulge in medicine-centric conversations whatever the occasion was. Once past the 'foreign objects in the rectum' anecdotes, it held little interest for others but little would her comrades register the annoyance of their audience.

So she had tried to keep away from the familiar crowd all evening. She first noticed him almost fleetingly while talking to a writer. He was standing at the other corner of the living room and even in the dimmed lights his features were noticeable. He was not very tall, about five feet nine, stocky built with a broad chest and muscles in the arms bulging out from under his inadequate T-shirt. His face was square with almost Mediterranean contours, his dark hair adding to the illusion. All in all he was a good-looking fellow and having made that small note she turned her attention back to the writer and his unpublished works.

The atmosphere mellowed as the evening tread onto the late hours. The alcohol had permeated quite a few blood-brain barriers and small, more personal conversations replaced the more loud and rabid discussions of the early evening. When the music changed to a softer tune it signalled to the keen souls to push the sofas against the walls and tuck the coffee table under the staircase to create space in the centre.

Puja had had a few glasses of wine to drink by then. Being a late starter to alcohol she was still in the infancy stage of developing an acceptable tolerance to it. As soon as the rotary vertigo began to take effect she parted company with her wine glass and slumped on the sofa.

'Would you like to dance?' A pair of dancing blue eyes asked her. It was the same person who she had noticed earlier in the evening standing in one corner of the room. He had noticed her too then.

She swore to herself that her lips had not moved but could not account for the 'yes' she heard herself.

His hands were warm as he took hers and slowly glided her onto the floor. They danced in silence. Her taut muscles relaxed to the warmth that flowed through their hands. The cushion of air between their bodies thinned and then became insignificant. The mellow music, the intoxication of the cerebrum, the smell of the after-shave, each was culpable but there was something more, indefinable, that made her arch into him. She closed her eyes as their hands disentangled and circled each other

'The name is Lennie?' he finally whispered into her ears.

'Puja,' she replied in a drowsy accent.

'I was dying for an introduction all evening but Carol kept ducking all my requests.'

'Typical Carol. Protects me from everything. My parents would have been proud to have her as my elder sister.'

'You two are very close?'

'Yes, she swears she loves me more than her boyfriend whenever she gets drunk but retracts it the next morning.'

'You of course do not hold your boyfriend in such contempt?'

Puja lifted her head and looked into his dancing eyes.

'You guessed right,' she said. 'I am single.'

His eyes smiled back though his lips barely moved. They relapsed into silence and tightened their embrace fractionally to acknowledge that revelation.

The lights were dimmed further as the first chemical reactions to prolonged body contact were beginning to manifest itself on the dance floor. Puja too felt Lennie's hand slip from the silk onto the skin. Then the faint ripple of the fingers on the nape of her neck. It was hard to hold back. She was desperate for a snog. She dug her nails deep in his back in acceptance and raised her face, eyes closed in denial. His hands uninhibited now, rubbed her neck with more vigour though now she needed no further stimulus. She lifted her eyelids slightly, to catch a blur of his face descend down to create total darkness as his moist lips locked onto hers. They kissed each other desperate and distrustful of the momentum that had propelled them into this frenzy. Their hands desperately seeking the skin beneath the fabric, muscles taut around each other, lips locked, heart and tongue flicking unstoppably. A few in the crowd paused to take interest in this undiscovered couple. It was Lennie who regained consciousness and withdrew abruptly leaving Puja in a daze. Her eyes still closed, her lips still ajar.

'You know what I do not like about kissing,' he said, acting to ignore the crowd. 'It kills the romance by sending blood to wrong parts of the body.'

Puja was still glowing in the warmth of that snog, but she could not help bursting out in a laugh.

'I am sorry I got carried away a bit,' she said.

'No, you can blame me. Girls always do.'

An awkward silence followed. They searched for the autocue on the floor below. Finally Lennie spoke.

'Listen, I know that I may look a bit superficial and shallow but that is not entirely true.' He hesitated. 'Can I give you a call sometime?'

She looked at his dancing blue eyes. They were quite deep.

'I would like that,' she said.

'You really mean it?'

'Sure, I do.'

'You have made my day.'

'Have a goodnight as well.'

Their bodies arched spontaneously for the momentary brush of the lips. Then she melted into the crowd.

A light brush on the lips, brushstrokes on the heart. An abstract, indelible imprint refusing to fade away.

Next morning the hangover cleared over the mind but remained over her heart. Something unlike anything before had disturbed every chord in her heart. Time failed to wipe away the images of the previous evening. Those blue eyes still sharp and clear, riveted upon her. She had been asked out and pampered by boys before but had always managed to shake them off without much thought. But this time a solitary stone in a becalmed pond was creating ripples, one after another. To her annoyance Puja knew that this time, for the first time ever, she was seriously infatuated.

Carol seconded her. 'That is infatuation,' Carol confirmed to Puja.

'Girls usually have it when they are thirteen or fourteen but you obviously are a late developer.'

Lennie's expected call did not come over the next couple of days and Puja's plight worsened further. Time stretched like an elastic band, each moment taking its toll. The dancing blue eyes, the bass voice, the fairly ordinary looks were beginning to hurt. As a week passed by, that hurt began to shift from her heart to her pride, her infatuation transformed into anger and bitterness. Twenty-four more hours and she would black him out of her thoughts forever. There was no point suffering in vain. Carol had been watching her friend with increasing concern oblivious of the reasons. She was quite used to Puja's many mood swings, but usually they were a flash in the pan and disappeared without trace. This one had been going on for a bit too long. And so one day she entered Puja's room, hugged her patronisingly from behind and asked what the matter was.

'Just ask your friend, Lennie, to keep his word and ask me out,' she confided without shame or embarrassment.

'O my God!' Carol exclaimed, withdrawing from Puja.

'What now?' said Puja, slightly surprised. 'Don't tell me you love him too and I cannot have him. Remember a bloke called Pete?'

'No!' Carol cried. 'He called in two days ago asking for you and I completely forgot about it.'

'What!' Puja jumped from the bed. 'How could you?'

'I don't know,' she said defensively. 'I thought he was just one of those creatures from the male sex for whom you hold no interest. He did say he wanted to ask you out.'

Puja was confused with emotions of anger and despair. 'Did he say anything else?' she asked Carol.

'Yes, he is going to call you on Friday.'

'Today is Friday?'

'So it is.'

'I forgive you.'

'Oh! Thank you. I shall do your ironing this week.'

From that moment the telephone became the epicentre and the earth revolved around it. She phoned home to ensure they did not call back and engage the phone. Carol now alight with guilt, marched down the street to make her own calls from a phone booth. She checked thrice to ensure the phone plug was in the socket. She cursed, she prayed, she begged and when the phone finally rang, she waited and counted till five before picking up the phone.

It was indeed Lennie. His cool voice filtered through the phone and warmed her heart. Puja was desperately trying to sound casual and composed. He was asking her out and she barely managed to muffle the shriek from her heart into a whispering 'yes'.

They met at Leicester Square that evening. He seemed to have had a hair trim since she last saw him which somewhat took the edge out of his sex appeal. They went to the 'Comedy club' and then to a pub. Puja was edgy, tentative, and nervous and it was obvious to her that Lennie suffered from none of her ailments. He was doing most of the talking. His parents were Publicans living near Dublin and were devout Catholics. He was the youngest of three children and had always attracted his parent's wrath for not devoting more time to the church. His brother was a priest and his sister had left home early after marrying a Protestant. He was never bright in studies and the home environment choked him. So he decided to try his luck in London. He missed Dublin initially but gradually discovered the Dublin circuit in London and from then on life was a bit less boring. He was learning rock sculpting and was gradually building up a reputation in the studio.

Puja watched him from across the table as he spoke. The synchrony of his moving lips and his dancing eyes. The careless laughter of an innocent child. He was holding her hands across the table without him knowing it whilst he told her about his college life, his circle of friends and his village life in Ireland. She never let his hands go even when she jerked way in peels of laughter.

Time flew that evening as if jealous of them. When the clank of the chairs being put on the tables distracted them, they looked at each other and let a sigh. They caught the tube and Lennie walked her back to her flat. It was a moonlit summer night and the stars hung like an expensive curtain across the skies. The reckless breeze picked up slightly forcing them to put an arm around each other. At the steps Lennie kissed her on the lips and retreated hastily saving her from an awkward moment.

Puja dated him with disguised desperation over the next few weeks. The highs and lows of meeting and separation had infused in her life a new spirit of happiness and excitement which had been erstwhile missing. She searched for one grain of deceit, one shadow of doubt, but there was none. Her ecstasy was mixed with fear for she knew that she might have crossed the line of infatuation into the vast unknown territory of falling in love. She was going down a slippery path of no return and she had to know whether it was the right path. The consequences were huge, for her parents would never have dreamt that she was going out with a white boy. She had been warned on several occasions that this was one line never to be crossed. There she was staring down at that thick broad line almost wishing for something to go wrong. But it was hard to swim against the tide when the currents were so strong. When the heart and mind fought against each other. Every time she was with Lennie or thought about him, another brick fell from the wall.

'Don't be foolish,' Carol had chided her. 'Don't even think in those terms now. Just take life one step at a time and enjoy while you can. Four dates and you have begun to think about your grandchildren. Do not give in that easily. You need a lot more time to decide whether he is the right person and whether it will work. Once you have crossed that milestone then only start to think about your strategy for dealing with your family.'

Carol's advice was logical but logic seldom permeates the heart membranes. Love often distorts the reasoning mind to further its own evolution unhampered. It hides its faults instead of correcting it and grows by deepening its roots into the two hearts. It is time and only time that lays it bare in its truthful nakedness.

But few young hearts have the patience to bide for time. The youth in them challenges them to dare and later sometimes despair. And Puja was no exception. Three months with Lennie and she had made up her mind.

So when they next met she invited him in for the proverbial coffee. Inside, as the silk crushed the satin and their lips dissolved in each other a tingling current went down her spine. They peeled off the layers of clothing that came between them. As he came into her she arched upwards to meet every inch of him. Their bodies now synthesized in perfect harmony and rhythm. There was a strange tenderness in the brute urge with which they sought each other. As if making love was personification of something more ethereal and sublime. But then the physical forces took over and steadily tiny bombs began to explode in her head, rapidly increasing in intensity and frequency to a deafening climax after which she could take no more.

Moments later they lay in bed, still. She looked down at Lennie in her arms, the world at her feet and closed her eyes to capture that moment in time.

V

England had one of its best summers that year for a long time. The sun barely hid behind the clouds lifting the grey moods to an exalted optimism. The trees dressed in new leaves swayed elegantly to the tune of the summer breeze. The countryside basked in uninterrupted sunshine and every strip of land that kissed the seas was strewn with revellers as if the whole nation had given up on clothing. The prolonged spell of good weather so unknown to ordinary Britons had lifted the nation's spirit as a whole. The high street was an ocean of smiles, the sales people joked more often with the customers, the car drivers did not press their horns in traffic tail-backs and even the news-broadcasters smiled occasionally on television. Sick leave absenteeism soared as some days were just too good to work.

But for Puja the misery had just begun. She had just become a junior doctor.

The workload itself had come as a rude shock. The long hours of toiling soaked the compassion out of her like a dried sponge. The idealism she had nurtured for the past few years was overwhelmed by fatigue. A chronic, constant ailment which she tried to fight back but always ended up in defeat. The therapeutic communal moaning in the doctor's mess helped slightly but the singular passion would still be to end the day and run out of the building. She felt guilty and ashamed but consoled herself that those very emotions were proof of some humanity left inside her. She forgave herself for rushing away from her expectant patients to do the jobs to help those very patients. On occasions when she would deliberately root her feet on the ward to spend some quality time with her patients, the bleep would draw her away.

The lack of practical knowledge was another shock in reserve for her. She remembered her first day on the wards when a nurse had stuck a sheet of paper in her face and asked for some intravenous fluids to be prescribed. She did not have a clue. After five years of hard work and imbibing all that theoretical knowledge, she did not have any idea of even how much fluid she should be writing let alone treating some one or writing any prescriptions.

'Well how much would you usually require?' she had mumbled.

'You are the doctor!' pat came the reply. The deliberate ploy to drown her in shame had worked instantly.

The overwhelming emotion of the season was guilt. Guilt for not knowing enough, guilt for not having the time to spend with her patients, guilt for cursing the patients for her overworked state. On one occasion she had received a call from a General Practitioner at four am, just minutes after she had hit her bed, about an elderly lady who was coming to the casualty after sustaining a massive heart attack. The GP had warned her that the patient was in an extremely critical condition and might not even make it alive to the casualty. She had closed her eyes and prayed for a few seconds. And the relief that had swept her when the phone rang to inform her that the patient was indeed dead on arrival. She had slept with not even dreams to disturb her for the rest of the night.

Next morning, rested and refreshed, she wept in guilt and shame. She had wept in front of her Registrar in the tiny doctor's cubicle at the end of the ward. The Registrar had been very sympathetic.

'You know,' he said, holding her hands. 'You are better than most of us. We would have felt the same way and not even thought about it.'

Things improved slightly after her pre-registration year. Her work became more clinical than clerical, the respect from nurses increased measurably and the Consultants sometimes talked to her on the ward rounds. Most importantly she had a houseman under her to do the donkey's work. Now she could despatch him to chase the results and draw the bloods while she could draw the curtains and hold the hands of her elderly cancer patient. For the first time after nearly a year the embryonic interconnections were beginning to take shape between her and her patients. Their smiles infecting hers, their hopes raising hers, their despair mirroring hers. The dam of fatigue was still there; big as ever, but in it were cracks and holes through which the positive tides were beginning to gush through. She was also aware of the good reputation she was building up, despite her own reservations, and worked harder to consolidate it.

But life still remained on an automatic conveyor belt. Work, catching on with sleep and then work again and catching on with sleep again. The same finished product day in and day out. She would sometimes step off the belt and reflect upon it in her bathtub like a detached psychoanalyst. Life, as she had dreamt it, hibernated hidden somewhere, scared to come out and face the glare of her professional life. Would it die before it was too late? She had not read a novel for eighteen months. She had not been on a holiday for nearly a year. Her friends had paled somewhere in the shadows as she barely had time for them. Until now the show had been fanatically about her. She had nurtured it, scripted it, loved it and envied it; until now, when she was just watching it drift away without a mast.

But across those dark clouds there was a constant rainbow. Lennie Riviera. In the vast desert she had set out to explore, she returned to the tiny oasis she had discovered for herself again and again waging war with time, fatigue and quite often her Registrar. Like a river emptying into the welcoming sea she would flow into his arms after a hard day's work and close her eyes to wipe off the day's memory. She would thump on the rising mound pressing against her body and tell him off without opening her eyes.

'Just keep me hugged for the next twelve hours and none of your silly antics you sad person.'

'Haven't they taught you about involuntary actions,' he would protest.

'Try thinking from above the waist sometimes,' she would reply.

The chemistry between them rhymed like poetry. Nearly two years down the line and she had given up on finding any major fault in him. All her aspirations, hopes and happiness had crystallised into that one person. Time subconsciously had sealed their relationship into something that was now inseparable and irreversible. Though they met quite often, their yearnings would stay afresh like morning dew drops. An unquenchable desire that went from thirst to thirst. A sense of happiness that was almost painful. Puja almost desired sometimes a row or a disagreement to touch its invincibility. She would pump up her defiance and then surrender to his surrender.

The whole affair was kept a secret from her parents with military precision. Lennie would be sometimes puzzled at the extremes she would go to cover her tracks. And he felt like a complete fool assisting her in that.

'What is so wrong that we are doing?' he would ask in exasperation.

'We are violating my cultural and family traditions,' she would reply.

'How?'

'It is too complicated for you to understand but basically my first relationship should be with my husband and virginity should be my wedding gift to him.'

'You are a bit stuck there, aren't you ?' he had laughed.

'Not really,' she replied, 'horse riding is the usual excuse but if you are smarter you should think of some other excuse as the boys I am told are half expecting that answer.'

'Any vetting for the men?'

'Don't be stupid, how dare you question their integrity.'

But in her heart of hearts she knew that she had kept that tradition alive. For now, she desired no other person in her life as her lover or husband. When the time came she would fight her corner, defy her parents and ignore the so called society for a prize worth possessing. As for the wedding gift, she was sure that he would want something more conspicuous to show off to his friends.

Chaudhary sahib passed away one hot summer afternoon.

It was Ramesh who had picked up the phone. It was the weekend and Puja, Ramesh and Savita were in the lounge leafing through the Sunday papers.

'...He was fine in the morning. He did his gardening in the morning, presided the *Panchayat*...,' Bacchan, his cousin was shouting at the end of the line. But he could hear no more. A sudden storm erupted from somewhere inside him shaking him like a dead leaf clinging desperately to an autumn branch. It was Savita who first heard the muffled choking voice and lifted her head to see Ramesh shaking violently with the phone in his hand. She ran towards him and snatched the phone from him.

'Hello! Hello!' she was shouting incoherently. 'Who is this? What is the matter? What happened?'

Puja was taken completely aback still not knowing what had happened. Ramesh was kneeling on the floor, clutching his stomach and shaking violently. Tears were streaming down his cheeks but he made no sound except a few muffled gasps. Blood had drained off his face and he appeared pale and ghastly. She had never seen him in this state before. He was crying like an unstoppable child.

Savita was wailing, still clutching the phone in her hand.

‘ *Bhabhi, Bhabhi,*’ Bacchan was now crying too at the other end. ‘We won’t cremate the body until *Bhaiyya* arrives here. *Chachi* is still unconscious but the doctor has seen her and said it is only the shock and nothing else.’ Savita put the phone down, still crying aloud and clutched Ramesh from behind urging him to stop crying.

Confused, puzzled and still stunned Puja did not cry. She ran to get the telephone book to contact uncle Girish and the Sharmas.

His earliest memories were from when he was about five. Dressed in a spotless white ‘dhoti and kurta’, few tufts of cloud floating in the sky, astride on his father’s shoulders, his tiny hands lost in his big hands, walking through the paddy fields. Men and women stopping work momentarily in respect, nudging each other to tell them who he was. Their eyes brimming with genuine appreciation and envy for that boy sitting on top of their Chaudhary sahib.

He was seven, when one day, while both of them were feeding the pigeons his father told him that he was going to boarding school.

‘For generations we have depended on this land to feed us,’ he had said. ‘No one in the family has even fully completed school education. I do not want you to end up like that. I want you to acquire knowledge for that is one wealth that never leaves you. I want you to become a doctor and come back to this village and treat the poor for free and look after them. This land should be enough to feed you. People respect me for what I have got. I want them to respect you for what you are. If there is anyone between God and ordinary people, it is a doctor. There is no profession nobler. Do you understand me my son?’

He had nodded.

He was twenty-two, young and strong, when his father had snatched the rifle from his hand after the Naxalites had burned their fields and hacked one of the labourers to death. A police case would ruin your career, he had said and walked out into the sun with the gun shouting abuse and firing into the air. What happened next was state news and took ten years of court battles to dispense with but not once did his father speak to him about it.

He was thirty-two when he left for England, optimistic and scared. His father had come up to Delhi. Both were fumbling for words till his father finally spoke.

'Look son,' he had said. 'You are going there to acquire knowledge so that you can serve your people better back here at home. May God and my blessings help you in achieving this noble task. It will be a new country and you may find it different and strange. If you run into any difficulties just come back. There is enough at home to feed even our future generations. So never compromise or suffer. Think this as a penance after which lies a glorious future back at home.' He bent down to touch his father's feet. No hugs or kisses. That was the only physical contact they ever had since he had grown up.

And then he had silently promised himself to live up to his father's expectations.

He had decided quite early on after arriving in England to settle down here but had lied to his parents regarding his plans with one excuse or another. Somehow he could not pluck the courage to tell them that their only son was not coming back. He had tried to drop subtle hints but his mother was impermeable to any ideas that ran contrary to her strong beliefs. Belief or trust. And yet when he had broken the news to them citing Puja's education and his career as reasons he had met with absolutely no reaction. Chaudhary sahib had kept his eyes firmly on the ground and mumbled something about a village meeting and walked out. His mother's eyes, he saw, suddenly went stony as she stared hard at the wall in front of her for a few moments and then slowly got up and left for her worship. The next few days passed as if the conversation had never taken place and when he finally prepared to return to England strangely this time his mother did not weep but gave her blessings with a faint smile. In the past her hope had always melted her grief of separation into tears but this time there was no hope and her grief was solid. He knew, for once and forever, he had failed his parents.

He had tried to persuade his parents to come and live with him but Chaudhary sahib had dismissed it with a laugh.

'It is easier to transplant a sapling,' he had said. 'But try doing it to a grown up tree, son, and you will end up killing it.

Fifty years, he had been a child to his father. Always secure in the knowledge that come the worst he could go back to him. And now without any warning he had walked away.

When death knocks on the door of someone you love, the sheer absurdity of it can sometimes transcend human comprehension and dominate over grief. Disbelief takes over in defence and there is almost a wishful desire to make it happen in stages to dampen the shock. But sadly it comes suddenly and with one swift movement severs all the bonds with the living left behind.

Just like that.

It is that password in life, 'never again', that lifts the gates and inundates you with grief and sorrow.

And then there was guilt. Waiting patiently in the queue. Gnawing at the emptiness. He could almost see his father calling out for him in his dying moments and the lowered heads of his cousins at the foot of his bed.

The house was beginning to fill up. Girish and his wife were first to arrive followed by the Sharma's and many others from the neighbourhood. Ramesh had finally fought back his tears and was sitting on the settee with his gaze fixed on the carpet. He would break down intermittently in a sob and then regain his composure. Girish was holding his hands and Nitish was coaxing him to take a sedative, which he refused.

'If Ma does not come with me this time,' he finally spoke. 'That's it then. I am not coming back either. Enough is enough.'

Savita was still inconsolable. Mrs. Sharma, who had been trying to calm her down started crying too. Savita's own parents had died soon after the wedding in a car crash and since then her in-laws had taken the mantle. *Bahu* soon became the most respected person in the household. She had to force her way into the kitchen as Chaudhary sahib employed new servants after her arrival. Ma handed her the keys for the storeroom and the family locker soon after, expressing her desire to devote more time to worship and religion. With the keys in her Sari she had become the undisputed leader of the household. Even Ramesh had to sometime beg for money from her when he ran out of his meagre salary. She fasted on Tuesdays and Chaudhary sahib would travel himself to the fruit shop three miles away in the town to pick up fresh fruits to break the fast. He told her that the servants could never be relied upon to pick up the right quality. He had told her not to keep the *Ghunghat* and cover her face in his presence as she was the daughter and not the daughter-in-law in the house.

'That makes Ramu the son-in-law,' he had laughed. 'Tell him, he better behave.'

She never did know whether they blamed her for the decision of settling in England. She never caught any hints in that direction but a guilty heart kept the mind unsettled. And now that guilt flame would remain alight forever.

Puja too had cried a little, locked in her room. She never was very close to her grandparents but the whole occasion had overwhelmed her. The grief of her parents had both surprised and saddened her.

There was a knock on the door and Auntie Patel entered with a cup of tea in her hand. She looked at Puja and knew that she had been crying.

'Come on Puja, have a cup of tea,' she said giving her a light hug. 'You have to be strong. Both your parents have been shattered by the news. You have to give them the support.'

Puja did not say anything. Somehow it felt nice to bury her head in Auntie's chest as a fresh stream of tears escaped from her eyes. After a few minutes she felt much lighter and collected herself. There were plane tickets to be arranged, packing to be done and traveller cheques to be ordered. But first she had to get to her mother. She left Auntie Patel to pack Savita's suitcase and went downstairs to look for her mother.

It was so hot in Delhi that sheer discomfort replaced any emotions of grief for a brief moment. Ramesh had always managed to plan his visits in the winter months and over the years his memory of the tropical summers had all but vanished. Crouched uncomfortably at the back of his Ambassador cab he cursed himself for coming in the summer forgetting momentarily the purpose of his visit. They were caught in a huge traffic jam at the Connaught circus on their way from the airport. The sun had parched the earth dry, peeling her skin off, to be pounded by the howling winds into dust, which rose in tandem with the smoke and soot to seek vengeance on every living being. The air was black in mourning shedding any pretence of invisibility. The sea of automobiles meant for human comfort exhaled with delight at having their own back. The smog hung over the city like a malevolent veil hiding the blue sky. Everyone was protesting with coughs and groans except for a group of labourers working at a building site, daring the sun with their bare skins in open sky, oblivious of the whole drama.

Ramesh felt slightly better on catching sight of those labourers. He returned his concentration to his original sport of 'spotting the changes', a game he always indulged in after landing in his home country.

Lutyen's Delhi was crammed with humanity in such great numbers that it was threatening to clog its very heart. There were people everywhere. In the buses, on the buses, between the cars, squeezing on the pavements, being knocked and shoved for daring to be stationary on one place for long. The boulevards were still lined with the tall Ashok trees but they had turned a pale grey with the sheen of dust that coated their leaves reflecting the general gloom. Every womb in the earth had opened up with new constructions. Multi-storeyed building with strands of land in between which were yet to be roads. There were more beggars lining the streets. Their bones threatening to break the skin barrier, men filing by looking straight ahead, avoiding the gaze to avoid the guilt. The dogs still outdid the urchins in extracting more food out of the scattered refuge beneath the election posters promising to eradicate poverty once and for all.

But somehow the faces betrayed the general atmosphere. There was calm and hope and even smiles as the vast multitude raced towards their own goalposts unaware of the heat, the smoke, the screeching cars and each other. As if he, an outsider, was the only one in pain. Even the urchins by the refuge were laughing after having chased the dogs with a shower of stones.

And still why it was, that he only felt at home only these few days that he spent in India every year after having lived in England for twenty years. The smell and the heat bred a familiarity which he disliked but could not disown. He could always extract a strange reassurance and identity from the sweltering heat and the swirling dust and feel elated with the bargain. Home was England but he always experienced homecoming here.

'As an Indian,' he remembered Girish's words vividly. ' If you work very hard, you can earn money, identity and respect in India but here, no matter how hard you work, you will only end up with money.'

But Ramesh considered himself far too ordinary for these exalted goals. He yearned for the more basic things that had been snatched off him in his quest for a better life. Lying on the roof on a cool summer evening...calling on a friend unannounced...eating and not washing your plates thereafter...waking up not wanting to go to work and actually not going to work...servant massaging the feet after a hard day work...the festivals of Holi, Diwali and Eid...the echoes of '*Pranam* Sir' as you entered your surgery...the traffic police-man bowing on recognising your car...friend's children touching your feet instead of calling you by your first name.

He glanced at Savita sleeping on his shoulders oblivious of any such conflicts or the dripping sweat on her face. He shouted at the chauffeur next.

'Why are you blowing your horn constantly when you know that next car cannot move because of the jam?'

'But sir everyone is doing the same,' he countered, 'Not everyone can be a fool.'

The logic defied him but he shut up anyway.

He had often tried to weigh the romanticism against the harsh realities of life in India. When the mosquitoes drew his blood in the darkness of a power failure, he would curse the country much to consternation of his relatives. When he compared the absolute denigration and corruption in public life in India against the trampling of personal and family values in the west, he did not know which was worse. From whichever angle he tried to look at it; the reflection always was that of a compromise.

There had been little conversation between him and Bacchan seated in the front seat. He was the son of the youngest of his four uncles. There was an age gap of seventeen years between them and perhaps because of the proportionate amount of respect that such age gap generates in village life there was always a formalness inbuilt into the relationship. Bacchan was only ten when his father died of a heart attack. The daily diet of meat and *Purees* dipped in *Ghee* had to take its toll at some stage. Chaudhary saheb had then taken the entire responsibility of his brother's family.

'How is Ma?' Ramesh asked and almost immediately regretted the question. How else could she be? All those years of fasting and praying to die a married woman had been in vain.

'She is better now,' Bacchan answered. 'But she is still refusing all food. She wouldn't wipe her *sindur* off till the doctor from the town came and certified Babuji dead.' Ramesh choked silently. 'Her entire life was around babuji.'

Indeed it had been. All these years she had clung like a shadow to her idol. Her whole world was him and she had never ventured beyond him in her life. And now lost with her loss, it was too late for her.

Their flight to Patna was four hours late thanks to a portly gentleman seated in the front of the aircraft. The plane had left Delhi on time but five minutes into the flight this gentleman declared he had urgent business in Varanasi and demanded that the plane make an unscheduled stoppage there.

The rest of the passengers were furious but surprisingly not the cabin crew. They were standing in front of him with folded hands trying to cajole him into agreeing to drop his ridiculous demand. But the gentleman was adamant. He had to go to Varanasi and there was no other plane scheduled from Delhi for that evening and hence he had boarded that plane.

Ramesh was seated in the fourth row and at first he could not comprehend what was going on.

'He happens to be a Cabinet Minister and also a local mafia of Gorakhpur,' another passenger seated across explained. 'Can't you see how the aircraft personnel including the Captain are standing in front of him like scared chickens.'

Grief within often seeks different emotional expressions to let go. Ramesh later blamed it on that. He got up from his seat and rushed towards the Captain.

'What is the matter Captain?' he asked sternly.

'This is Mr. Umer Yadav, Cabinet Minister,' he said. 'He has got some urgent business in Varanasi and wants the plane to be diverted. I have explained to him that it would be extremely inconvenient to the rest of the passengers and also against the rules. But he is insisting.'

'Why are you doing the explaining? Can't you just say no?'

'Sir, please go back to your seat,' the Captain mumbled, 'we are trying to sort this out.'

The Minister looked bewildered by this daring intervention from a non-entity.

'No! I am not going back,' Ramesh exploded all of a sudden. 'Why are you even listening to his nonsense demand? I have paid for my ticket from my own money and so have the rest of the passengers while this man is almost certainly travelling free of cost, courtesy of the tax payer. Would you take me to Srinagar now if I demanded to? Is there no law? Are there no rules?'

The Captain was at a loss for words. The Minister, who was in two minds initially to join in the conversation as English was not exactly his forte, decided that it was time to stem the rebellion.

'What matter? What problem?' he addressed Ramesh directly. 'I am a Minister.'

'I know,' Ramesh replied in Hindi giving the Minister some rope as he knew that the Minister's English would only wind him up further. 'But this plane is not going to Varanasi.'

'Who are you to object?' the Minister was now in full stride in his native language. 'I am travelling on urgent government business.'

Ramesh laughed at the stupidity of the argument. It almost appeared funny. The passengers behind were getting increasingly restless but none else ventured forward.

'Throw him from the plane when we are over Varanasi,' someone shouted from behind and quickly hid himself. A few other less daring suggestions followed.

The Minister was visibly irked. Quite clearly he had not expected this kind of resistance from the lesser mortals.

'Look mister,' he raised his index finger to Ramesh. 'I suggest it is something you would not want to be involved in. I am speaking to the crew and this plane will definitely go to Varanasi or else the consequences will be dire.'

'Are you threatening me?' Ramesh was equally indignant.

'I am telling you that if you continue to interfere, I shall have you arrested at the airport.'

Ramesh went berserk. 'You do that,' he shouted, 'and I shall make sure that you are headline news on every newspaper and television channel. It is because of you politicians that this country has no hope even in hell.'

The Minister just glared back at him. There were whistles, booing and clapping from the back seats. The co-pilot poked his head from behind the curtain.

'We have fresh instructions to stop at Varanasi, sir,' he addressed the Captain.

There were muffled gasps of disbelief. The Minister smiled with satisfaction and returned to his newspaper. The captain began to retreat into his cockpit when Ramesh gave him a tug.

'When you get to the airport captain, get a bucket of water and drown your head in shame.'

The captain had had enough of abuse from both sides.

'When I am suspended for being righteous and brave, sir,' he hissed back shading the word 'sir' with obvious contempt. 'None of your testimony is going to get back my job or food into my kid's stomach.' He raced back into the cockpit.

Ramesh was still in a foul mood by the time they left for Bishanpur by car.

Savita also had not taken kindly to his intervention on the plane.

'Your *Bhaiyya* should join politics as well,' she was telling Bacchan. 'He always likes to be the torchbearer. There were a hundred other passengers in the plane but only he had to get up and engage in a confrontation.'

'Bhabhi is right *Bhaiyya*,' Bacchan said. 'These people are hardened criminals and often above the law.'

Ramesh did not reply. He knew they were right. Politicians were the pseudo 'Raj' still enslaving the population.

Bishanpur was four hours by car and it would be dusk before they reached the village. The sun was in full glare and the mercury was boasting another high. The warm dry air through the car's open windows did not let the sweat stay for long but made the airways distinctly uncomfortable. The heat had melted the bitumen in several places on the road and created blisters on its surface trying to emulate humanity. The thinned air hugging the surface created small puddles of water, which disappeared on approach. While humans sought any hint of shade, the animals were rolling in the tiniest collection of water visible, in an attempt to cool down. In the fields on both sides of the road, farmers were desperately pumping water to save the crop while urchins danced in front of the strong jet coming out of the pumps. He used to do the same as a child and often got told off.

'It must be the mango season,' he suddenly remembered.

'Yes,' answered Bacchan. 'The *Biju* and the *Bambai* are nearly over but the *Maldahs* are just beginning to ripen. We were not very lucky this year as we had a few hailstorms in February.'

'Enough to eat though I hope.'

'Oh! Eating is never a problem but the sale of mangoes from our grove could have been better.'

As the car crossed the bridge over the river five miles away from the village, Ramesh felt a strange sense of nervousness. For the first time he was entering his village with no joy or excitement. He wished the driver drove a bit slow. They turned into the semi-metalled dirt track that prided itself in being the village's connection with the outside world. Five hundred yards further their mango groves would start. Whenever he came from England, Chaudhary saheb would meet him at the edge of the groves.

'Had some important work down here,' he would pretend.

'There are no mangoes in the winter, Baba,' Ramesh would speak to himself.

He waited for the groves to appear then pass by. It was true then. He clutched Savita's hand and squeezed hard. He was sweating excessively even for the heat.

The car had come to a halt. There was a big crater in the centre of the road filled with dirty water. The driver wanted to wade through the puddle to assess the depth and wanted the passengers to get off to make the car lighter. A dark skinned figure ran towards them from across the fields.

'It is Madho!' exclaimed Bacchan. Madho was the one of their cousins. He stopped, panting in front of them and touched everyone's feet.

'They took Baba to the cremation ground,' he informed them. 'Everyone is waiting for you there and so we better go straight to the *Ghat* from here.'

'Why this rush?' asked Bacchan. 'Couldn't they wait for us to arrive?'

'We were expecting you by mid-day. It is so hot today that even the ice slabs were failing...'

'Okay, okay,' Ramesh intervened. He did not want to hear the rest. He felt strangely relieved that he would not have to face Ma for another few hours. Women did not come to the funeral grounds.

The *Ghat* was swelling with people. The wet sand had turned into swamp under the trampling feet. Chaudhary saheb was a well known and a respected person and people had travelled from afar to pay their last respects. They were outnumbered by those who were there just out of curiosity. Ramesh was in a daze when he got out of the car. Savita stayed inside. The crowd surged towards him. There were people touching his feet, some thumping on the shoulders, some hugging him, some crying wildly, some watching him with pity, but he barely took notice. His eyes searched for the pyre. It was far down by the riverbank. He could see a face from under the wood logs but could not make out anymore. He desperately wanted to get closer but was scared at the same time.

His arrival unleashed a flurry of activity as everyone began to prepare for the last rites. The noise from the crowd drowned under the chant of the Brahmins. The cousins held a wall of sheets as Ramesh changed into a *Dhoti* from his suit. A Brahmin led him to the river where he washed his feet. Water from the Ganges was sprinkled upon him to purify his body for the last rites. He was still in a daze. The wailing grew louder. Then with a blank expression and a nod of the head, the Priest asked him to proceed to the pyre. He turned to face his father.

Near the pyre the *Dom* was haggling with one of the uncles for more money for the cremation. The uncle quickly thrust a wad of notes in his hand and in a low voice threatened to give him a thrashing after the funeral. The Dom took the money accepting the risk. Ramesh heard none of that.

The chant grew louder. *Ghee* was being poured on the pyre as the Brahmins prayed for the peace of the soul. Ramesh inched forward to have a closer look.

But he always looked like that whenever he was deep asleep. He had seen him so many times. The lips hiding a glint of a smile under the thick moustache. The face serene and calm. Handsome as ever. He had always woken up afterwards.

There was a nudge from behind. The priest was beckoning him to take the torch to light the pyre. The chanting reached a crescendo. *He was always a deep sleeper. Ring a bell by his ears and he would not budge.*

The priest nudged him again.

He waited.

Bacchan came from behind and held his hand. Ramesh touched the pyre with the torch.

Baba was still smiling.

His vision began to blur even before the flames and the smoke leapt skywards. His legs could no longer bear the weight of his grief and he sagged on his knees, trembling, as he wept aloud.

It was dark before the last flames began to die off. Everyone had left except for Ramesh who requested to be left alone. A gentle wind had begun scattering the ash around and smearing his face with it. It felt nice and warm. A few tiny sparks detached themselves from the luminous logs in pursuit. Since growing up into an adult he had never hugged or touched his father except for his feet. He ran his hands through the pile of ash with his eyes closed.

They had never before been this close or this far apart.

You, who, is wailing, haven't even learnt the art of crying,
Tears are for holding back, and not for letting it stream by.

But Parvati Devi was beyond crying. Her eyes were dry, parched like a desert, which soaks everything that seeks to rejuvenate it. Tears could melt her grief, her last gift from her husband. When Ramesh touched her feet she lifted her both arms pointing at her wrist without the bangles and with a grimace asked 'why'. When he had hugged her she wondered why her son was shaking so violently and asked whether he was hungry. Then she kissed Savita and retreated to her room for her prayers. She seldom came out of her room, one of the servants informed Ramesh.

The Hindu soul is different from others in the sense that it is far more vulnerable to go to hell if everything is not carried out according to the *Diktats* of the priests after the death of its body. The post funeral ceremony, the *Shradh*, extends up to thirteen days and is so elaborate and hectic that it seldom gives one space or time to grieve for their beloved. May be that was the original purpose behind it. The whole effort goes into organising the *Shradh* successfully rather than grieving in solitude to ensure the smooth journey of the soul to the heavens.

The worshipping for the soul began in earnest from day three onwards. Ramesh was isolated from the rest. He was not to touch anyone and no one was allowed to enter into his room. His eating utensils and all personal items were to be kept separate until the purification ceremony on day thirteen. Savita slept in a different room and was also not allowed to touch him. He was made to fast on various occasions as the Brahmins commanded. Meanwhile nearly the entire village dined twice daily at his house. Special kitchens had to be erected and new cooks were drafted in to cope with the situation.

On day seven was the *Mundan* ceremony. All the uncles, their sons and Ramesh sat in a single row on the floor while the village barber shaved their heads.

On day thirteen the final *Pooja* began. He finally gained purification by personally serving food to twenty-one Brahmins and giving them generous amounts of gifts and money. The village dined at his place for the last time. People praised the quality of food they had been enjoying for the last few days and winced at the thought of going back to their normal diet.

With his touchability regained and his father's soul safely securing a place in heaven, Ramesh went to the village post-office the next day and sent a telegram to Puja.

> *'Coming back on the 24th. Ma coming with us to stay. Get Plumber to fit bidet in downstairs bathroom. Love, Ramesh.'*

VI

The clouds continued to pile its wealth like a greedy businessman on the earth below. Layers of snow on top of each other. The flakes drifting and dancing in the gentle breeze, transiently iridescent under the neon street lamps before lying down with unhastened grace. The night hushed the stars to retreat as the infant rays made the darkness paler. The carpet of thick snow as yet a blackish white. The tiny leaves spruced up to meet the first sun rays shaking off the snow flakes gently. The full moon remained defiant.

Twelve men raced silently through the snow. Like a team in a boat race wading in perfect harmony. They all wore black balaclavas. Their eyes glinted even in the dark. They were carrying different objects in their hands which were hard to discern in the darkness. Cans, axes, base-ball bats...and a few other things. They communicated in sign language even though there was no one around who could have heard them.

They stopped at the first building at the edge of the open field. They had no specific targets but this seemed ideal. Easier to retreat and disappear into the cover of darkness. The falling snow nearly occluded the sixty-watt bulb flickering over the signboard.

"JARNAIL PUNJABI DHABA."

Their eyes glinted with excitement. Like a cat's eye in the headlights of a passing car. These were no ordinary people. For it takes a lot more to hate and maim someone who you do not even know. To affect someone's life so profoundly when he or she has not even touched yours. For just to note the colour of the skin and black out everything else. The person in it, the soul, the heart, the history, the family, children...all snapped in one moment of a violent act. To achieve so much in just that one moment. No Sir, these were no ordinary people.

They looked at each and nodded to confirm the target. One of them detached himself from the group and sprayed on the front door with a can.

PAKI SHIT GO HOME OR DIE.

Then they set into motion, non-meticulously, shedding all pretence. The baseball bats against the glass panes, pick axes for the wooden doors, match-sticks for the Molotov cocktails.

Cocktails shall it be as a toast to their conquest. They raised it in the air, cheering, before throwing it through the broken windows.

He was having a bad dream again. The same one. Even in the dream he wondered why again. The summer heat, the smog of fear. Ugandan troops thumping in the streets. He and his pregnant wife huddled in the tiny room with no windows. A suitcase stuffed with cash and jewellery.

Troops looking for cash to loot, women to rape, men to shoot. They fulfilled all the criteria.

The banging on the door. Troops or Naseem.

Naseem.

They were running through the plantation. Bending to get cover from the maize crop. Running fast without looking back. Fear propulsion. Miles away from the windowless room.

Why wasn't the banging subsiding? Why were the cries getting louder? Why was the sun so hot all of a sudden?

Jarnail Singh opened his eyes.

Fear snapped it shut again until the smoke knocked at his senses. He shrieked convulsively as he ran out of the door. His wife was sleeping in the other bedroom with his daughter. They were at the door shouting hysterically. Downstairs the Restaurant was by then in full-blooded fire. The hiss of fire and the shouts of abuse fell on the ears like molten wax.

He was trying to think for a route of escape except he could not concentrate. His wife grabbed him and pushed him towards the bathroom at the back. He knew now why. All three got into the bathroom and he quickly opened the window. He looked outside. A ten-foot drop onto the garage roof. A forty eight year old wife and a twelve year old daughter.

Fear propulsion. Always works.

His heart was pounding so loud that it was threatening to break his rib cage. He lowered himself first. Next his daughter. A free fall and he caught her safely in mid air. He almost let a cry slip as the weight of his daughter transferred to his broken ankle. He could see the shadows and they just had to lift their heads to see him.

Just from ten yards.

The heat from the fire did nothing to stop the blood freezing in his arteries. His wife lowered herself down next. With a thud on his chest. Another drop of ten feet but this time it won't hurt because of the snow on the ground. He almost felt happy for a second.

They began to run fast, away from the shadows luminescent in the raging fire. As fast as they could with a broken ankle, an old woman and the thick snow clinging at their feet. Hand in hand dragging each other away when they heard a shout.

'Look the bastards are getting away, catch the bitches and kill them.'

Bitches !...Bitches !...Kill them !...Kill them !

The words resonated inside his skull. From one side to the other. His daughter a bitch, they had called his wife a bitch. The frost of fear transformed almost immediately into a fire of rage. He stopped thinking.

He turned back and ran towards those men shouting the traditional Sikh battle cry.

He did not feel the first blow of the baseball bat on his forearm. Rage absorbed it with just a crackle and no pain. The second one he did and all the rest thereafter. The blow on the skull, the bones caving in and squeezing a spurt of blood through the nose and the ears. The punch on the abdomen and he took instant revenge by throwing up blood on his aggressor. The boot on the scrotum and the total solar eclipse. The rod on the leg and the thud and the click. The knife through his viscera, the least painful of all.

As consciousness ebbed out of him, he began to dream again from where he had stopped. Of Uganda. Stopping to catch their breath under a tree.

'Let us go back to Punjab,' Bimla was saying.

'No we will go to England. There are no Idi Amins there and we can run a good business. It will be better than Punjab,' he promised.

The dream finished and the lights switched off.

The blood ran away from his body as if in fear, in tiny rivulets away from him till they clotted.

Like icing on the ice.

The snow continued to fall, unstirred and undisturbed, like God himself.

There are two types of very nice people in this world. Complex nice and the simple nice. In these modern, fast paced times the latter are threatened with extinction but if you meet one by accident or design, there is a benign urgency to feel and explore them and draw them into your own life. Mostly for the simple joy of knowing someone like them.

Normally Ramesh was more reticent of his Asian patients. Mainly because they often attempted to cross the professional line of a doctor-patient relationship and tried to lure him into a friendlier bond on the presumptions of a shared culture and skin colour. And if he resisted, as he always did, he would be dubbed as arrogant and proud.

But with Jarnail Singh, he had sought to cross that line himself. Just to know him and draw him into his own life.

He had not thought much of him the first time he saw him getting out of a Mercedes car, dressed elegantly in a black striped suit outside his Surgery. But three hours later, after seeing the last patient in his afternoon session, when Ramesh spotted him again behind the reception counter answering his Surgery phone he had stopped and looked at him more intently.

'I am a new patient at your Surgery, doctor,' the man was saying, 'I had just come to request some nicotine patches. But your receptionist's son had an epileptic fit at home and she had to leave. I offered my services to Mr Hancock, your Practice manager to look after the reception for a while and he let me do it. He knows me well. He is regular customer at my restaurant. My appointment was two hours ago but it was chaos here with the patients coming and the phone ringing.'

It was not only that act of pure selflessness, nor the way he said it or only the innocent sincerity in his eyes; but a defying summation of all of that which hit a tender spot somewhere inside his heart.

'You need not have done this,' Ramesh had mumbled.

'It was no trouble at all Doctor. You bring smiles on so many people's faces each day. This is the least we can do in return.'

In truth that was a lie but Ramesh was flattered nevertheless.

'Thank you,' he had said.

'Any chance of getting some nicotine patches Doctor?'

'You are a very demanding patient,' Ramesh had laughed.

But that compliment and that encounter had had a lingering impact upon Ramesh. In a small measure it had dented the cynicism which had changed his vocation into a chore that had to be done till a reasonable pension allowed him to abandon it. He did not feel tired when he got back that evening and Savita was pleasantly taken aback by his unaccustomed cheerfulness.

When that effect began to wear thin, he took Savita to Jarnail's restaurant one evening. Jarnail's eyes lit up when he saw Ramesh come in through the door. He refused to entertain them as customers and took them upstairs to his flat above the restaurant.

At the end of the evening Ramesh could not bring himself up to offer to pay for the meal. But when they had shaken hands and looked in each other eyes, there was an understanding that would soon bloom into an enduring friendship.

On that eventful morning when Girish had rung him and told him about the incident, Ramesh had squeezed his eyes and clenched his fists in despair. Not at the racist violence but at the regret that it's victim was Jarnail.

He cancelled his morning surgery and headed for the hospital.

Ever since the British National Party had won a council seat a week ago, tension had been running high in many areas of west London. There was further provocation in shape of a victory rally in Ealing which had turned violent after a clash between rival factions.

Soon after two shops were looted and ransacked in Ealing. Both the shop owners were whites and had no connection to the far right. It was the handiwork of a gang of Asian youths called 'The Knockers', who in peacetime were a ragtag collection of unemployed youths engaged in petty crimes and drug peddling. They had also adopted in their charter, the vow to protect their community and did not hesitate to indulge in violence to counter the far Right.

Southall is one of the few places where an Englishman fears to tread upon his own soil. The day's incident had knocked the 'Knockers' pride but there was no sadness or despair. For evil, even when pitted against each other are just but friends in disguise who feed each other with their loathsome acts. This violent act has just sanctified their cause.

But the hurt and despair was felt by the gangless people of Southall that morning. As if they too had been individually beaten up. That hate in the aggressor's heart often baffles the victim's mind. The same 'why' bounces back at him multiple of times, each time without an answer till he sinks low or rises in anger. Vengeance becomes the balm for the ordinary people, forgiveness for the brave.

There was a heavy police presence at the hospital. Jarnail did not have any immediate family in Britain and so when Ramesh introduced himself as his close friend and his family doctor, he was swiftly ushered in by a police officer. Jarnail had just been shifted to the recovery unit after a three hour surgery but was yet to wake up from the anaesthesia.

The surgical registrar briefed Ramesh on their condition. Jarnail had to undergo abdominal surgery for stab wounds and Internal fixation for two compound fractures but was now stable and out of danger. His wife, Bimal, had suffered severe blood loss and a punctured lung from a knife stab and had to be admitted to Intensive care after surgery. Their daughter, however, escaped with only minor injuries and was presently by her mother's bedside.

He tiptoed silently to where Jarnail lay in his bed. He scanned him slowly, restricting his vision to one part at a time, to be able to withstand the shock. With the screen of drips and tubes and the camouflage of plasters and bandages, it was difficult to recognise him at first. His face was sunken and darker but still looked peaceful.

As if nothing had happened.

Jarnail began to stir and Ramesh reached for his hands. Jarnail squeezed his eyes in a few vain attempts before finally opening them to see Ramesh by his side.

'Hello Doc! How come you are here?' He managed that welcoming smile again.

'My receptionist's son has had a fit again.'

Jarnail's smile widened as laughter would have been painful. Ramesh squeezed his hands.

'How are you feeling Jarnail?'

'Violated and small,' Jarnail answered.

A lump rose through Ramesh's throat. He could say no more and just nodded.

'Bimal?' Jarnail was asking.

'She had some surgery too. Now completely out of danger.'

'*Bitiya*?'

'She is fine. She was not even admitted. Just a few minor scratches. She is by her mother.'

'She will be alone in the house for the next few days,' Jarnail said hesitantly. 'It would be really kind of you if you could drop by sometimes to make sure she is okay.'

The lump resurfaced again. 'Don't put me to shame Jarnail,' he begged. '*Bitiya* will be living with us till you come home. I will not accept anything else that you say.'

'God should make a few more human beings like you Doc.'

Ramesh smiled back deciding against repeating the same words.

There was an uncomfortable silence as they ran out of words. Ramesh was thankful of the nurse who came around to record some observations. When she left he turned around and told Jarnail that two of the culprits were in police custody.

Jarnail smiled at him, as if thankful of that attempt to cheer him up.

'It does not matter anymore my friend,' he said. 'The damage has been done.'

That same morning a slip of paper extracted from a brown envelope unfolded to announce that Miss Puja Singh was now a member of the royal college of Physicians. She had finally passed her MRCP exam.

A fountain burst high inside her heart spreading through her chest and freely escaping from her eyes. She sagged on her knees kissing repeatedly the print on the letter. This was her fourth attempt. Each time success had eluded her, sometimes blatantly and sometimes by a whisker. She had walked out this time from the exam hall with tears in her eyes. She had fumbled again in the short cases and was certain of her failure. The exams appeared unassailable and she was ready to call it a day once the result came through.

She was alone in the flat. She paced across the rooms and waited for all of it to sink down and then shrieked at the top of her voice.

And then again.

A gentle breeze rushed in from the open window to share the excitement and the cat in the corner remonstrated.

Where was the world today? She ran for the phone.

She was still breathless with excitement as she relayed the news to Lennie on the phone. Lennie was both ecstatic and relieved. Ecstatic for Puja and relieved for himself as their love life had been a perpetual misery over the last few days while she awaited the results.

'Where are you darling?' Puja was asking.

'At my flat. I was about to leave for the studio.'

'Don't bother, call in sick today.'

'Puja?' Lennie tried to protest

'Lennie, I shall die from the shock of joy if I am left alone at this very moment. We have to meet.'

Two years of courting Puja had taught him the art of giving in.

'Will I be allowed to take advantage of the royal physician?' Lennie said. 'Making love to the royalty was a long cherished ambition of mine.'

'Wrong time of the month sado,' Puja laughed at the other end. 'Let's meet in Covent Garden and grab some lunch together.'

'Puja this is a great achievement. I am so pleased for you. We have to celebrate this with a party.'

Puja was laughing. 'Half an hour then?'

'Half an hour. I cannot wait to see the smile back on your face.'

'I love you Lennie.'

'Not as much as I love you sweetheart.'

'Shut up.'

'See you soon. Don't make me wait. Bye!'

She tried home but the answer machine was on. The news was too important to be relayed by an answering machine to her parents. She looked at herself in the mirror. Hair a mess, still in her night clothes and she had thirty minutes to reach Covent Garden. She ran for the bathroom. The excitement was still adding precious seconds to every chore. The buttons and the bra hook played mischief, the kettle took longer to boil. Only the watch seemed to be running faster than before. At the end of the thirty minutes she was still trembling and still at the flat.

She decided against taking the tube and hailed a cab. The morning peak hour was just executing its daily ritual of grinding jams and smoke therapy totally unaware of her exam results. She fumed in silence as the watch notched another half an hour.

She got off the taxi at Covent Garden and searched frantically for Lennie. Had he left already? He dare not. Then she caught a glimpse of him. His face hidden behind a bouquet of flowers, his trademark black T-shirt that she had unsuccessfully tried to throw away thrice, giving the game away. Wordlessly they flowed into each other's arms and kissed with desperation. The joy finally beginning to thaw inside. It is amazing how happiness shared multiplies instead of dividing. She fleetingly opened her eyes to see her lover's face. A flicker of triumph before the heavy eyelids shut her eyes again. The tongues joined in.

She opened her eyes again when her jaws began to ache and caught someone familiar. Their eyes met momentarily without acknowledging each other, turning away sharply.

Girish Patel walked briskly disappearing into the heavy crowd, his face sweating in the cold weather.

Puja's heart continued to thump but for a different reason. All her joy vanished without trace.

The next two nights were thoroughly dreamless. The morphine blended the pain with sleep somewhere in the darkness and deterred the dreams from breaking that union. Pain and sleep. That morning he felt strangely at peace. His head felt light like a reservoir of cool air. He raised his hand and let his finger cut through the mist on the window pane to create a weird inscription.

'What is it?' asked the blonde nurse laying down his breakfast.

'It is "Happy Birthday" in Punjabi,' Jarnail replied with a smile. 'Today happens to be my wife's birthday.'

'How wonderful,' the nurse beamed with genuine delight. 'And I have some good news for you too. Your wife has this morning come off the breathing machine and is also off her sedation. She is now completely out of danger. Completely.'

He tried to speak but his lips gave way to his eyes as tears welled in them. The nurse bent forward to squeeze his hands.

'And yes you can see her this morning. Have you got a present?'

The lump in his throat and his poor English, both conspired to keep him speechless. He nodded and scrambled to open his bedside drawer. There in lay a small package wrapped in gift paper. His daughter had brought it in the previous evening.

'How sweet,' the nurse said. 'You finish your breakfast and I shall fetch a wheel chair. Then we could go to the Intensive care ward.'

He raised his hand to give a blessing. The nurse slightly confused by the gesture, clutched it momentarily and left.

The excitement killed his appetite instantly. He tried to force a few spoonfuls of the cereal down and nearly choked on it. He gave up the effort and rested restlessly on his bed. A few minutes later the nurse turned up with the wheel chair.

The first emotion was of shock as he entered the intensive care. There was his wife behind a web of tubes and drips piercing her body. Her face was swollen with a lattice of stitches behind the oxygen mask. Joy trickled in form of a single tear from the corner of her eye as she caught sight of her husband. The nurse left them alone.

The lump in his throat returned as he grappled for words. He desperately wanted to hold her hands but felt shy in the presence of other people. He brushed his fingers against hers and smiled.

'Happy Birthday.' They always spoke to each other in Punjabi. 'From today you are officially an old woman.'

'Are you in pain?' she asked.

He shook his head. Then to reaffirm his lie he knocked on the plaster cast on his leg.

'I am also in no pain.'

They both were lost for words for a few moments.

'The nurse told me that *Bitiya* only had minor injuries?'

'Yes, yes, she was not even admitted,' he reassured her. 'She had been coming to see you everyday while you were asleep.'

'God must be listening to all our prayers. That is why we are all so lucky to be alive.'

He smiled as the irony struck him. An awkward silence followed again. He fixed his gaze on his wife's heart rhythm on the monitor and tried to make sense out of it.

'Is the food here any good, ji?' She asked.

Jarnail smiled back on discovering the next worry that weighed on her mind.

'Bimal, I have a present for you,' he said taking out the small package from his jacket. His hands trembled as he handed it to her.

She carefully undid the gift-wrap till it revealed the white envelope. She extracted the small rectangular booklet with the picture of an aeroplane on the cover. She flipped one page and then another and began to cry soundlessly without inhibition. She brushed aside the pall of tears that had blurred her vision with her hand to reconfirm the words printed below her name.

LONDON

DELHI

VII

Each word seeped inside and scalded his heart. Emotions of grief, anger, disbelief, embarrassment lashed against each other creating a tide over which he had no control. Then thoughts intervened and blocked his vision and hearing. He drifted away.

Happy memories flooded in.

A wriggly mass staring at the ceiling with amazement. Taking sides with him against everyone's wishes by being born as a daughter. How he had refused to take her in his arms out of the fear that he might drop her. The vote of confidence by the village grannies that her eyes, upper lip and toes had taken after her father. Only the nose went to her mother.

And how she had grown, in his heart, on his back. No dinner could be eaten until she had her piggy ride.

Till yesterday. Or very close to yesterday.

The tiny pair of eyes bright as a bulb in a sunken face came into focus. How his four year old daughter begged him not to let the other doctor insert the intravenous cannula for the fluids she needed. And how his heart cramped between love and logic let out a cry.

He had adored her beauty as it blossomed under the gaze of her puberty. He had dreamt about her marriage several times in all its lavishness, pomp, joy and sorrow. He had boasted about it from even before she had begun school. He had felt the sadness several times at the thought that one day she would be leaving for her *Sasural.* He had opened an account to save for her marriage on the day she was born.

And now Girish was saying all this. All his investment of love and hopes over the years had come to a naught.

He tried to search within for the answers. The fruition of his Karma? The blood splattered pheasants he had shot in the marshy grasslands of his village. The starving labourer he had beaten lifeless for stealing some rice from the storage. The God he had forgotten in his good times. Were these sins so great to merit such punishment? Perhaps they were.

And then it came to him. Through the haze of his conscience, clear as a crystal.

His parents.

Oh God, the merciful, why are you so exacting in your punishments?

Someone was shaking him. The veil of thoughts lifted and the tide set in again. The three persons in the room came back into vision. He sank on the sofa under the added weight of his emotions.

'Ramesh, you have to tackle this in a sensitive way,' Girish was saying.

'Like what?' he retorted. 'Hug my daughter and give her away to that white chap. Tell my folks that this son-in-law shakes hands and does not touch your feet. Never mind he won't understand your language any way. Look forward to his Christmas cards in my health authority nursing home?'

'Don't jump to conclusions straightaway. I am only saying that those times are gone when you could shout at or hit your children and force them to do things your way. You have to treat them as grown up adults and talk your way out.'

'This is what happens when you leave your home and settle elsewhere,' his mother began to weep.

'Oh! Please shut up Ma,' Ramesh responded angrily. He was well aware of the sarcasm behind the grief. 'As if everyone in India is bathed in milk. Do you want me to recount for you how many boys and girls that you know of have run away from home, how many have had abortions?'

'It still does not happen in reputable families.'

'Ma, do not make me open my mouth.'

His mother finally shut up.

Savita was confused. Her own sense of shock hid behind the fear for her husband's anger. Ramesh was a sea of tranquillity with a dormant volcano beneath which rarely exploded. But when it did, it knew no boundaries nor cared for the consequences.

'Let me to talk to Puja, ji?' she begged of her husband.

'No,' Ramesh was emphatic. 'She can talk you out of anything. Let her answer to me. Give her a ring and order her to come home immediately.'

Girish sensing that his role was over got up and left after mumbling his good-byes. His mother kept quiet but was breathing audibly to register her displeasure. Ramesh kept staring at the perfectly clean carpet below his feet. Savita wanted to hold his hands but waited for his mother to leave the room. The ticking of the wall clock made the silence louder. Thoughts and emotions raged invisibly in that awkward silence which had gripped its occupants. Someone picked up the remote and switched on the television. Their eyes converged in the same direction but continued to stare into the blankness.

Savita took the initiative and rose to make some tea. As she crossed the entrance hall she caught a shimmer of green and yellow behind the frosted glass of her front door. She ran desperately to open the door before the ribbon of brown reached the doorbell. She knew the colours even before the door parted to reveal the secret. She lunged at the shadow putting one hand on her mouth, signalling for silence and dragged it upstairs to her bedroom. She then shut the door behind her and started to breathe again.

Puja stared at her mother intently. For her the moment of reckoning had arrived. For three days she had waited for the phone to ring. Never wanting it to ring. She had woken up in the middle of the night imagining it to be ringing. But only silence had greeted her. She had not told Lennie about the episode at Covent Garden. This was too personal. The tension within left it footprints on every second that had passed by till she could take no more. Whatever the consequences it had to end.

Savita was trembling as she faced her daughter. She was not sure how to start.

'Ma?'

'Is it true that you are seeing a white boy?'

Puja hesitated and then slowly nodded her head. She watched her mother's eyes open wide in disbelief. Somehow Savita had hoped that her daughter would come in and dispel it all. The last straws floated adrift.

'Do you realise what you are talking about?' Savita began to tremble even more as she clutched Puja's arms and began to shake her. Her fingernails dug deep into her skin but Puja refused to flinch. 'Have you no shame? Have you no honour?'

'Ma, I love him and I will marry him.' Each word, cubes of ice with grit of steel.

Savita's hand lifted spontaneously in mid-air. Puja did not move. There was a knock on the door. She quickly lowered her hand.

Ramesh entered. His face was calm and impassive. He walked across to the window and stared at a car passing in the street. Only the incessant tapping on the window pane gave a hint of something amiss. The silence screamed at them for a few moments before he finally broke into words.

'What has happened has happened,' he paused. The red car had stopped on the double yellow line. Right in front his house. Bastard. 'The past cannot be amended but the future can be. What you have done will bear heavy on our souls till the day we go to our graves.' Guilt arrows. She knew it would come. 'But from this day onwards all this should be history, strictly history. Do you understand?'

The chill in his voice left no one unscathed. He waited without turning for his daughter to reply.

Puja walked up to him. He did not turn. She wanted to touch his shoulder but decided otherwise.

'Papa, you cannot blame Lennie for being born white. He had no control over it. We have been together for three years. We love each other. We make each other happy. We want to marry and live together for ever.'

Ramesh slowly turned around and looked into her daughters face. He searched for his four year old in vain. Those vulnerable eyes were now a fire of defiance.

'You did not hear me Puja. It is past tense now.'

'Papa,' her voice frayed. 'Why do you want to snatch away your only child's happiness?'

'I could ask you the same question but I won't. Do not be confused Puja. This is not a request. This is an order.'

'No Papa, you did not hear me. I love him and I won't walk away from him.'

It is difficult to define the hurt felt by a slap on your face. As to why the pain is so disproportionate to the force when struck by someone you love than when by a stranger. Why the weals on the heart take much longer to disappear than the weals on the skin. Why tears well up in two pairs of eyes instead of one.

But the damage is always done.

Ramesh was raging and crying. Savita and Puja were only crying.

'Papa,' the defiance persisted between the sobs. 'I am not stupid to let the love of my life go because of your false beliefs, your false ego, your false prestige. You are ready to barter your daughter's life for them. You really thought you could bring me up in England, educate me and then tie me up like cattle with anyone you wished.' That one slap hit again and again and anger took up defence instead of hurt.

'Am I cattle? Is your father cattle? Are ninety-five percent of all Indians cattle?' Savita shouted back. 'In your world of human beings one in three marriages end in a divorce. If only your two cattle parents fought and divorced you would be today in care or sleeping in the underground. Do you understand what marriage is? Do you understand what raising a child means? Do you know to whom you owe your very existence? Do you even know the meaning of sacrifice?'

'So now it is pay back time? Is it? For the favour of bringing me up and giving me birth, it is time I sacrificed the rest of my life to feed your false pride and uphold this family name that no one has heard of or bothers about?'

'No Puja. It is time when you walk out on your own family for the sake of some person you have barely known. It is time when all the dreams we had nurtured of your marriage, our son-in law and our family have come to an end. The Chauhan family clan will in the future be known as a Smith or a Jones. It is time when you have dared to raise your voice to your father like no one else in the family.'

'Ma, what family tree are you talking about,' Puja tried to plead with her mother. 'We are not descendants of a royal family. When we die even the house round the corner won't be bothered about it. All we should try is to lead a normal and happy life. My life. That is what I am trying to defend here today. I am pleading not shouting. I cannot even dream of being disrespectful to you or papa.'

'Puja let me make it absolutely clear,' this time Ramesh spoke. 'There is no question of you marrying a white boy. Generations of family tradition are at stake. We will never be able to raise our head in the society. This thing cannot simply happen.'

Puja looked up to her father. There was a strange look of innocence on his face but there were no lines of doubt. She knew there was no point in arguing further.

'I am sorry Papa, but I am not willing to give him up and it would be nice if we had your blessings.'

'Get out of my house,' hissed Ramesh.

She turned slowly on her heels waiting for someone to stop her. The heavy heart made her drag her feet. The flowers on the wallpaper bade her farewell. She stopped in the hall and turned around to see the walls stare back at her. One last time. She looked at the open door upstairs and yearned for a face to peep through.

No one came out to stop her from leaving.

Outside the air felt fresher than before. She took a deep breath to fill her lungs with the cool air. The salt from her eyes was beginning to irritate the skin of her face and she splashed her face with cold water from the outside tap. Tiny snowflakes slid down invisible strings and rested on her shoulders in solidarity. She scooped the snow in her hands and gazed into the crystal ball intently.

She was sad but there was no guilt. She was right in principle and about that she was not in any doubt. She loved them too but would have never imposed her will on them. She would now get Lennie and then her parents eventually. It will all work out well in the end. She even let a victory smile to stamp on her sorrow as she flung the snowball and watched it disintegrate between her and the open sky.

The city of London raced by her in unwarranted haste as she pressed her foot on the accelerator driving towards Lennie's house. Her father's face kept interrupting her vision. It was true that she had never raised her voice in front of him. But something today had snapped within to make her to cross that line. She knew that her daring to do so had set her mother aflame. Ramesh was her God and rightly or wrongly, she could not brook anyone showing disrespect to him.

She wondered what Lennie's reaction would be. The usual cultural dumbfoundedness? Or would he show more understanding? He would be pleased anyway. He had refrained from proposing so far as he did not want to place her in an awkward situation. Now the risk of that had diminished. Her face blushed red as the thoughts of marriage crept in. At last she could begin to contemplate it. Her parents won't come to the wedding. That she was sure of. It would take something more to bring them around. The traditional British-Asian way of reuniting families. Her hands instinctively reached to her stomach as she began to laugh dislodging a few tears on to her cheeks.

She looked up and saw the small lumps of cloud coalescing in a bid to cover the mighty sun. The sun continued to train its guns on the ground creating holes of green on the snow-covered ground.

She prayed that Lennie be at his flat after all this.

But it was Sunday and it was only mid-day. Decision time for him. Whether to leave the bed or linger a bit longer. At best he would be searching for his toothbrush in the pile of rubbish in his bathroom. That stinking bathroom of his that she cleaned every so often. Then eating the cereal without milk. How can anyone eat cereal without milk?

As usual there was no vacant parking slot left outside his flat. She parked her car on the double yellow lines and said a small prayer. Being fined on this day would be a divine joke. She raced up the stairs with barely concealed delight. A big smile extended across her face and she lowered her eyes to avoid the bemused stares from the people descending down the stairs. Her mind raced ahead of the body conjuring scenes which were about to follow. Her heart raced with a double boost of adrenaline from the physical exertion and the growing excitement.

She paused in front of Lennie's door to catch her breath. Then she paused again to listen to the sound of heavy breathing unsure of whether it came from her own lungs. There were muffled sobs and groans as well. The gasps of ecstasy pierced her ears. Her heart stopped momentarily and then raced faster than ever. She silently turned the key in and opened the door. The sounds magnified.

From behind the mist in her eyes she saw flesh unwrap, startled by her arrival.

Long golden hair fanned on the pillow like wings of a peacock. The naked truth staring at her with stark simplicity. His head buried in his hands, she saw only his back, like a wall of high tide drowning her in an instant.

The air was still but every one shook in their own individual storms. In rage, in shock, in shame, in guilt. Then the deafening silence melted as the glass vase by the window narrowly missed his head and crashed into the wall. She ran outside and rushed down the stairs. She stumbled at the last few steps and crashed against the iron railing. She hurt her legs and her head and began to cry because of the pain.

She kept on crying long after the pain had gone.

How swift was God's retaliation. Betrayal for betrayal. It was now only in the flashback that she could see the pain on her father's face. Those lines and those unspoken words which she had misconstrued for anger. How she had broken his heart in quest of a goal that was never hers.

Deceit inflicts both pain and anger as it hurts both the heart and the intellect. Blinded in love for so long, the harsh glare of truth blinded her once again. In one stroke she had cut all her ties from the world that was hers and now she had nowhere to go to.

Absolutely nowhere.

The clouds above had won the battle and the earth was plunged in an eerie grey darkness. The silver lightening unzipped its belly and it poured on the ground like a widow's tears. Puja staggered out of her car and the heavens still not satisfied from its vengeance, drenched her from above. But somehow it did not matter now. She could barely drag herself from under some unknown weight to the front of her flat's door. It was dark inside and she stumbled and hit her shin against the coffee table. It hurt but she ignored it and limped to the bathroom. She emptied the tablets from the bottle in the cabinet till they occupied half of the small glass and then filled the rest with water. She stared at the tiny bubbles bursting at the surface of the water for a moment and then slowly brought it to her lips.

She limped across to her bedroom and opened the windows. A cool draft rushed in and wiped her wet face dry. The rain had stopped and it had begun to snow. Tiny flakes drifting down without purpose. The sky a dark blue now, more dark but less threatening.

It was beginning to feel better.

Just before her eyes closed, she saw the three fairies entering through the window. Their magic sticks with sparkling stars at its end. Just like the movie.

She was glad she had left the window open.

VIII

She remembered flying between the trees. Tall, naked, stark. Jutting up to the grey sky. The smaller branches in a maze like a cobweb hinting towards extinction. Dead leaves crushed at their feet. The rain painting a darker coat on them. One by one they peeked at her through the glass as the ambulance sped her by.

Just onlookers, curious like everyone else.

She saw a face staring at her. Blurry but familiar. The face kept calling her name. There were other voices too. None of them familiar

Silence! I am dying.

But the sounds suddenly grew louder. Footsteps banging at her head. Many more blurry faces.

Someone stabbed her in the arm. Someone else was trying to choke her. They were trying to kill her. She laughed at the irony but felt violated as well. She contracted her throat muscles to resist the tube like object in her throat but felt it sliding further inside. She tried to jerk her limbs in protest but they felt flaccid and paralysed.

Then the pain began to recede. The voices grew distant. A picture began to float in. Greens by the river Thames. Savita spreading out the picnic basket on a small mat. Ramesh, much younger and thinner, playing Frisbee with a young girl of around ten years dressed in jeans and a polo neck jumper with horizontal stripes of red and navy blue.

A jangle of laughter echoing back again and again.

She closed her eyes to that.

Puja kept her eyes closed even when the mind switched on. She wanted to collect her thoughts before she let the world in. Something hurt in her throat. She eased the furrows on her forehead to continue the deception.

Her head felt heavy like lead. She tried to exercise her mind but only with great effort. She remembered coming into the flat and swallowing the tablets in the bathroom. Then she had staggered back to her bedroom.

Was she still there?

She let her eyelashes partly ajar to let some vision in. The windows had changed. Suddenly her brain resonated with the chime of a clock she knew too well. It was the Big-Ben. She had been admitted to her own hospital.

O' Lord! Kill me now before I die of embarrassment.

She opened her eyes wide open and the light green walls with the dark green curtains of the intensive care came into focus. She now knew the cause of discomfort in her throat. She was connected to a ventilator. Tubes emanated from her body like head of the Medusa. She glanced at the monitors and checked herself out.

Heart rhythm normal, blood pressure lowish, oxygen saturation ninety two percent.

She was doing okay.

The nurse at the foot of her bed was immersed in the observation charts oblivious of the fact that her patients had regained consciousness.

Though the head throbbed and the throat hurt, Puja felt strangely at peace. Like a volcano which had erupted and spewed its lava out and was now cold and empty inside. The treachery and Lennie were still there but somehow transferred to a blind spot that she was aware of but could not see or feel. She was glad to be alive but could not reconcile to the stupidity of her attempt to end it. She had always considered herself to be much smarter than this but perhaps she was wrong. Then she rewinded a bit more and her parents came into focus.

Guilt twinned with that peace now.

The curtains parted and Carol came in.

'How are you feeling, Honey?'

She spread her mouth open around the tube to hint at a smile. She was pleased to see Carol first and not her parents.

'Don't worry, the Anaesthetist should be coming any moment now to take the tube out. You are doing fine now.' Carol sat down and took her hands.

Both friends were silent, their hands clasped together. Carol also had a block in her throat now, in parity with her best friend. They looked at each other eyes searching for themselves. First the bravado, then the giving in. Puja's head between her breasts. Their bodies rocking to stifle the sound. Hugging carefully, not to touch the wires.

The Anaesthetist stepped in. It was Mark, three years her senior in the medical school. She had had a brief crush on him as a medical student after she had spotted his convertible Mercedes. He smiled at her. A condescending smile which mocked her for her stupidity. Puja turned her eyes away.

'You are a lot better today Puja. You had a brief arrest in casualty and had to be shocked out of it and subsequently ventilated.' His hands were already steadying her neck as the nurse took out the pillows from beneath her head. 'Your vitals have been steady for some time and we desperately need your bed.' He eased the tube out gently as the nurse placed an oxygen mask on her face.

Puja coughed at his face as he quickly retreated from her bedside.

'We shall be transferring you to the high dependency unit soon,' said Mark. 'Be prepared to stay in for a couple of more days. Psychs would be giving you a visit sometime today as well.'

Puja interrupted him hastily. 'I do not need to see the Psychs Mark. I am fine, believe me. I do not need to see them.'

'You know the rules Puja. Besides the threat of seeing the psychiatrist again might just deter you from taking any precipitate action in the future.' He disappeared behind the curtains.

Carol diverted her attention.

'You have ruined my blouse,' Carol said. 'I bought it from Harrods.'

'I am not paying for it.' Puja coughed to break the croakiness.

Carol looked at her tenderly. She ran her fingers over Puja's chest lightly to see if she would wince. Just sixteen hours ago she was thumping wildly on that chest when she could not feel a pulse. She had put her lips around Puja's foaming mouth and breathed into her chest through the vomit in her mouth.

'I found you in the flat. You were unconscious and barely breathing.'

Puja had to pause as the shock returned momentarily to block off her words. 'Lennie was cheating for I do not know how long. I caught him red-handed at his flat yesterday.'

Carol registered it with shock and then with anger. 'I would have appreciated if you had attempted to kill him instead of yourself.'

'I had also just walked out of my parent's house to live with him.'

Carol did not say anything, just hugged her tightly again. There was silence as Puja picked up her courage.

'Where are they?' asked Puja.

'Sleeping in the visitor's room. They were by your bedside all night long. I had to force them to go and get some rest.' Carol paused. 'You should have seen them last night Puja. I almost felt angry at you for putting them through all this.'

Puja just looked at Carol but did not say anything. To put into words would have been futile.

Just then Ramesh walked in. As if a few years had rolled into him overnight. He looked tired and older. Gaunt and defeated. The skin under his eyes was leathery and had many more lines. But his eyes lighted up as they met hers. Puja pursed her lips tightly but the lower lip trembled and gave way. Hot tears welled in her eyes.

Ramesh grasped her hands tightly and raised it to his heart. 'Everything will be okay now Beta, everything will be okay.'

She made several attempts to say sorry but broke down before she could complete the sentences. It somehow felt nice to cry and she did so clutching her father's hands and turning her face away.

Ramesh reached out and wiped her tears carefully from her face. His face glowed with relief undeterred by her daughter's tears. He grasped her hands firmly in his own hands. 'You are the most valuable thing I have got in my life. Try snatching it from me again and I shall kill you for that.' He bent forward and hugged her, his lips brushing her eyes to lift them into a smile.

The grapevine of Southall dripped with juicy speculation about Puja's suicidal attempt. The Chauhans were a respected household and often looked upon as a torchbearer of the traditional Indian family values. Now jealousy and curiosity combined to widen the first chinks in the fortress. In the absence of any credible lead there were many rumours, ranging from logical to the ludicrous. Thus she was made to marry in secret to an English boy and a Muslim boy. She was made pregnant and also made to terminate it. Even Ramesh and Savita were made to divorce leading to Puja being stressed. Phones buzzed in the houses of the neighbours trying to share information of any sightings or suspicious activity. It was almost like life in the village back home.

The ladies had more restless nights than their spouses. Mrs. Sharma convulsed in her ignorance and prodded her husband to gather more information. Her daughter even tried to access the medical records in a futile attempt. Family friends tried empathy, sympathy and various other armaments but could not break down the wall of silence. Girish proved to be a true friend. He had not even told his wife, fully knowing her potential for keeping secrets. Slowly people gave up, subscribing in their hearts to one theory that appealed to them most and hoping it was the right one.

The winter thawed soon after the last of the snow and nature adorned newer garments to prepare in earnest for an early spring. The last of the Siberian winds blew the gloom with the clouds and cleared the dead leaves to remove the last hints. The air still had the chill but with a pleasant freshness and the new leaves fluttered with excitement amidst the teasing breeze.

Puja was left untouched by the changing seasons. She tried to draw some sense out of her second lease of life. She was glad that she had lived but was not sure what to live for. She would lie for hours staring at the ceiling trying to solve some unknown arithmetic and always give up in the end. She tried to manipulate logic to mould some sense but always ended in despair. Sleep often came late, usually in the early hours.

Carol visited her regularly. They would sometimes venture out to do some shopping or see a movie but mostly they stayed indoors chatting till the late hours.

'Look at it this way Puja,' Carol told her one day. 'You too had your loin share and had a good time and now that scumbag does not deserve any second of your thoughts.'

It had brought laughter to her eyes. Carol's humour was one of the few positive things she had in her life at that moment.

Puja and her parents stuck together as a family in face of the unseen onslaught unleashed by the friendly neighbourhood. Even grandmother had turned sensible and hidden her quiver of sarcasms. When Puja had told them about Lennie's deceit, she was surprised to see pity instead of vindication on their faces. The first few days were difficult at home. They feigned normalcy until it became real. The hurt had created a crater which they did not try to fill. Instead they built around it. With effort and passion, into a beautiful memorial that stood for their resilience and love for each other. For there is no hurt without love and one can draw strength from both. They acknowledged without acknowledging each other's pain and unspokenly nursed each other's wounds.

Time slowly in its mundane fashion began to heal the wounds while guilt gave birth to a seedling. The cactus often pricked Puja as it grew but that was the only thing that seemed to thrive in her arid life. She reasoned against it, she argued against it but the farcical plant took no heed and continued to grow and grow.

Till one day it burst from inside her.

'Papa,' she told him with no overtones to upset the flat monotone of her voice. 'I want to marry and I want to marry the boy of your choice.'

IX

The town of Sitapur writhed like an eunuch in search of an identity. Though it had been promoted two years ago to a subdivision and hence officially a town, the sceptics argued that it was more due to political patronage than on grounds of merit. The local MLA was also a Cabinet Minister and he had worked hard to get this subdivision status to ensure his re-election. Proximity to the Nepalese border had ensured flourishing cross-border smuggling, which in turn had created a local market larger than the neighbouring District town. Even the hut to house ratio had been usurped in favour of the houses after the dark yellow government houses and offices were completed for the sub-divisional bureaucracy.

But what about the Paddy fields interspersed between the housing estates? What about the daily evening march of cattle on the High street returning from the grazing fields? Well, just bid for time, the modernisers argued. One could already see the cement pillars protruding skywards from amidst the paddy crops. One could hear the mighty tractors at dawn rolling into the fields, not for ploughing but to deliver the bricks, steel and cement. The shiny backs glazing under the sun in the mid-day were not of the farmers but of the builders and the labourers. The traditionalists who argued vociferously in favour of the village identity secretly sold their land as the real estate prices soared. The unstoppable march towards progress had begun. Television had come a few years ago and the arrival of the telephone was almost a certainty. In fact there was already a telephone in the village post-office. But the patience needed to get connected through the antiquated system could often test even the most patient. The additional necessity of bribing the post-master meant that it was seldom used.

Through the centre of the town ran the only metalled road affectionately called the Bazaar road. From the air it resembled a moth eaten shaft of wood, puckered with craters created due to the collective consequences of scandalous construction, cattle hoofs and the bullock carts. Dirt track offsprings divulged from its belly on either sides into the paddy fields and the housing colonies. They changed colours with the weather. In the summer it was dusty, in the rains swampy and in the winters, just bearable. These orphans had been promised a makeover several times in the past. A few inaugural marble plaques erected along the sides were testimony to it. Some had even stone chips laid on them as the first phase. But then the second and third phases always melted as cash in the pockets of the contractors and the Engineers of the Public works department. The stone chips with time in true Christian spirit returned to the dust without trace. On paper the road would have been showed to be constructed and then washed away in the rains. Who could argue against the power of nature.

Historically the Bazaar road had also served to divide sharply the two communities that inhabited the town. The Hindus on the north and the Muslims on the south. But lately that division had been blurring with mixed localities coming up mainly in the south. It had nothing to do with advancing modernity or rising intellect but with the laying of a railway line in the south which brought with it huge commercial advantages. The traders, mainly Hindu Marwaris, flocked to open their warehouses and Godowns. That raised the real estate prices to values as high as those in the north and the Muslims cashed in on the boom forgetting the centuries old animosity. The communal compartmentalisation had scaled down now to streets rather than whole colonies and that is where it had stopped for the last decade. No one was willing to stoop below that.

Harivansh Singh was an exception in the sense that he was not a neo-settler in the south. He, and before him, his forefathers had been living there in the same house for as long the town's history stretched back in anyone's memory. The 'Durbar' as the house was affectionately called was almost hundred and fifty years old and had withstood the test of times though not in a perfect manner. It stood in a vast expanse of land that touched the railway track on one end and kissed the shores of the Bagmati river at the other. The original design was unmistakably Victorian but the latter flat roof extensions had rendered the whole architecture meaningless. Digvijay Singh, his great grand-father, was the Diwan of the local king in the middle of the nineteenth century. He had travelled with his master to England where he was captivated by the houses he saw in the countryside. He and his king were worshippers of the British Raj and he tried to impress them by building the 'Durbar'. When designing the house he had employed an English architect and great care was taken to blend the open verandas and balconies with the Victorian mansions of the Home Counties he had seen in England. He often invited the British officials for organised hunts in the jungles of Nepal and entertained them at his mansion by the shores of the river Bagmati. His descendants however proved less refined in their tastes and concentrated more on building accommodation for the cows and the burgeoning family.

Time had conspired with nature to denude much of its physical glory. Plaster had peeled off in obvious places revealing the differential ages of the bricks behind it. The tiled canopy of the Victorian roof lay unwillingly like a worn out hat, bleached in places where the algae and the moss had spared its tiles. There were cracks in the wall, deep and random as it stood in defiance of the laws of physics. Small plants emerged from the gaps as flag-bearers of optimism. There were feeble attempts at repainting and repairs whenever the funds allowed but the house was simply too big to be maintained adequately in the modern inflationary times by a middle class family. This was one inheritance, Harivansh Singh had cursed all his life.

Still he could not bring himself ever to sell it. To part with the legacy would have been too much to bear. The hosting of the durbar, the assembly of the dancers, the toasts of the English Sahibs. The house had not only given him shelter but pride and respect that went far beyond his status of a simple homeopath Practitioner. People talked about those glorious days as if it were yesterday and bestowed reverence upon him which he accepted without guilt or reservation. A few souvenirs which had survived the auctions and the neglect of the times were displayed unashamedly in the living room to preserve the freshness of those memories. His own roots were as old as the one embedded in the cracked walls of the house. He was born there, grew up there and practised his homeopathy from the little out-house which used to be the stables when keeping horses was affordable.

When his father had died he had inherited five hundred acres of agricultural land. After donating a substantial chunk to the '*Bhoodan*' movement of Vinobha Bhave, he continued to sell land in fear of the Government's land ceiling act and the menace of the Naxalites that was growing in the countryside. He used the money towards the education of his two sons and sent them to English medium private schools. Avinash, the elder son became a doctor, but Bharat his younger one displayed no aptitude or inclination for academics and continued to struggle at every juncture. Harivansh feared that Bharat might end up becoming a farmer and engaged private tuitions along with parental coercion and threats but to no avail. Avinash too tried to inspire his younger brother with his own academic brilliance but when it did not have the desired effect was forced to recourse to less acceptable measures. He had stood under the hot sun on many a day outside the exam centre writing the chits and bribing the officials to pass them over to Bharat. Not that Harivansh Singh approved of such measures but under the circumstances there was no other way to secure a better future for his untalented son. Both son and father maintained a dignified silence to legitimise the underhand tactics and keep the moral head high. Once the Intermediate results came through he sold another large chunk of land to pay for a large donation to get his son admitted in one of the private Engineering colleges in south India.

He still had a hundred and fifty acres of land left and had decided to safeguard it for passing on as inheritance to his two sons. Both his daughters were married now and so the last of his responsibilities were taken care off. Avinash had opened his clinic in Sitapur itself a year ago and was doing reasonably well for a beginner, earning on an average fifteen to twenty thousand rupees a month. But Harivansh Singh had greater plans for him. He wanted his son to go abroad and get a higher degree before settling down in Sitapur. There was only one FRCS in the hundred and twenty odd doctors that practised there and he was minting money. And that was on top of the respect and fame he had earned. The four letter word on the signboard with England in the brackets promised imported clinical care and instilled a faith in the average villager no less than he had for the BBC world news service. He needed no further reassurances. Harivansh had told Avinash that he should be the next one but he had only shrugged and laughed.

But Harivansh Singh continued to plot for his son's departure to England. He had meticulously saved every penny that Avinash had given to his mother every day from his practice earnings. He had also recently written to an old acquaintance who lived in England for help. He was a friend and also in some sense a relative as his sister was married in that friend's village. Their last contact was more than twenty years ago and at the time of writing the letter he had wondered whether such dormant ties could be rekindled. In the end he decided that it was worth a try.

Ramesh Chauhan, as he recalled, was a generous man with the kindest of hearts. If time had served to preserve him as he was when they had met last, he was sure that he would come forward to help him. He had heard about the lust and curse of the foreign lands changing many such innocent souls and had kept his fingers crossed with his eyes rested in the direction of the post office.

That morning as usual he woke up before dawn. Just a few sun rays splintering through the dark skies across the horizon. He tried a few minutes of his '*Sita-Ram*' recitation in a failed attempt to rouse the other family members deep in slumber. His wife, Radha Devi, though would be up and in her kitchen. There were two kitchens in the household. One, exclusively for the vegetarians, which only included her in a strict sense and the other where the sin of cooking meat was permissible. She would get up every morning before the crack of dawn and personally paint her earthen stove with an emulsion of cow dung in water before lighting it up with the wooden logs and coal. The stove in the other kitchen was accorded no such dignity. She would then cook her own food, as anything made by a lower caste servant was unacceptable to her for consumption. If any of her utensils was even touched by a servant by mistake then it had to be purified by water from the holy Ganges before being put to use again. The verbal torrent of abuse and the occasional thrashing of the servant apart.

The trembling bass horn of a diesel train engine signalled that the Janata Express was arriving on time that day by mistake. Harivansh Singh stepped on to the veranda and surveyed the world in front of him. He looked around for any human presence, stretched his arms and noisily let go off some air. The pigeon on the guava tree, startled, took flight in fright. The parrot in the cage tried to mimic the sound and he angrily remonstrated at the caged bird. The air felt crisp and cool on his cheeks. The morning mist hung undecidedly in the air. He drew a deep breath in and the smell from the morning ablutions of his neighbouring slum dwellers hit his nostrils and immediately fouled his mood. The shores of the Bagmati river provided an ideal latrinal retreat for the men and women in the *Basti* and despite numerous protestations by him, the lure of the sandy beaches and plenty of water proved too strong a temptation for his neighbours. A public toilet was erected in the *Basti* by the Rotary club two years ago but it had made little dent into the claustrophobic reservations of the traditionalist to void in nature, a call from nature.

Once Harivansh Singh was so enraged that he got up early one morning, picked up his rifle and fired in the darkness in the general direction of the Offenders. He was cautioned by the District Magistrate later in the day not to repeat his act as the majority of the offenders were Muslims and it could provoke a riot. Till then a fanatic secularist, the first seeds of hatred had been sowed.

He wiped the thoughts disturbing his mood and settled for shallow breaths. He shouted at a servant to announce that he was ready for a bath and then waited for him settling on the cement slab by the Well. The servant rushed inside the house to get his master's clothes, soap and towel. Harivansh began to hum an old Sehgal tune. Old songs always brought the nostalgia of the good old days.

The servant emerged from the house with his clothes and he stopped humming the tune abruptly. The last thing he wanted was his servant gossiping behind his back about his abysmal singing talents. The servant perched the clothes on a wooden bench and began to draw water from the well and then poured it gently over Harivansh Singh's body. The water was cold and made him recoil as it splashed on him. Mohan, his servant, flinched back himself thinking he had erred. Then sensing the lack of any rebuke he summoned his courage back and continued to pour the water over him.

The bass horn, as if a hundred bamboo shoots split apart, signalled the departure of the Janta express after shedding its load of morning hawkers, their baskets filled with fish and vegetables. His own association with the train went back to the days when he was crossing the thresholds of adolescence. But then the Janta express came at a different time. Right in the middle of the noon and then it was mostly on time. It also used to be the lunch recess at his school and he and his friends would be on the railway bridge just a few hundred yards away from the railway station. As the steam engine hissed out of the railway yard they would hold their breath, shivering with the cold and the excitement in their underpants and wait for it gather speed as it approached the bridge. The bridge was only thirty metres long and as the first of the wheels rolled on to it they would jump off the edge with a shrill cry. Floating on their backs, carried under the bridge by the downstream current, they would watch the tiny sparks leap at them from the underbelly of the train only to be extinguished in mid-air. That was the only sport at that time in the village apart from *Kabbadi.*

Through the lather in his eyes and the mist in the air he saw a roundish figure bumping along the dirt track in the general direction of his house. He poured water over his face to clear the soap and squeezed his pupils to ascertain if it belonged to someone other than the Postmaster and concluded against it. The silhouette, the incongruous bolting of thin limbs and an oval head to an expansive torso, was unmistakably his. The flaps of fat pouches hanging unflappably over his groin from the abdomen were testimony to a general rebellion by his fat cells to migrate evenly to other parts of his body. It was a rare disease, he had claimed but most concurred that it was a joke of God. The bribes he took and the extortionate 'reading' fee he charged the illiterates for reading their letters were cited as additional contributory factors.

It was funny to watch the man hurtling towards him but Harivansh Singh was surprised as well. The post would still be lying at the Station after just being unloaded off the Janta express. Why was this man running towards him with such urgency? Unless there was a telegram. But again no one he knew was about to die or wed. He waited with eager anticipation for the man to cover the distance and signalled the servant to begin wiping with the towel.

But Kirpal, the Postman, was running buoyed by nervousness and excitement as something had happened at the post-office that morning which had never happened before in the thirty odd years of his service. He was munching the chickpeas which he had soaked overnight in water with his legs spread comfortably over his office table when the telephone rang. He had stayed immobile in that posture of absolute luxury and waited for the caller to hang up in exasperation. He hated these trunk calls as it usually meant carrying a message to one of the village folks on behalf of the caller. And at this hour of the morning it would be an absolute inconvenience.

But the phone continued to ring and he cursed himself for not taking it off the hook earlier. In good Samaritan spirit he decided to answer if it lasted longer than the four chick peas left on his plate. He lost the battle and picked up the phone.

The crackle at the other end sounded something like 'England' and he froze. He had never received a call from outside the country. There was a female operator at the other end of whom he did not understand a single word. He raised his voice and repeated 'hello' in twenty different ways to camouflage his handicap on a perfectly clear line. The shouting probably did the trick as the operator at the other end connected him to the caller without much further ado after receiving an entire months' quota of 'hello' greetings. Kirpal continued to shout undeterred even when the voice changed to a male one speaking perfect Hindi. This was his day of *Nirvana* after thirty years of a monotonous job that carried little excitement. He had handled a call from England and spoken to a foreign operator. He was now officially a part of the technological revolution. Why should he shut up but the voice at the other end told him to do so and he did exactly so.

'Now listen carefully,' the voice at the other end took full command after the initial confusion, 'My name is Ramesh Chauhan and I am calling from England.' Kirpal stood up from his chair in attention. 'I want you to go to Harivansh's ji house and tell him that I wish to speak to him. If you call him to the Post-office, I shall call back in an hour. Now do you understand?' He spoke as plainly as he could but still was not convinced that the message had gone through.

Kirpal replied with a 'yes' and a string of 'Sirs' and '*Huzoors*' to make up for his earlier stupidity but Ramesh asked him to repeat the message back to him and then finally reassured, hung up the phone.

He was still perspiring after he had put the phone down. Was that woman operator impressed with him? Probably not. But she would be calling again in an hour. He had one hour to inform Harivansh ji and brush up his English. He was determined to be smarter the next time around. His toileting reflexes quickly suppressed on that note he abandoned his morning chores and ran out of the post-office.

Presently Harivansh Singh stood up watching this strange figure emerging from the mist. He encircled his body in the white *Dhoti* and jiggled his lower half to get rid of the wet under-clothing. Kirpal came to a complete halt in front of him but after uttering the word 'England' ran out of breath and began swallowing the atmosphere around while Harivansh Singh stood in suspense. Finally with air replenished in his lungs, he narrated the whole story.

Harivansh felt the wet hairs bristle at the back of his shoulders. His eyes gleamed with joy as his dreams came more sharply into focus. He asked his servant to skip the oiling of his hair and walked briskly into the house to inform his wife of the news. He found her in the kitchen trying to ignite the stove by blowing into the wooden logs which seem to be resisting her repeated attempts. When he told her about the telephone call she failed to share his excitement.

'I don't understand what kind of a father are you. How can you send your son across the seven seas and feel happy about it?'

'Come on,' he retorted. 'He will only go there for a degree and come back to become an even better doctor than he is now.'

'You make it sound so simple. How many have you seen coming back? Your friend has been coming back for the last twenty years? I do not want to lose a son for some foreign degree.'

'*Arre Bhagyawan* if he settles in England,' he joked, 'you can become an English *Memsahib* and wear skirt and blouses like in the movies.'

His words made her flush and she instinctively drew the Sari over her head. 'God has given no control over your mouth. You just blurt out anything that comes to your mind. Go and wait for the phone and I will tell Avinash not to even consider going away from home. You fathers' hearts are made of steel or else you are too dumb to understand a mother's feelings.'

'*Bhagyawan*, Avinash is no longer a small boy tied to his mother's Sari. You have to let your children go sometimes if that is in their best interests. Don't be selfish.'

Radha devi kept her eyes on the floor as they moistened despite the lack of any smoke from the coal and the wood. She knew that though she had the liberty to rave and rant, her words would bear no weight on the final outcome.

Outside Kirpal had recovered much of his breath and composure. Harivansh hastily shoved a ten-rupee note in his hand as tip and asked Kirpal to follow him to the post office. Inside the single room office they waited in silence. The old ceiling fan whirred noisily above without generating much air. Sipping the ginger tea, both men crafted their thoughts and rehearsed their lines. Harivansh could not understand why he felt nervous and chided himself in silence. Should he be informal or more measured to reflect the breadth of the years that had gone by since they had last seen each other?

The phone rang before he could make up his mind.

Kirpal was disappointed as this time the operator was different and male but he carefully substituted his previous 'hellos' with a single 'yes' and quickly handed over the phone to Harivansh Singh.

Ramesh's voice was loud and clear. His voice still had that inaudible halo of laughter that Harivansh remembered so distinctly from twenty years ago. Ramesh switched from Hindi to *Maghi*, their local village dialect and Harivansh was overwhelmed. Ramesh was asking about Radha and the children. He nodded his head and then remembered to speak into the handset. Were the Mango orchards still yielding the same good crop they did twenty years ago? He remembered how they had sat and devoured a whole bucket full of mangoes after a hunting expedition. Harivansh mindful of the phone bill his friend might be incurring kept his enquiries to a minimum but Ramesh was chatting with no haste or urgency. Then the talk turned to Avinash and his practice. Harivansh launched himself in a tirade of praises for his son and the hopes he had nurtured for him. Training in England would give him the boost that would take him to the very top in Sitapur. Ramesh concurred.

Then Ramesh started to talk about his family. The death of his father, Savita and then about Puja. He told him that she too had become a doctor. Harivansh had seen Puja when she was about three or four.

'It only seems like yesterday,' said Harivansh. 'It is hard to imagine she is a big girl now. Have you married her yet?'

There was a pause at the other end. 'Actually Harivansh ji this is one of the main reasons I am calling you today. Do you think Avinash and Puja will make a good couple?'

It was so sudden and unexpected that it knocked all sense out of Harivansh. He sagged down on to the chair, still speechless. Ramesh waited for a few seconds and then broke the silence.

'Harivansh ji this was just a suggestion. If you disagree it will not change anything between us. Avinash can still come to England and do his degree. I just could not think of a better family for my daughter but I shall understand if you have any doubts.'

A guilt wave was already flushing his face red. 'No Ramesh ji, please do not misunderstand. Who would not be privileged to marry into Chaudharys saheb's family. Puja is like a daughter to us but marriage is not a game to be completed in haste. Don't you think that they should see each other first? Times have changed since the days when Parents decided the whole thing.'

Ramesh was relieved. 'I could not agree more. The final decision should be with the children themselves. Harivansh ji we were thinking of coming to India next month if it is all right with you. Puja will come too. The two can meet each other while we reminisce about the good old days.'

Harivansh was overwhelmed with excitement. 'That would be excellent Ramesh ji,' he shouted over the phone. 'It will be the Mango season as well. Radha will be so pleased when she hears about all this.'

They continued to chat about matters more mundane to render a natural end to their conversation and then after exchanging pleasantries bade each other good-byes. With a spring in his steps he almost ran back to his house to share the news with his wife.

That morning Avinash had woken up earlier than anyone else. He had three operations scheduled for that morning and he wanted to start at the crack of the dawn.

It was desirable to finish the operations before the mercury peaked with the late morning sun. The heat and sweat and the anaesthetic often made him nauseous. He had sneaked into the kitchen and helped himself to fresh yoghurt and beaten rice. It was too early an hour for his old Ambassador car to wake up and he had to cajole Mohan to give it a push to bring it to life. He had hated this car ever since he had inherited it from his father. The 1960 engine soaked petrol like a sun-dried sponge and regularly spent its weekends away from home in some garage. It had a mind of its own when to start and when not to and would often stop in its tracks spluttering and coughing. Every part of the car made a noise except the horn, which has been out of order for a long time.

But he had to cling to this car until he had enough money to buy a new one. A Doctor's car parked outside the clinic was an important indicator of one's prosperity and status and was crucial in attracting patients to the practice. Those doctors without a car would often beg the relatives to park their cars instead and would intermittently come out of their consulting chambers and honk the horn to press their lies home.

And then there were the *Dalals*.

He winced at the thought of such people and pressed his foot on the accelerator. He remembered being approached by these men when he was first trying to establish his practice. Spotless *Kurta-Pyjama*, betel leaves in their mouth and the red saliva dripping from the corner of their mouth. They offered to bring patients from the far-flung villages in lieu of a commission. They were the unseen catalysts for all the successful practices in the town, they would claim. This was almost wholly true. Most of the Doctors had indeed compromised their integrity in lust of a quick buck.

But he had chased them out of his clinic. It was more pride than integrity. They had threatened him that he would long for patients without their services and indeed such was the situation for the first few months. But then word began to spread and slowly but surely the trickle became a steady flow.

He drove slowly to land gently in the potholes mindful of the car's suspension and his own vulnerable back. He could see the smoke permeating out of the thatched roofs from the earthen stoves being lit for the day. It was still darkish and he could see shadows disappearing into the Bamboo groves. Women still had shame unlike the men who would defecate in the bright morning with their backs facing each other while they discussed national politics.

The diesel engines of the morning buses to the capital roared by with their passengers dozing off on the rooftops. Only last month one of the passengers was electrocuted by an overhead electric wire. But then he knew men who would travel on the rooftops even when there were seats inside the bus.

Mohan, for instance. He felt suffocated inside, he would say.

He drove on the bridge over the Bagmati river. The early morning devotees were taking the dip in the river with folded hands towards the rising sun. Disrupting their prayers were the laundry men and women with their stacks of clothes banging against the stone benches. As if scaring the dirt away from the fabric. The harder you hit, the cleaner it got. He always panicked when on the bridge. That bridge was intact as a miracle of God rather than a feat of engineering. It made a strange noise, somewhere between creaking and splitting every time any thing heavier than a human being or a buffalo stepped onto it. A noise he could never get used to. This was the only temple Avinash prayed at for a few seconds every day. Buses were banned by decree due to the inherent risks but the alternative route was a long one. A five-rupee bribe was fixed therefore and collected by the traffic policeman who was on duty there to prevent it from happening.

He thanked God again after negotiating the distance and breathed a sigh of relief. He weaved his thoughts around the operations he had that morning. The one he was concerned about was a sixty year old man with cancer of the large bowel. There was extensive involvement apparent on the Barium X-ray and he had initially wanted to refer him to the nearest teaching hospital. But the man had begged to be operated upon by him. It was not faith in Avinash but lack of money that drove him to take the risk. It was simply beyond him to afford the treatment at a bigger centre.

The tyres screeched and he stood on his brakes as he caught the blur of the young lad running across in front of his windscreen. Applause followed from the group of urchins standing by the road as the boy successfully ran across the road without being crushed by his car. It was not the first time it had happened to him and each time it gave Avinash a small heart attack. Once he had got out of the car and ran after one of the boys and had slapped him viscously across his face. The lad had not cried but looked back at him in amazement. Why was he being thrashed in his moment of triumph? That look had revealed a stark truth to Avinash. This was the only spark in that urchin's life. Running at the last moment across a fast approaching car, timing it accurately enough not to be crushed like pulp and that roar of applause from fellow sportsmen. That surge of ecstasy at not dying one more time. In that moment of glory everything abated- their hunger pain, their homeless status, the pain from their regular beatings. Who was he to snatch it away?

From that day on Avinash suffered his heart attacks silently.

His male nurse, Rajaram, was waiting for him at the steps of the clinic. He quickly stepped forward to open the car gate and took charge of the briefcase. Avinash drew in deeply the cool fresh morning air in anticipation of the anaesthetic vapours for the next few hours. A small crowd of three relatives attempted to intercept his way and Rajaram tried to brush them away rudely.

'What is the matter?' asked Avinash.

'Nothing Sir,' said Rajaram. 'This chap is the uncle of the first case. We have already reduced the operation fees by hundred rupees but he is insisting on a further reduction. Says he has got no money but I know he is a liar Sir. He lives in the village next to mine and owns nearly ten acres of land. I have told him he will have to come with the full deposit.'

The eldest of the three whom Rajaram had pointed out as the uncle fell prostrate on the ground forcing Avinash to stop. Embarrassed he asked him to get up but the man stuck to the ground encircling Avinash's feet with both his arms. It was difficult to see if there were any tears in his eyes but he wailed aloud attracting onlookers to arouse sympathy.

'*Huzoor*,' he pleaded, 'I have already sold my land to treat this nephew of mine. His father died fifteen years ago. We spent two thousand rupees with the other doctor and there was no benefit. I have ten stomachs to feed in my family and yet all the money is going in his treatment. I should have left him in an orphanage the day his father had died. I swear *Huzoor* this is the last thousand rupees that I have got. I beg for your pity *Huzoor*.' He was still holding tightly to his feet.

'He is lying Sir,' Rajaram pleaded too. 'He has money to spend every night on the booze in the village but not for treatment.' His income was based on percentage of total earnings and hence any deduction was unwelcome.

This was nothing new for Avinash. No one wanted to pay the full price for the treatment and everyone used poverty as an excuse. His problem was differentiating the genuine ones from the fake and it was not always that straightforward. But this morning he was in no mood for argument. This person was asking for a fifty percent reduction in fees, which was simply not acceptable.

'Charge him two hundred less and that should be the end of this matter,' he delivered his judgement and walked briskly inside his chamber leaving Rajaram to deal with the relatives. Both parties were reasonably satisfied. Rajaram, because his boss was less generous this time and the elderly uncle, as a two minute prostration had saved him two hundred rupees after the impossible haggling with the nurse.

Inside the Anaesthetist was devouring a plate of hot *Samosas* and *Jalebis* after administering the pre-medications to the first patient. Avinash quickly picked up the last *Jalebi* from his plate before it disappeared into the dark caverns of his friend's bulging stomach. Ashok remonstrated and groaned and then resumed munching again to clear his mouthful and regain his speech.

Avinash was quite pleased with his work that morning. The operation on the cancer patient had gone very well. The barium enema x-ray shadows of extensive involvement turned out to be half tumour and half faeces and he was able to resect the cancerous part without much difficulty. By the time he had finished his list for the morning he felt drained both physically and mentally. Hunger added to his misery and he waded through his outpatient consultations with unreasonable haste. It was nearly three in the afternoon when he finally finished and left for home. His car engine pre-warmed by the hot sun did not demand an extra hand to start.

On arriving home he slid into the bathroom for a cold shower. He scrubbed his body hard with the soap to get rid of the smell of salt from his dried sweat and shampooed his hair to undo the gel effect of the summer dust. Freshened, he slipped into the kitchen where the food was already laid out in the steel *Thali* and took it across to the sitting room where he could eat and watch the Cricket Test match on the television. Soon after, his father and mother came in and sat down on the sofa opposite him. He was a bit surprised at their newfound interest in cricket but did not say anything. It was a few minutes later when he found them looking at him rather than the television that he concluded that it was more than an aberration.

'What?' he exclaimed.

They both looked at each other gesturing for the other to make a start but it was his mother who finally spoke.

'We had a very good marriage proposal today.'

'Oh Ma! There is nothing new in that. I have told you that I am not interested in marriage at the moment.'

'You do know Chaudhary saheb from Bishanpur. His son Ramesh phoned from England today. He wants you to take his daughter's hand.'

Mentally Avinash switched on but still maintained a blank expression. 'I do not know Ma, I think we should not rush to any decision.'

'No, I need to rush,' Radha devi raised her voice. 'I am fed up with your delaying tactics. Even if you do not need a wife, we do need a daughter-in-law. And do not think you are still in your teenage years. In a few years time you will be out of the marriageable age band.'

'Wouldn't that be lovely?'

'Yes, and so will be the rumours that the boy either has epilepsy or leprosy.'

This time Harivansh spoke. 'We could not have asked for a better family, son. They are coming next month with their daughter. We are not forcing you into any decision. All we are asking of you is to meet her and the family and then make your decision.'

'Well she is a girl from abroad Ma,' Avinash taunted. 'She might even reject me.'

'Only a fool will reject my son.'

Avinash laughed and focussed his attention on the leg before wicket appeal. He could not concentrate as despite the pretence, a strange excitement began pulsating within his heart.

The photographs arrived two weeks later. There were two of them, both coloured, one in a Sari and the other in a *Salwar-kameez*. There were no stamps of a studio at the back of them. When Harivansh and Radha devi opened the photographs together, they did not utter a word. There were no doubts to air. They had sat in the courtyard on their cane chairs for nearly an hour, with one photograph each, staring at it wordlessly. Radha devi picked her eyes and lips but chose her son's nose and cheeks for her first grandson.

By the time Avinash arrived back from work the photographs had already been circulated amongst the neighbours and relatives and the conventional praises been heaped. Avinash too had a brief look but was not allowed to take it away by the assembled women. So he had carefully copied it on to his mind and crept upstairs cautiously holding his head still. He slowly lay down on the bed and closed his eyes to darken everything except a fluorescent screen. He kept his eyes closed for a few minutes and concentrated hard with the furrows converging on his forehead. When he opened his eyes again, he smiled, clearly elated by what he had seen.

In the evening Radha devi took possession of the photographs and crept up to her bedroom. She opened her steel *Almirah* and unlocked the small safe inside. She put them back in the brown envelope they had come in carefully placing it between the jewellery boxes.

Unlike the tens of other photographs with their horoscopes crammed in a polythene bag behind her Saris.

X

That year spring arrived early treading on the toes of the winter which had been miserably cold and rainy. The seasonals unfurled their sprightly colours in an early bloom and covered the landscape with shimmering beauty. They swayed in the gentle wind under the sunny blue sky and teased the human souls to join them in their ecstacy.

Spring had arrived even earlier in the Chauhan household judging by the shades of happiness and excitement so apparent on their faces. Though Puja had failed to be a part of it. As the tide of guilt receded, the question marks on the sand became more apparent. The sheer absurdity of the notion of getting married to an unknown stranger stared her in her face. She had walked from one mess in her life to another and it had her own footprints all over it.

And yet the happiness and fervour she had unleashed in the family scared her from taking any precipitate action. She tried to drop hints on occasions but subtle expressions were simply not registered in that torrent of euphoria. Grand plans were being weaved about the marriage, the shopping had begun in earnest and the phone bills to India had rocketed through the sky. The winter of sorrow had thawed into an irreversible flow of happiness and Puja could not bring herself to dam that flow.

The walls of the house would have cracked had the news been contained any longer and so one day Savita picked up the phone to Mrs Sharma. That ensured proper dissemination and in came the womenfolk followed by their less inquisitive spouses. An air of festivity began to take root. Puja tried to put some perspective by reminding her parents that the boy could reject her, his family could reject her and also she had the veto power but their optimism would not be reigned in. On occasions when the feminine gender exceeded a minimum number they would spontaneously burst into a folk song and Puja would run upstairs in despair.

Both her friend Carol and her foe Nisha were cross with her. Carol, for she was unable to comprehend her friend's decision and Nisha, for setting up a precedent for arranged marriages.

'Now you will be cited as a shining example in every lecture we get from them,' Nisha had said.

Ramesh had been cautious enough to indicate that the negotiations were still not final but Savita and his mother dropped all such pretences and engaged wilfully in talking up the groom and his family. Harivansh Singh's Haveli assumed palatial dimensions and Avinash's academic record shamed all the past and present son-in-laws of Southall.

Finally the day came when the Photographs arrived. Two of them. One a 'black and white' in a cardboard frame behind which there was a bold stamp of 'Rama Studios' and the other a much smaller, colour photograph with no stamp to take credit for it. The black and white was taken from a closer angle and included only his face and shoulders. His features appeared obviously sharpened by artistic intervention when compared with the colour one. The hairline, the eyelashes, the moustache all placed in perfect symmetry. The valiant attempt to smile somewhat masked by the apparent nervousness of the occasion. The nose was somewhat large but the big dark eyes compensated for it and were indeed the focal point of the photograph. The double chin was only faintly visible but was more prominent in the colour photograph taken from the side. This was a more casual picture of him standing in a garden with a more convincing smile on him. It also divulged the beginning of a bulge at the abdomen. He was much darker than Puja and probably a shade taller.

Having analysed the groom, attention now shifted to the background in the photograph. One could just catch the corner of the house. The archways over the veranda, above which were the terrace rails with their inverted flasks shaped supports. Clean yellow to dirty yellow, enough to have Savita ponder whether to share it with Mrs. Sharma. Vegetation seemed abundant from banyan trees to rose plants and at the bottom right hand corner a bushy tail of what must be a cow. There were no marks of cow dung cakes on the wall despite the presence of a cow much to the relief of Savita. It reflected a certain degree of a modern ethos present within the family.

In her bedroom, alone, Puja had stared hard and long at the photographs. Trying to make them speak, trying to make some sense. And then when no answers came forth, she had wept like a child. Hugging the pillows, scared like a hunted Hare, she let the tears flow. Often when she would be having a bad dream she would let it continue knowing it was a dream and would open her eyes when it became unbearable. This was one nightmare she was trying to shut her eyes to but it would not go away.

In the evening a mini tea-party was hosted to introduce the photographs to some more close friends. Every one praised the looks of the groom irrespective of whether they were impressed or not. There would be a second conference behind their backs for a more critical appraisal. Past and present son-in-laws would be compared. Mrs. Sharma was perturbed after detecting something unusual.

'Are these small pox marks on his face?' she had whispered in her husband's ear.

Nitish had to strain his eyes to detect the two marks on the colour photograph.

'I do not think so darling. Small pox was eradicated before he would have been born.'

'How can you be so sure?' his wife mocked him.

People, throughout the evening in subtle undertones sought to find out about details of the dowry. While Ramesh ignored the oblique references, Savita was playing on inflated figures in the other sitting room where the women had grouped. Somehow perversely a higher dowry reflected upon the status of both the families tying the knot. The truth was that neither of them knew, as it had not figured in their talks till then. Ramesh felt awkward about talking on such matters over the phone but then again he needed to know the amount of money he would have to take to India.

That evening he phoned India and spoke to Harivansh Singh. He told him how everyone had liked the photographs and that Avinash was already becoming a popular son-in-law in England. Having flattered him sufficiently he gently raised the issue of dowry.

There was a stunned silence at the other end for a moment as both men listened to each other's heavy breathing.

'I have not even thought about it,' Harivansh lied at the other end. 'Don't you think it would be appropriate to talk about it after the boy and girl have seen each other.' He and Radha had already discussed the issue. They had taken into account their own family status, their son's qualifications and Ramesh's estimated income as ascribed by a friendly neighbour whose brother too was a doctor in England. Then they had made a minimal allowance for the fact that the girl was professionally qualified. The figure, they had concluded, was slightly inflated but desirable and it would leave ample room to negotiate a notch or two downwards if need be.

'That would have been ideal,' Ramesh was saying, 'but I need to have some idea about the amount I need to bring when coming to India.'

'Around nine to ten *lakhs* for the *Tilak*.' The bombshell dropped with equal emphasis on each word.

Ramesh drew a deep breath in. The shock had knocked out any strength to raise a protest. The initial enthusiasm was erased without trace.

'I shall be honest with you Ramesh ji,' Harivansh was saying, 'I have had much higher offers for Avinash but I was never the one to compromise on my son's life.'

Ramesh had wanted to laugh aloud but checked himself. Suddenly he felt too tired to carry on the conversation any further. After a few pleasantries he hung up.

When Savita heard about the dowry she was furious. 'Have they gone mad or what. They just think that money grows on trees in England and America. Pluck away as much as you want. Our daughter is more qualified than their son. Have they forgotten that?'

'Darling remember we are the bride's side. In our culture that hardly gives us any position to bargain from.'

'But if you give away twenty five thousand pounds in dowry alone how will you manage the marriage expenses, the jewellery, the travel expenses?'

'We will take a small bank loan.'

'As always.'

'As always.'

It was decided to keep this bit of information from Puja. At least till after the wedding. Knowing that money was conditional to her marriage might well be the excuse she might use to back off from the whole thing. Besides the compulsions of the dowry system would escape her comprehension, they told themselves.

Finally the flights were booked and a departure date finalised. The very next day Puja went to St. Thomas's to submit her resignation. Professor

Camm eyes were riveted on the piece of paper long after he had finished reading it. He had nurtured Puja from her student days as his personal disciple. He liked her as a person. There was this cool professionalism within that cloak of a vulnerable personality that made her, in his eyes, so human and full of life. He had endured her tantrums on a regular basis for a long time before chastising himself for a delayed diagnosis of premenstrual tension. But those three weeks of black humour that preceded it made him look forward to his weekly ward rounds with Puja. Deep down he knew that she would make a great physician some day.

'You do know Puja that you are taking the wrong decision.'

'Yes Prof I know that but I am not spoilt for choices either. Besides I might need to stay in India for a few months before my husband comes over to England.'

His eyes were still fixed on her resignation letter.

'What is this nonsense about arranged marriage?' Professor Camm raised his head. 'I thought you were much smarter than this.'

'I too had thought the same Prof.' Puja smiled.

He waited for her to speak more but there was silence.

'Do you want me to speak to Dr. Chauhan?'

'Thanks Prof, I do not think that would be necessary. This was my own decision and my parents did not apply any pressure whatsoever.'

Professor Camm looked unconvinced. He softened his tone.

'I do not wish to delve in your personal life Puja but I am vaguely aware of the background leading to this. This is life. Of lows and highs. People get betrayed, people get let down. But is it wise to let that one incident in life ruin not only an excellent career which beckons you but a wonderful whole life which you most certainly deserve.'

She felt a surge behind her eyes. They had never been at such a personal level before.

'Prof I cannot even begin to thank you for....'

'Cut it Puja,' he raised his hand dismissively. 'We have known each other long enough to spare the thank-yous'. I will have to accept your resignation, albeit reluctantly, but I would urge you to think over it again. When and if you do come back there should be a job for you if I am still around. Now if you will excuse me I have a medical board meeting to attend.'

'Thank you Prof,' she turned to go as the professor stood up but his final words arrested her feet.

'I know that it is not exactly tradition but may I have a hug before we part.'

She ran to him like a long lost child.

She did the countdown from thereon with remarkable nonchalance. She would wake up each morning and then wait for the day to pass by till darkness descended again. The stillness of time in equilibrium with the blankness of her emotions as life passed by.

But life is too endearing to endure such suffering for long. Darkness beyond a point gets scared of its own darkness and seeks light in sheer exasperation. This is human nature which confers upon us a remarkable ability to comeback against the most adverse circumstances. A pleasant curiosity tickled the fear. Sadness got illuminated with a few flickers of excitement. Despair gave way to hope. She clutched on to that hope and just hoped for the best.

Carol had stood by her in those testing times like a true friend. There was no one else Puja could have turned to and Carol was there for her whenever she needed her support or counsel. When Puja first showed her the photographs, Carol looked at it intently for a few moments. Then she tried to see it from Puja's eyes. She could not better it. She looked up to see Puja smiling at her discomfiture and then both of them said spontaneously, 'it is the heart that matters.'

'Look at my Pete,' Carol added. 'All heart no looks.'

'He is not too bad,' said Puja. 'He has got a nice bum.'

'I do like men with moustaches. My father had one.'

Puja insisted that she come to the wedding in India. Carol was flattered by the invitation but had her own reservations.

'Puja, I shall be a total misfit out there and will end up looking like a fool. I do not know your folks, your ceremonies, your customs.'

'It is time you broadened your knowledge about the different cultures in this world. Besides I do not know my folks, my ceremonies, my customs and I am the one who is getting married. You are just a bystander.'

'You are an idiot, I am not.'

'Carol I need you there to go through all this. Treat this as a vacation. Visit the places after the wedding. There is so much to see in India. It is a tourist Mecca.'

Carol could not bring herself to decline the invitation. When Ramesh heard about the plans he too was apprehensive. A single white girl in the midst of village folks was sure to attract unwelcome attention. But Puja was adamant and he did not put forward his case. However he insisted on paying her fare and after some initial reluctance Carol agreed to it. It was decided that she would fly in a week before the marriage date, which was yet to be finalised.

That lifted Puja's spirit enormously. The nascent recovery took some giant strides. Her dormant instincts of shopping and spending resurged back and she took great interest in choosing her wedding dress and the jewellery. She was in peels of laughter at the shocked expression on Carol's face staring at herself in the mirror after having tried on a *Lehanga-choli* for the wedding day at one of the shops. Carol pleaded permission for a formal black dress but the new clothes were thrust upon her.

'When in Rome, dress like a Roman,' Puja said laughingly.

The night before departure, Puja, Carol and a few friends went out clubbing for what was to be the official Hen's night. They were all in a rampaging mood and drank heavily and danced wildly. For those few hours Puja was able to snatch back her present from her recent past and the future and enjoy every second of it.

It is amazing what alcohol can sometimes do.

XI

Puja first thought it was the heat from the plane engine but when the prickly warmth persisted and chapped her clothes tight onto her skin she knew it was the weather. The sun burnt her skin, melted her make-up, which along with the sweat drifted down in a trickle. For some reason the chutes at the airport had malfunctioned and they had to alight onto the tarmac to make their way to the airport building.

'This is the national sauna service provided free to the rich and poor,' Ramesh whispered into her ears as she almost ran to cover the distance.

Inside the air-conditioning in the lounge whirred noisily protesting against the amount of work it had to do. So did the pedestal fans strewn at random in the hall and she stood in front of one of them to get some relief. Her parents though joined an elongating queue at the immigration desk and asked her to join them.

The person at the immigration desk must have been in his forties and was obviously born in the era of small pox, the marks of which had extended on to his triple chin. The bald patch at the occiput was making fresh inroads to the front and the sides in a random manner. He had dense hair though protruding from both his earlobes which he had carefully combed in a perfect horizontal plane. The expression on his face could be construed either as depression or boredom.

He looked at her and then at the photograph in the passport, yawned, and then looked up at her again and then again at the photograph. He could not make up his mind and decided to give her the benefit of doubt.

'Business or personal,' he raised his eyebrows in a questioning manner without raising his eyes.

'What?' Puja snapped under the added pressure of his sheer looks.

'Purpose of visit?' he raised his eyes too on this occasion.

'Both.'

'What?'

'The business is to get married and as you can appreciate it is a very personal matter.'

The man woke up, gave her a startled look and quickly stamped her passport.

They waited in the arrival lounge for their luggage to arrive. The conveyor belt was switched on to raise hopes during the tortuous wait. Everyone had their gaze fixed in anticipation at the tiny hole in the wall till the eyes began to hurt and the mind began to despair. A few irate words were flung at the airport officials in frustration who looked on bemused with fixed smiles on their faces. A single suitcase emerged and did the rounds for the next couple of minutes with no one claiming it from the waiting passengers.

'I bet this is a plant just to calm us down,' one of the passengers shouted.

There was a ripple of laughter and a few faces turned crimson with shuffling of the feet and change of hand positions from the trouser pockets to the hips or vice-versa. But they did not move and the smiles remained pasted. A few more grunts followed and a few trolleys were pushed around in protest but then the wait again relapsed into silence.

It was nearly three quarters of an hour when the luggage belt suddenly creaked to a halt, drew some abuse from the crowd, and then stuttered again on its journey but this time with the baggage. The crowd burst into applause and whistles and the officials joined the celebration to disguise their embarrassment. The tide then flowed hastily through the green channel with the customs giving them all a clean chit in compensation.

Outside Puja got her first glimpse of the teeming millions. England ended suddenly at the 'Exit' door. A wave of humanity surged forward as the few constables tried to push them back with their batons held horizontally in both hands. Curious onlookers outnumbered the people who had turned up to collect their relatives and friends. She felt her stomach churn as she was flung into the crowd. Tyres screeched, horns blared, cab drivers tugged at the bodies and the belongings to lure the passengers into their cabs. Visitors were waving one arm once they spotted their loved ones and flinging the other arm in a kind of a swimming action to ward off the hawkers and wade through the crowd to reach them.

'What is the emergency?' Puja shouted over a few shoulders to her dad.

'Wait till you see one.'

Suddenly there was a hissing sound from within the crowd. Normally she would have survived the onslaught but the intense heat, the sweat, the claustrophobia conspired against her and as the pungent odour hit her nostrils, her head began to swim and her legs turned jelly. Ramesh caught her before she hit the floor. The crowd compressed at the edges to create space in the middle. Savita started waving her flight magazine furiously in front of her face and Ramesh sprinkled the remains from the mineral water bottle on her face. People stopped moving to satiate their curiosity and different diagnoses of epileptic attack, simple faint, heat exhaustion began to be whispered. The fartist too had stopped and was looking on innocently.

Puja recovered quickly as the effect wore off and stood up embarrassingly trying to avoid the converging eyes of the crowd. She was the only one who had gone down. She clearly lacked the great Indian spirit.

Meanwhile the space closed again like a batting eyelid and the general push and shove drifted them towards the outer ramparts. It was Ramesh who spotted Bacchan first around fifty yards away and looking in a complete opposite direction. He yelled at the top of his voice to no response. Finally a few shouts later he did manage to reach his ears over the din of the car horns and the general commotion. Bacchan leapt forward to touch their feet and then looked at Puja with amazement.

'My God! She has grown up fast. Do you remember me at all young one? This Chacha used to take you for a swim in the river when you last came here.'

'Of course I do,' she lied without hesitation as she bent forward to touch his feet.

Bacchan touched her forehead lightly and gave her a blessing. 'You do not need to touch my feet Puja. When children grow up they become more like friends.'

'How is everyone in the village?' asked Savita.

'Everyone is well Bhabhi. Everyone is waiting eagerly to see you all again. But this time it is Puja who is the VIP not you two.'

'I bet she is. It is nearly twenty years since she last came.'

Puja felt uncomfortable rather than flattered.

Bacchan went away to get a cab while they collected their luggage in one place. Soon a car screeched to a halt in front of them and Bacchan alighted from it. It was distastefully painted with the body in black while the hump of a roof was coloured in yellow. The Sikh driver opened the boot which looked woefully inadequate for the amount of luggage they had. Ramesh suggested they take a second cab but the tall Sikh quickly dismissed his suggestion.

'This old woman can take more than that *Saabji*."

He opened the front door and produced a long nylon rope from beneath his seat. This he presently wrapped around his neck as he took the first three suitcases and fitted them in the boot. The boot refused to close and he sat on it to produce some compression. The Samsonites lived up to their reputation and refused to buckle under pressure. The lid still wouldn't shut down. Exasperated he drew out a knife and the startled Chauhans withdrew a few steps. He cut around two feet of the rope still hanging from his neck and tied it round and round the handle of the boot lid, which still gaped with it contents visible, and the steel bumper at the back. The next two suitcases landed with a thud on the roof and the purpose of the rope became more apparent now. The two large airbags were sandwiched between the front and the back seat on the floor so that one had the option of sitting either with their legs spread apart, which reminded Puja of the pelvic exam posture or with one's feet on top of the bags gently crushing their contents. The vanity cases were thoughtfully spared a seat between the driver and the front passenger. With his job accomplished, he stepped back rubbing his hands in satisfaction and looked towards his customers for some well deserved appreciation.

'This is art,' Puja mumbled to her father.

'Think what he could have achieved with a little bit of education,' replied Ramesh. 'Don't worry this will last only twenty minutes of your life. Get in and get over it as soon as you can without further grumbling.'

The old woman, fully pregnant with its contents, lumbered precariously out of the terminal building.

They raced through agricultural land and then through some half built housing estates as they reached the outskirts of the city. The hot breeze removed the sweat from the faces and coated it with dust, which rose in miniature whirlwinds at the edges of the road. As they reached the centre of the town the blaring of car horns rose in crescendo to a maddening cacophony. The smoke spewing from the Auto rickshaws coloured the air and the faces took another coating, this time of soot, which blackened the clothes as well. The cocktail of heat, dust, smoke in rhythm with the howling car horns whipped up such frenzy that Puja was momentarily scared for her life. She shut her eyes and tried to remember the tranquil serenity of her English countryside.

Once in the hotel, she ran into the lobby and sprawled on the sofa letting the air-conditioning sap away her misery. It was only after having a cold shower that she felt human again.

The tropical siesta urge and the jet lag inflicted a deep slumber that lasted the whole afternoon. When Puja woke up it was nearly dark with the sun struggling with the last few rays it had in its quiver. She looked down from her twenty-first floor room's window. In the light of the twilight she could see the dark cars with their headlights on weaving through a lattice of greenery and concrete. Dots moving at a tardier pace. It certainly looked greener than London. The noise seemed to have died down. At that moment her mother stepped in and asked her whether she wanted to go out to do some shopping. Puja opened the window and extended her arm out to feel the air. It felt cooler and breezier and a shaft of air pleasantly brushed her face.

'Yes,' she said.

They went to Karolbagh, which was crowded with her own species in such large numbers that she started to feel faint again. She clung to her Mother's arm who dragged her expertly with intermittent mumblings of 'give way, ladies!' Once inside the shop it felt far more comfortable and spacious. It was a different experience from her London crusades as they settled comfortably on the sofa and the shopkeeper displayed his wares whilst giving a running commentary. Savita selected a Banarasi Sari and asked for the price.

'Six thousand and seven hundred Madam.'

Savita moved her lips but the audible words came from Bacchan. 'I would not give more than five and a half thousand.'

The shopkeeper turned his attention to him cleverly hiding his irritation. 'This is a pure Banarsi sir and the embroidery is in gold threads.'

'Oh come on,' challenged Bacchan, 'no one uses gold threads any more. It is just gold polish.'

'I swear by my mother, sir.'

'Good luck with your mother but I still would not give more than five and a half thousand.'

With his mother cremated a few years ago, the shopkeeper did not feel dejected by the comment. In the past it had worked often with other customers. He turned his attention to the less demanding customer.

' Madame, you are one of my last customers tonight. As it a bad omen to let you go empty handed, I am willing to sell this at six and a half thousand.'

Savita looked at Bacchan for guidance. She clearly liked the sari.

'Five thousand and six hundred is the most I would give,' said Bacchan.

'Come on Madame,' the shopkeeper urged, 'What difference a few hundred rupees would make in Pounds or Dollars. I bet it costs more to have your hair done where you live.'

That ruffled Savita completely. 'How did you know that we lived abroad?'

'You still have the hand baggage tag on your purse.'

She scrambled to take the tag off but she could not, instead she covered it with her hands. It was not the Pounds but the principle. The pleasure of haggling, the delight of getting a discount which someone else could not have extracted.

'We live here. We were just visiting abroad.' She transferred the ball back to Bacchan's court.

'Okay I won't take any profit on it. Six thousand and three hundred.'

'Five thousand and seven hundred.'

'Do you expect me to sell at a loss?'

'You will never sell at a loss.'

'Six thousand and one hundred and that is the final price I can sell at.'

'Five thousand and eight hundred.'

'No that is impossible.'

'We are going then.'

'Let us settle on a round figure. Six thousand.'

'Fifty-eight hundred.'

'I can't.' There was an emotional appeal in his eyes.

'Let us go Bhabhi.'

The shopkeeper drew a deep breath in and held it while he thought. Then he let it go accompanied by a sigh.

'Okay Madame, in the name of God I shall accept that price.'

He packed the sari while Savita counted the money. The shopkeeper handed her the package and made a last request. 'Next time you come Madame please do not bring this gentleman with you. He drives such a hard bargain that I shall go bankrupt in a month.'

Savita laughed aloud. 'I promise, I won't.'

The flight to Patna was uneventful and lasted for just over an hour. Puja tried to get a feel of the new country from her window seat but the clouds often came in the way. The countryside appeared less uniform and patterned than back in England and she could see a meandering river coming in and out of her sight. As they approached their destination the clouds below coalesced in unity. The plane skidded over its belly for a few minutes before dipping to explore into it. When they emerged below the clouds it was raining heavily. Their plane landed without problems but they had to stay inside till the rain stopped. Once the mighty downpour diminished to a drizzle, they made their way hastily towards the terminal building.

Outside her mother's elder brother, PremShanker, had come to receive them along with his wife. They rushed forward to greet their guests with tears and hugs. Hugging was purely gender based with merely a folding of the hands to acknowledge the opposite sex. Puja waited at a distance, awed somewhat by this free flow of intimacy, for them to disentangle so that she could touch their feet. Now attention turned towards her and she trembled slightly with concealed nervousness under their gaze of amazement.

'My God she has grown up so fast,' said Premshanker.' Only yesterday she was running around in her frilly frocks.'

'And grown up to be so beautiful as well.' His wife said clutching Puja's hand and dragging her towards herself to give Puja her share of a hug.

In the ensuing embarrassment she forgot to touch their feet and was later to be reprimanded by her father before going to bed.

Presently they sat in the car and proceeded towards her uncle's residence. Ramesh's mood changed instantly in his now familiar surroundings. That calm grave veneer peeled off without trace and he was like an excited child chatting animatedly, laughing at the silliest of humour and every so often poking his head out of the car window to point out unimpressive landmarks from his impressive memorabilia. In the limited space of the front seat both the bodies of her father and her uncle contracted and expanded and swung unpredictably with each spasm of laughter displacing the third person, the poor driver of the Ambassador car. He uncomplainingly shrunk towards the car door with his hands clutching at the steering wheel at an extremely acute angle and his legs stretching to reach to the foot clutch. The poor man dare not grumble. In the back Puja was a wall of silence between the two ladies who leaned forward constantly to direct their voices.

Meanwhile the town contracted continually upon them. The open airport had emptied into a wide road lined by trees and tall government buildings. As they drove further the trees disappeared, the buildings began to shorten and the road narrowed. The traffic increased but the road continued to narrow, broken in places and sometimes disappearing altogether. The congestion increased. The non-living traffic slowed to catch up with the living traffic, which swarmed between the cars, the buses and the auto-rickshaws in the forms of human beings, cows, dogs and even pigs. The distinction between the road and the pavement was lost and the pale yellow structures housing the shops converged upon them.

Then in a gesture to symbolise the triumph of man over machine everything ground to a halt except the pedestrians snaking through the standing vehicles. The rising mercury gave rise to rising tempers. One of the occupants of the car junta got out and started shouting abuse to the masses in general. Since it was directed at no one, no one took offence and the stalemate continued. Another occupant stepped out and converted into a traffic policeman. He produced a magic stick and began directing the cars into different directions. The drivers obeyed and momentarily there was some movement till it dawned on everyone that he was only interested in getting his car out from the jam. They all fell back in their original formations. Then a genuine traffic policeman appeared with a whistle and a stick. He appeared genuinely confused too. He surveyed the jam in front of him, appearing to be thinking, blowing soft whistles as he exhaled through it. Then all of a sudden as if stung by 'Eureka' he pounced upon a Rickshaw-puller and started abusing and hitting him, blaming him for all the evils. He had to be seen to be punishing someone for the jam. The rickshaw-puller begged for mercy but to no avail. A crowd flocked to see the *Tamasha.*

Meanwhile quite a few passengers baking in their steel ovens decided they had had enough. Premshanker was one of the first to get out. They made eye contact and proceeded unanimously towards the policeman. One portly gentleman dressed in a safari suit ripped the policeman away from the Rickshaw-puller and berated him loudly. The policeman was stunned by this verbal abuse in front of the crowd. He glanced over his shoulders and saw a few well-dressed men standing behind him. He was unsure about their official status but the sheer fact that they had the guts to shout at him in public rang alarm bells in his mind. A wrong move could lead to his suspension. He withdrew with his head hung down and began his job of dispersing the traffic. In the next few minutes the traffic resumed its former snail pace.

The road shrunk further as it entered the residential areas. Huge chunks were gnawed out of its belly creating craters upon which the car jolted merrily unaware of the discomfiture of its occupants. Open drains ran parallel to it straddled by small shacks, which sold goods from Betel leaves to bicycle spare parts and repair shops. The housing panorama extended from the freshly painted to the weather-bleached yellows and the yet unplastered. The pavement was conquered by the vegetable hawkers and the meat sellers, who displayed their slaughtered goats hung upside down on iron hooks attracting flies and customers alike. The open-air supermarket buzzed alive with the advertising chants of the vendors and the honking horns of the cars trying to reclaim its lost road. Once off the main road both the bazaar and the road itself disappeared.

'The monsoon swept it away,' Premshanker was explaining as the car turned onto a flat track of land that once proudly was a metalled road. 'The present government has neither the will nor the money to repair any of the roads. Last year boats came out in the colony because the drainage packed up during the monsoon season.'

To Puja it felt like a trip back from the Promised Land. She was trying to absorb all this with deep inhalations followed by prolonged expiratory sighs. Savita nudged her to breathe normally to avoid offending the hosts.

They finally stopped in front of a house. A large two-storey structure almost bulging over the road with its name boldly inscribed in gold on a black marble slab by the side of the gate.

ASHIYANA.

The driver pressed on the car horn to announce their arrival and a crowd of strangers rushed out from behind the front door of the house. They milled around the car, slightly confused and then formed a proper queue to touch Ramesh and Savita's feet. Ramesh and Savita, overwhelmed by the numbers sprinkled their blessings without being even sure about their identities. Premshanker began introducing them one by one and then Ramesh would go hugging them individually once he realised they were all offshoots of his larger family tree and a mere initial wave of his hand would not suffice.

Puja felt a tug at her side and turned to face her mother.

'Bhabhi's mother lives here,' her mother whispered. 'Be sure to touch her feet. And call Premshanker and Bhabhi, mama and mami.'

'Got it Mom.'

She felt another tug and this time she turned to face a smiling girl in her early twenties dressed in a plain white salwaar-Kameez.

'Hi, I am Rama. One of your twenty-three cousins that you will be meeting over the next few weeks. But believe me, one of the most mature and sane of the lot.'

Puja smiled broadly. It was a relief to meet some one from her own age group at last. Besides she appeared to speak fluent English.

'I am Puja and it is so nice to meet you.' She leaned forward to brush her cheek.

The small crowd followed the guests into the house. The town ended abruptly at the door as the luxurious expanse of the interior struck a familiar chord, belying its impression from the outside. Ramesh sprawled onto a sofa while Savita went inside to meet a few other members of the family. Puja settled on a leather chair and inspected herself on the wall mirror in front of her. A curious expression of awkwardness, dumbness and nervousness. She tried to adjust it in vain. The smirk remained securely glued.

An old woman walked in and Puja promptly got up and touched her feet.

Everyone laughed.

'She is our maidservant,' explained Rama trying to suppress her giggle.

Puja by now thoroughly embarrassed looked for her familiar escape territory. Once inside the bathroom she let out a deep breath. She sat down on the marble floor with her back against the wall, closed her eyes and tried to blank out the past few days.

What was she doing here sitting on the floor in a bathroom with closed doors, seven thousand miles away from home? Was this just a dream that has gone on a bit longer? The last few days had rolled on like reels from a movie and she a spectator but now that distinction seemed to have gone and so had the fiction from the truth. She was actually in India to enter into an arranged marriage with a complete stranger.

But she could still wake up. She pinched herself hard and let a shrill cry out.

She got up after a few minutes and washed the tears out of her eyes and put on a light make-up. She practised the words 'mama' and 'mami' a few times till the anglophile accent came off it and adjusted her *Dupatta* to cover the cleavage of her breasts. She drew another deep breath in and then walked out on to foreign soil once more.

She caught a glimpse of her cousins peeping through the door but she chose to ignore them. The lead on her eyes was beginning to bear down and as the cool draft of the whirring air-conditioner hit her face, sleep overwhelmed her instantly.

She dreamt she was driving through Trafalgar square. There was barely any traffic. Clutching the steering wheel she concluded that she must be dreaming. Driving towards the suburbs she was surprised to see that most of the houses had flat roofs. Only the posh houses had the slanting tiled roofs. Most of them were painted yellow. She never seemed to have come to this part of London. There were fewer white people, almost no blacks and lots of Asians. There was an open drainage in one place. She searched desperately for more English people but could only see a few. It was definitely not Southall. She saw her grandmother on the street pavement chatting to a white woman with shopping bags hanging in her hands. Puja waved to get her attention but grandma remained oblivious. Then all of a sudden the slums started. White men and women dressed in Indian clothes going about their normal chores. She saw her father with his medicine bag walking towards one of the huts. It said 'London' on one of the signboards hanging over a shop.

It just did not make any sense.

She opened her eyes.

The earth had rotated away from the sun since she had fallen asleep and she was startled by the darkness when she opened her eyes. There was a low intensity buzzing around her which she could not understand until it stung her on the face. She slapped herself reflexively and killed the offending mosquito in one stroke. Her own freshly drawn blood, squeezed out of the dead mosquito, smeared her cheek. She ran outside in fear and disgust to search for another human soul but was met with only silence and darkness.

Where was everyone?

A dimly lit bulb illuminated the corridor but none of the other lights were switched on. Silence hung in the dark stillness of the air as she concentrated her senses to detect any signs of life. She began to hear faint voices and she tiptoed towards the sound with some sense of relief. It led her to the stairs and then up till she emerged on the roof.

And there was everybody.

Her father and mother were at one end of the roof with mama and mami and another gentleman. They were sitting on cane chairs with a cane table in the middle on top of which a duty free whiskey bottle stood elegantly in place. On the far end there were mattresses spread on the ground covered with white cotton sheets and stacks of pillows. Rama was in that corner chatting animatedly with the other children on some topic, which appeared to provoke both disagreements and laughter. Darkness had largely engulfed the horizon with the last tinge of orange fading into it. The hot dry air of the afternoon had blossomed in a gentle cool breeze which felt pleasant on the face. She looked at the dense cluster of rooftops around her which had come alive with its inhabitants. They were lying, sitting, chatting, pacing or simply gazing at the stars. The last of the kites which had survived the sky battles were being brought back to the roofs. The birds were also bolder singing at the top of their voices.

She stood hesitantly at the entrance when mami caught sight of her and asked her to join them. The tall burly gentleman who must be in his fifties rose to acknowledge her.

'Meet my neighbour. Retired Major Ranbir singh,' Premshanker started the introductions. 'Retired early as he could not stand the sound of gunfire.'

'Do not listen to this corrupt civilian, *Beti*,' he courteously shook her hands and offered her a chair. 'If only everyone was as honest as an army man your father would not have to leave his own country.'

Everyone laughed and so did Puja without grasping the exact humour. English humour was definitely different.

Mami was telling everyone about the experiences of Ramesh's mother who had flown in two weeks earlier.

'Oh Babuni, she would say, they are so poor in that country. They do not have enough clothes to cover their bodies. Government employees look after the old people instead of their children. And the younger ones shake hands with their uncles and aunties. When they dance on television it appears as if they are having a fit.'

Everyone laughed again. Ramesh's mother was a famous for her caustic sarcasms in her village and her victims would try their best to stay away from her as sometimes she would combine that with a foul temper to devastating effect. At times, Ramesh was recounting, he could remember his mother armed with a broomstick, shouting over a neighbour's fence till his father came over and calmed her down. Few people spoke back to her because of her husband's status. But as the years advanced her heart softened with her bones and skin. She became much kinder and would go out of her way to help other people. Religion and menopause took the sting out of her sharp tongue. Women from the village began to flock back to her house to endure her lectures on God and Hinduism and take a share of the daily offerings of sweets and nuts made to the Gods at her morning worship.

Ranbir Singh changed the topic and asked Puja about her impressions of the new country since her arrival.

Puja held her breath back momentarily to prevent an outpour. 'I am still to form one but so far it has been good.' She avoided committing blasphemy with effort.

'Don't form an opinion very soon *Beti*. The complexities of this country unravels in layers, the worst' strike at you first. There is lot more that is good. Unseen and subtle, felt with time. Just give it some time.'

Rama tugged her from behind and asked her to join them. The younger cousins were shyly huddled at one corner of the mattresses as she approached them. On her approach everyone stood up. Puja asked them to sit down.

'All day they have been waiting to be introduced to their foreign *didi*,' Rama was saying, 'they tiptoed several times in your bedroom while you were asleep. And what's more they all speak English and go to English medium schools.'

The formal introductions began with her Indian cousins. Chintu was six and youngest of the five present and Babli at twelve was the eldest. Rajeev at eight, was a keen cricketer and had already made up his mind to settle in America. Then there was Sweety, age ten, who was always top in her class and wanted to be a scientist. Pinku was eleven and boasted of having a girlfriend. Rama then tried to explain the family tree to place the five offshoots in the right perspective but Puja simply failed to grasp the intricacies and merely nodded.

An awkward silence followed as they all settled down on the mattresses. The cousins glanced at each other sheepishly and prodded each other to say something. They were visibly nervous and trying their best to hide it. Rama began to gently massage Puja's legs and she protested but Rama dismissed her with a wave of her hand. The night swallowed the crimson at the edge of the horizon and the breeze became gentler and cooler. Puja finally broke the silence.

'So Pinku tell me about your girlfriend.'

'Oh *Didi* do not listen to him,' Sweety replied instead of Pinku. ' He is only trying to boast about how smart he is. I go to the same school as him and I can tell you not a single girl even glances in his direction. And do you know he is the only boy in the school who has a comb in his bag and he keeps doing his hair in the toilets.'

Pinku was visibly embarrassed and retaliated immediately. '*Didi* they are all jealous of me and they all want to know the name of my girlfriend. That is why they keep teasing me.'

'Imaginary girl, imaginary name.'

'Is England better or America Didi?' Rajeev asked.

'England, of course.'

'But Papa says that America is much bigger and richer.'

'But they do not play cricket there.'

'Oh damn.'

'What is wrong with India?'

'It is so boring here. So dirty. There are no video-game Parlours here in Patna.'

'I listen to Michael Jackson didi. Have you heard him?' asked Chintu.

'He is good isn't he?'

'Chintu tries to dance like him and one day he sprained his ankle. Uncle had to take him to the doctor,' said Sweety.

'Would you like to come with us to the ice-cream parlour tomorrow?'

'I would love to.'

'Will you pay?'

'Shut up Chintu,' shouted Rama.

'Yes I will but only if you show me your town tomorrow.'

'She is not a miser like you Rama didi.'

'It has been a long time since I have thrashed you Chintu. You are almost missing it.'

'We always talked about you,' Babli finally opened her mouth. 'Mummy always quotes your name when we do not study. She says that we should work hard to become a doctor like you.'

'I am sure you won't have any problems.'

Dinner was served on the roof by the servants. The children soon went to sleep weighed down by exhaustion of an exciting day and a sumptuous meal. They sprawled themselves in zigzag lines on the roof itself and a mosquito net was hung over them attached by thin ropes to every pole and chimney shaft available on the roof. Rama urged her to sleep on the roof that night and she could not resist the temptation. They chatted late into the night. Long after Rama was fast asleep snoring safely by her side she lay there, her eyes wide open, staring at her new starry sky with its halogen moon covering this; her whole new world.

XII

There were rumblings alike in the clouds and Harivansh Singh's stomach. His constipation had flared up again after a row with his wife. He cursed his belching which interrupted his train of thoughts. Ramesh had been phoning him for the last few days in an effort to arrange a meeting for the two families. Harivansh had invited Ramesh to come to Sitapur which he had graciously accepted. But now Radha devi kicked up a storm which upset every plan.

She had recoiled in horror when he disclosed that the Chauhans were coming to Sitapur.

'Have you lost your mind,' she had shouted. 'How can a girl step in her in-law's place before marriage? You have forgotten your own culture in this quest to marry abroad.'

Harivansh had not thought of that at the time but refused to admit it to her. 'They can stay in a hotel here, can't they? The whole of Sitapur is not your private property.'

But Radha devi was not relenting. She quoted her ancestors, scripts from the *Ramayana* and his own mother to insist that the sky, the air, the soil and all the people of Sitapur fell under the category of *Sasural* or the bride's in-laws country. She kept rolling the pancakes in the kitchen and arguing at the top of her voice long after Harivansh had left the *Aangan* to sit in the front veranda.

He decided to seek advice from Pramod, his wife's brother, who had been especially summoned to facilitate the negotiation process. Usually in a village there is one person who distinguishes himself in fixing matches and Pramod had rightly inherited that title over the past few years. He had time and talent and enjoyed the attention from both sides; both in flattery and the culinary bonuses that came with it. His own father had noted the absence of any other talent early on and had toiled hard to accumulate two hundred acres of land which he passed on to his son after his death. Since then he had managed to feed his family by piece-meal selling off the land and sub-contracting the rest to someone else who would till the land and give him half the produce. Over the years the land had shrunk and so had the income but it did not bother him in the least. Or not enough for him to get up and do some work himself. His wife often coaxed him to go to the fields and do some farming himself as their daughter was growing up and they would soon need a dowry but he would pay no heed. On days when he was not on a tour fixing marriages, he would sleep after breakfast and then after lunch. In the evenings he would stoke his pipe and crawl over to sit under the *Pipal* tree in the village centre where the village elderly gathered to talk politics and village affairs. Except for a brief interval when he had contracted TB, every year had deposited its own layer of fat around the belly and the chin. For the first time he had confided to Harivansh that he was finding it difficult to carry his own weight and his legs buckled if he stood up for long. Harivansh often feared that he would die prematurely of a heart attack or some other ailment and it would be left upon him to marry off his daughter.

Presently he threw the question at his brother-in-law who was casually chewing a betel leaf in his mouth at the far end of the veranda.

Pramod paused before answering to pretend putting some thought behind his answer. When he tried to speak thereafter, he couldn't as the betel leaf juice left little space for his tongue to swing around in his mouth. He got up and the spat the contents of his mouth with a projectile force intended to fall into the neighbour's backyard but instead it ended up splashing against the freshly painted wall creating tiny islands of red. He grunted in dissatisfaction at his work of art and started chewing again vigorously to take a second attempt at the neighbour's house.

'Radha is absolutely right,' he said. 'Besides what if there is serious disagreement on any issue like, lets say, the dowry. You would not be able to say no to people who are your guests. It is safer to meet on neutral territory.'

'You are still living in the last century Pramod.'

'I would also say that the dowry negotiations should be concluded before you see the girl. Once you have seen her it will hurt their prestige and yours if the marriage does not happen.'

'I won't be asking any for unreasonable amount anyway. Only what is commensurate with the going rate for a doctor from a decent family.'

'Yes, but your perception can vary from theirs.'

'I am telling you now Pramod and remember this carefully,' Harivansh raised his finger at his brother-in-law. 'You can extract the maximum dowry that you can using your negotiation skills but dowry should not become a sticking point in this marriage. I am not willing to loose Puja or a family like that. I do not care how much dowry I get in the end. Besides much of Avinash's future depends on it.'

'Yes you do care how much dowry you get,' said Pramod. 'That is why you have called me here. I am only saying that do not be generous enough to gift you son away for nothing.'

Harivansh was drained out of any stamina to argue further. He got up quietly and left for the Post Office to telephone Ramesh.

Over the next few days the new country was beginning to firm its impressions upon Puja. The first thing that struck her was the strange mosaic of unparalleled wealth and absolute poverty that had it marks on the whole society. They coexisted so blatantly besides each other that she was surprised that it had not triggered a revolution of some kind. As she whizzed around with Rama in her air-conditioned car, she saw poverty in all its shapes. Tin plate roofs. Bamboo shoots and torn rags to form the walls, no rags to cover the human body itself. Naked children urinating into and drinking from the same stream. She felt like getting out of the car to touch them, to confirm that they were from the same race but could not gather the courage. She sank further into the security of her leather seats.

Rama took her to the local state Medical College Hospital. This was supposedly the premier institution of the state and she almost choked with shock when she entered one of the wards. The cocktail of odours overwhelmed her senses. The smell from the urine, the open wounds, the undisposed rubbish, the unbathed patients. Once again it was only she who seemed to be affected by it. Everyone else went about their business completely oblivious of anything amiss. There were doctors in the ward just like her, wearing the same white coats and flashing their stethoscopes, going around examining the patients, writing on the drug charts just like she did in England. But no one like her had their hands on their noses.

Rama introduced her to one of the junior doctors who on the introduction seemed extremely gratified to be in the presence of a foreign qualified professional and took her immediately into what was known as the doctors' room. It was a small cubicle tucked away in one corner of the large ward, and separated from it by a green curtain on which was boldly inscribed "No entry – Doctors only". The room had no windows and was sparsely furnished with a small wooden table and four wooden chairs and nothing else. There was a newspaper spread over the table, which acted as the tablecloth. There were two bricks placed on the newspaper sheet upon which was an electric stove which had an aluminium pan with water boiling in it. There was a jar of familiar Nescafe coffee and some loose tea in a small polythene bag. In one corner of the room there were two other doctors and a balding elderly gentleman who looked quite senior chatting animatedly over some medical topic. The junior doctor who had escorted them in introduced Puja to the rest of his team one by one. Caught between the Indian customs and foreign courtesy, the boys were hesitant initially as to whether shake her hand or just say hello till one of them bravely put his hand forward. The elderly gentleman turned out to be a professor in general medicine and he later divulged to Puja that he had trained as a junior doctor in England for five years.

'Pontefract in Yorkshire my dear,' he said trying to resurrect an accent which had faded away quite a few years ago. 'Lovely countryside, lovely people and a lot of our people as well.'

Puja tried to put the place on the map but could not work it out and just nodded vaguely.

Tea was served as the professor bragged about his achievements in that medical College despite the lack of proper facilities or finance. He had three papers published in the British Medical Journal, he boasted, since he had joined that institution. She was later told rather sheepishly by one of the junior doctors that all three papers were published on Kalazaar, a disease which was found nowhere else on the planet. Hence any external peer review would not have been possible nor would anyone outside the state or country be in a position to challenge or verify the facts. Ginger had been added to the tea to mark the special occasion and together with the heap of sugar there was barely any taste of the tea. It would have been discourteous not to finish the tea and Puja sipped it with great effort as the junior doctors quizzed her about ways and means of finding a job in England.

Tension buzzed like a constant tinnitus increasing each day in pitch as the

Chauhans approached the D-Day to meet the groom and his family. Everyone reacted in a different manner. Savita became nervous, Ramesh was irritable and agitated and Puja continued to live in denial. There were plans and counter plans, hotels selected and deselected, negotiation strategies discussed and discarded almost on a continual basis.

One of the major controversies was about Puja's dress to be worn on that evening. The males did not have any particular preference but the women folk were strongly in favour of Puja wearing a sari. Puja tried one for a dry run. The thick heavy silk with embroidery was wrapped around her by her mother at the end of which she was left with the feeling of being trapped in a plaster cast. She tried to move her hands and feet around and when she could not, she declared her firm intention of not to wear it.

'You have to stop being so obstinate Puja,' her mother said. 'In your Sasural you will have to wear a sari most of the time.'

'Those days are gone,' Premshanker intervened. 'Now it is not uncommon for daughter-in-laws to wear *Salwar Kameez* or even long skirts in the house.'

'Didi should wear jeans,' cried out Babli.

'You shut up. If the kids had their way none of them would get accepted in a decent family.'

The eventual consensus was for a *Salwar Kameez*. Puja and Rama went out shopping that evening and bought a beautiful dress made of white silk with artificial pearls and shells embroidered on it. They had to return it the very next day as it was pointed out that white was a colour for widows and hence would be most inauspicious for the occasion when marriage was being discussed. Red or pink was suggested but both Puja and Rama were so irked by the incident that they bought a yellow dress in defiance. Savita too went on a shopping spree buoyed by a weak rupee against the Pound. Ramesh and Premshanker scoured the local hotels for a suitable meeting place. Harivansh had insisted that they meet on neutral grounds and not at Premshanker's house.

The constant resonance of marriage often drove Puja out of the house but there were few places to explore in Patna. Movie theatres were deemed unsafe for girls to go on their own and Rama almost laughed herself to death when Puja asked if there were any nightclubs in the town.

'If there was a night club in this town it would be a venue for daily rapes and kidnappings.'

'But you have night clubs in Delhi?'

'Oh yes, but we are still quite east of Delhi.'

Despite everyone tugging at the rope to slow down the days passing by, time sped towards the day of reckoning till it finally arrived. It heralded itself by the loud ringing of the phone at 6:30 am and everyone jumped out of their bed and ran for the phone in the lounge fearing bad news at such untimely hour of the day.

'I could not sleep all night, Bhai Saheb,' Harivansh was saying, 'the first rays of sunlight and I could not help but giving you a ring. I am nervous like a newly wed bride.'

Ramesh laughed. 'I am glad that I am not the only one. Savita and I were up talking very late last night. It is strange to see how fast our children have grown up.'

'Leave aside the marriage. It has been such a long time since we last met.'

They talked for a further few minutes to finalise the timings and the venue and then hung up. The phone had disturbed everyone's slumber and the household creaked and yawned to wake up to what was to be a momentous day. That realisation hung like a thick cloud as everyone went about their normal morning chores. They smiled at each other without reason and especially so at Puja whenever she crossed their ways. She also unwittingly acknowledged those smiles with a brush of blush. Everyone was content with that pall of normalcy till Chintu ran into the lounge and shouted, 'today we shall see didi's husband, today we shall see didi's husband.'

Then all hell broke loose. Puja sought her familiar escape territory and darted into the bathroom with Rama in pursuit. Premshanker and his wife started laughing aloud as the all the children started running around and banging on the dining table repeating what Chintu had said again and again. The servant dropped the tea tray on the floor as Babli crashed into him and Premshanker's mother came darting out of her room hurling abuse at the children on being disturbed in her morning worship.

Soon after breakfast, relatives and friends began to assemble at the house. The adults soon segregated on sex lines, the men occupying the living room while the ladies sprawled in Savita's bedroom. Tea was being brought into the men's zone at regular intervals as the helpful suggestions and general discussions began in earnest. Ramesh's mother arrived with Bacchan by the morning train from Bishanpur. After a semi-tearful reunion with her son and daughter-in-law to mark the two weeks they had been apart, she produced a gold ring that had belonged to their ancestors and had the blessings of the family God of the Chauhans. This was for the groom to ensure that he does not die prematurely leaving Puja a cursed widow.

Crisis erupted in late afternoon when the beautician from the beauty parlour failed to turn up to do Puja's make-up. Savita went berserk with anger and anxiety and the gossipers in the men's zone scrambled to their feet in an effort to search for the missing beautician. Cars and jeeps raced to the beauty parlour and the beautician's house. She was finally traced to a local private hospital where her father had been admitted that very morning with a minor heart attack. The beautician was very tearful and expressed her inability to leave her father's bedside in such a critical situation. The men's delegation tried to convince her that her father was completely out of danger and even made one of the attending Physicians say the same. She was promised extra cash all of which was given to her in advance and a mobile phone thrust in her bag to phone the hospital whenever she wished to. After much persuasion she finally relented and an audible sigh of relief swept the room. Back at home a general applause was accorded to her for being such a brave woman which sure enough wiped away any residual guilt and she went into Puja's room with a broad smile on her face.

Inside turmeric paste was being applied all over Puja's body carefully avoiding the hands where henna had been applied expertly the previous night. The women were humming a marriage folksong while the kids looked on excitedly with wide open eyes. Her hair was first washed with yoghurt and then shampooed to leave a glowing effect. Sandalwood oil and a scented herbal powder were mixed in her bath and Puja was stunned to find a few women insisting on giving her a bath. No thank you, had little effect and finally Savita had to intervene personally to rescue her.

After she emerged from the bath she looked at her naked self in the mirror. Her skin was radiant with a golden hue. Her long silken hair flowed carelessly downwards over her breasts to kiss her navel. She breathed in to absorb the sandalwood fragrance of her own body and slid her hand down the silk of her thigh. She looked at her proud eyes and smiled at them. With great effort she turned around, put on her bathrobe and walked out of the door.

Back in her bedroom, she was frozen into a mummy as the artisans began their delicate work. Rama dressed her, delicately adjusting the folds and the sweeps while Savita compared different sets of jewellery to suit her daughter and took a vote from the house. The beautician worked on her face and rubbed special oil in her hands that turned the intricate patterns of the henna from orange-red to a dark crimson.

Premshanker shouted at the top of his voice from the lobby that they would be leaving within the next hour. The women recoiled in horror, as everyone had been so engrossed in decorating Puja that they had had little time to do their own make-up. Despite Savita's reminder that it was only Puja whose looks mattered on the day, they slipped away one after another on one pretext or another.

When the beautician had finished, she gently rolled the *Dupatta* over her head and asked Puja to face the mirror. She turned slowly under the weight of the dress and the jewellery and then saw someone in the mirror. For a few moments she tried in vain to recognise her. From under the silken cloak and the glittering diamonds she searched for a girl in jeans and a T-shirt. She concentrated her senses to look for that carelessly tossed hair, to hear that unabashed laughter, to feel that bursting fountain of freedom inside but all that came out was a single pair of tears as she quickly turned her face away. The beautician panicked thinking her effort had not been good enough but Puja gave her a reassuring smile. She then asked the beautician to leave the room and slowly walked to the window and waited for the call.

Through the metal grills and the window net, fragments of her life flashed before her. London, friends, college, hospital, pubs, Southall. Some general life, some specific moments floated outside her cell's window. She wept knowing that the mascara would have to be redone now. But she kept on crying as if in revenge for everything that had gone wrong with her life.

Avinash felt like crying too but could not come to tears. He tried laughing instead but to no avail. Anything to release the vice of nervousness that was gripping him tighter as the evening approached. He had looked at himself a thousand times in front of the mirror to ensure his appearance lived up to the occasion. He smiled at himself a few times and also spoke a few lines in English to the unprotesting mirror. He was not satisfied either with his English or the suit he was wearing. The Jacket clung around him like a wet wrap and he could not even lift his arms freely without risking the stitches coming apart. He had crossed over the border to Nepal to buy the fabric for the suit. The other knotty problem was the knot of the tie itself. His practise in wearing a tie was at best once a year on average and his collection accordingly was restricted to the one which he had bought on the eve of his admission to the Medical school as it was required for the interview. First he struggled with the length at which to tie the knot as the final outcome varied from falling on to his crotch to up to his sternum. He finally solved it by doing a double knot but then the size of the knot occluded his whole neck. At one stage he was so exasperated that he decided to do without the tie but then shame set in and he sat down patiently in front of the mirror till he was rewarded by the right knot and the right length.

He sat on the bed and closed his eyes for a few moments. To regain some calm, rehearse some lines and recite a prayer. Last evening he had sat with his friends and tried to arrange in some ascending order the importance of looks, nature, family and professional status to help arrive at a decision but could not arrive at any conclusion.

There was a soft tap on the door and his mother stepped inside. She detected the small beads of sweat on her son's forehead in excess of the warm weather and gave him a gentle pat on the shoulder.

'Remember we are the Boy's side and so we have the upper hand. All the tension is theirs,' she said searching her son's eyes for some glow of confidence. 'Your father is calling you downstairs. Time to go.'

Downstairs Harivansh was standing by the door ready to go while Pramod was still comfortably slumped on the sofa. They had obviously interrupted some heated argument that resumed again instantly.

'I still say we should be deliberately late in reaching the hotel,' Pramod was saying. 'We are the groom side and we might be seen to be too willing a party if we arrive on time.'

'I do not need to have lessons from you in customs and conventions Pramod. Just move your heavy bulk from that sofa and keep moving. And try not to come up with such helpful suggestions while we are there.'

Pramod huffed in protest creating a gurgling noise through the mouthful of betel leaf spit and rose reluctantly.

Hotel Magadh Sheraton was the only five star hotel in Patna. It was similar in standards to many other hotels in the town but since it boasted a swimming pool and a shopping complex, it had been awarded a five star status. It had started with a big bang and high hopes a few years ago but since then it had succumbed to the general spirit of degradation and downfall that had gripped the entire state of Bihar. The bars and restaurants were mainly frequented by politicians and criminals turning the civilised population away and the rooms were often occupied by top bureaucrats for prostituting purposes. Non-payment of bills by the politicians and officials and the regular monthly bribes to the same politicians and officials gradually made the financial situation untenable and consequently affected morale and the services.

But still it was the pride of the town. The only five star hotel in the town. So when respectable people needed to select a venue for any occasion, it always popped up as a strong contender. Lack of fresh paint, algae, moss and rain had dabbed the bright white building with ugly patches of pale yellow but then a few years on the whole building was engulfed by that pale yellow and did not look as bad as before.

Ramesh had booked a conference suite and a private room for the evening. He had already tipped the waiters in advance to ensure complete attention. Puja was kept in the room with Rama, only to come out when requested. The management sniffing the possibility that payment would be in foreign currency had arranged for complimentary flower garlands to welcome the groom party and played a wedding shehnai on its music channel.

Nervousness was palpable in the air and showed itself in different ways. Some could not sit down, some simply sat down and remained immobile while others paced up and down the lobby. There were painful attempts to start conversations but none lasted beyond seconds and then the silence of the wait. Suddenly one of Ramesh's nephew ran up the stairs to announce the arrival of the guests.

There was a sudden burst of activity. The men-folk rushed to the lobby door with garlands in their hands to welcome the guests while the women huddled in one corner to draw strength.

The heads first emerged on the horizon of the staircase and the women craned their necks to catch a glimpse of the groom. Harivansh rushed towards Ramesh and gave him a big hug and almost lifted him off the ground. Avinash shifted uneasily on his feet in this mayhem of greetings.

'Only the hairs have gone grey, the eyes are still young,' said Harivansh to Ramesh.

'Believe me, so is the heart,' Ramesh laughed out loud.

Harivansh turned to Savita.' Bhabhi ji Namaste.'

'Namaste, Bhai Saheb.'

You have not met my wife Radha before?'

'No we have not had the pleasure before.'

'I remember now, you stood me up on my marriage?'

'No Harivansh, this is unfair. I did write to you about my exams.'

'Meet my son. Avinash.'

Avinash shifted warily under the glare of so many gazes, undecided still whether to touch their feet or simply fold his hands. He caught from the corner of his eye his father's head flicking downwards in a gesture to go for the feet option. He gave himself the benefit of doubt and touched Ramesh's and Savita's feet. They caught him in mid air and spared him the full stoop. Savita looked carefully at the man who would wed her daughter. Nothing startling, but then merit was more important than looks in a prospective groom. She just prayed Puja thought the same.

As they settled in their seats, formality thinned and then disappeared. Premshanker's wife and the other women indulged in the traditional ballooning of the groom's mother ego by praising her sari and her jewellery. Harivansh and Ramesh reminisced about the good old days while Pramod and Premshanker diplomatically weighed each other in anticipation of the talks in store. That left Avinash exposed to the long stares from Savita to which he responded by alternately staring into the space and smiling back at her. She was still trying to focus on some handsome trait but apart from her conclusion that he would look fairer in sunlight, was not making much headway. It was certainly a step down from the photographs that were sent to her.

She decided on an impromptu interview of her would be son-in-law and changed her seat. Avinash straightened his spine to signal his increased attention.

‘So how is the Clinic running back at home?’

‘Very well, thank you. It is the grain-cutting season at the moment so most of the village patients are staying back for the crops.’

There was definitely something in his voice. A thick measured resonant voice that demanded attention.

‘Of course,’ she said. ‘We have these seasonal fluctuations here.’

‘We make up for it,’ Avinash laughed. ‘Once they have sold their grain in the markets they have plenty of money to pay for our fees.’

She was relieved at some sense of humour. She knew her daughter ranked it above love or loyalty. In her burst of spontaneity she had forgotten to frame her test questions.

‘Is it general surgery you are interested in?’

‘I am veering more towards Urology nowadays. I find it more stimulating.’

‘Yes indeed, there is plenty of scope in that branch.’

‘Particularly here, as it is still in its infancy as a sub-speciality on its own.’

‘So what are your plans for the future, Avinash ji?’

‘Well in the immediate future...’ his voice trailed off as he picked up the conversation on the other side where his maternal uncle, Pramod had just asked Ramesh his monthly income in England. He picked up the glass of water and sipped whilst gently turning his head to focus his ears in the right direction.

Ramesh was taken aback by the abrupt question from Pramod. It surprised him how often people in India would ask about salaries and income without any qualms. Strangely it was not considered rude to ask that question but it could be construed as rudeness if you declined to give an answer. And if one gave the answer in Pounds or Dollars they would want to know the latest conversion rate as well. He weighed his response. The dowry demand might be directly proportionate to his answer while on the other hand an impressive figure might sway them to send their son to England and approve of the wedding. Undecided, he decided to go for the truth and hope for the best.

‘Enough Pramod ji to live and feed well.’

‘Come on Ramesh ji, don’t be modest. Give us a figure.’

‘Five to six *lakhs.*’ His voice echoed in the emptiness of the sudden silence.

Avinash put his glass back on the table. 'I think in the immediate future, I would like to get some advanced training at a specialist centre either here or abroad. Then I can think of settling somewhere with my own establishment.' In his mind he doubled the sum he had just heard for himself and Puja. He compared it to his current earnings and felt his heart skip a beat. Then he chided himself for being so silly and greedy and turned his full attention to Savita.

Meanwhile Pramod was wallowing in the virtues of his nephew. 'Since he entered medical school we must have had at least a hundred proposals from interested parties but we turned them down. One party, he was a contractor laid his chequebook open before Harivansh and asked him to fill any amount he wanted to. He would not leave the house until we gave our word. But we would not compromise on the family or the bride. Bhai Saheb was absolutely adamant on that.'

Ramesh squirmed inside at the fat ugly person spewing those words and something must have shown on his face that made Avinash shuffle uncomfortably in his seat. Harivansh smiled in approval. Avinash felt embarrassed as he knew that the background was being laid for the dowry negotiations. He opposed dowry in principle but after being a victim twice in his sister's weddings, he knew that his father was not going to relent in his case.

'It is true,' Harivansh was saying, ' We have had so many proposals in the past few years that now we are simply fed up and just wish to close this chapter. But Radha kept nudging me that I should wait for the right girl. If I had my way he would have been married a few years ago.'

'Hmm,' muttered Ramesh.

There was a distinct unease beginning to spread in the air as the groom took charge of the proceedings oblivious of the dents they were making in the other side's egos. Despite being the bride family, the non-resident Indians were not used to be talked down by resident Indians.

'Puja graduated from St. Thomas's hospital in London,' Savita announced. 'It is supposed to be one of the best in the world. She has also passed her MRCP and was offered a cardiology registrar post in the same hospital. She always came top in her class.' She lied at last.

Radha devi could not quite grasp the whole detail but wondered if an over-qualified daughter-in-law would remain under her control. Pramod came up with the obvious question.

'How much was she earning in London?'

Savita had had enough of him for the evening and decided to respond in kind. 'You will have to ask her this question, Pramod ji. We never discuss our earnings with each other.'

Pramod's jaw dropped initially at the blunt response and then his mouth shut completely.

Picking up the temporary lull in the conversation, the waiters began serving the snacks and the second round of drinks were served. Savita resumed her interview.

'How do you feel about a career woman for a wife?'

'I do not see any conflicts arising just because of that. In fact I shall respect her more for having achieved more than the traditional woman.'

'So if both work outside, do you think it is only fair that they both share a burden of the household work as well?'

Avinash hesitated. Modernism clashed with chauvinism and egotism. 'I think it is harder for a man to supplement a woman's role in the house than it is for the woman to supplement a man's role outside the home. But one should always try.'

'Yes one should always try his best,' Savita said emphatically to drive her point home.

As the evening progressed the groom's delegation showed physical signs of restiveness almost in coordination signalling their desire to see the bride. Ramesh nodded in agreement and Savita got up adjusting the sari over her head to fetch Puja.

Everyone relapsed into a silence as they waited for Savita to come back. Avinash's heart began to thump and he clasped his hands firmly together as if they had some control over his heart. He was both scared and excited, not sure in what proportions. He closed his eyes and prayed like he always did in the exam hall before the papers were given out.

First the jangle of the anklets, then the flash of the yellow silk and then his future personified. Held nimbly by her mother and sister; escorted gently across the hall. Though he had seen her photographs a thousand times, he was stunned by what he saw in front of him and could only nod numbly as she stopped by him and greeted him with *Namaste*.

Radha devi on the other hand had inspected her prospective daughter-in-law carefully as she made her entrance. She searched carefully beyond the obvious beauty which had stunned her son. No squint, no limp in the gait, tall neck, full breasts, narrow waist. Height just short of her son but that was acceptable as long as she was shorter. Once her checklist was complete, her vision changed. That girl in front of her would be the bearer of her grandchildren, the daughter-in-law of the household. Her heart melted and tears swelled into her eyes as Puja bent forward to touch her feet. She embraced Puja unashamed of her tears.

'Be blessed with many sons,' she mumbled to her and then turned to Savita. 'Your daughter looks like an angel.'

Envy, joy and sorrow conspired to wet Savita's eyes too. For one moment she wanted to snatch her daughter from Radha's embrace and walk away with her out of the hall but the moment of truth had arrived. Just like she had flung the rice in her palm behind her back twenty-nine years ago and stepped into her new world never to look back again, so would her daughter. She looked at her daughter's new guardians and smiled feebly at them.

Puja sat down calmly on the sofa and slid the *Dupatta* further over her head to shield herself from the piercing gazes from all directions. Rama held her hand firmly in moral support. She angled her eyes to bring Avinash in her view but caught him staring directly at her and so quickly lowered her eyes. First impressions. She tried to assemble her thoughts. Avinash was positively ordinary looking, Radha devi was an ugly emotional wreck, Harivansh was the handsomest of the lot with a lovely thick moustache and half-greyed thick hair. Who was that fat person slouched on the couch at the far end? No, she was being far too critical. Let's start again. But then the question round began.

'How are you finding India?' Harivansh started breaking the silence.

'So far, so good,' Puja replied lightly completely missing the strategic significance of the question. Ramesh shuffled uneasily.

'You must be finding the weather completely different? It is so unbearably hot in this country.'

Puja just smiled.

'Ramesh ji told me that you have done your MRCP. Are there any further studies left for you to do?'

'I might decide to do a couple of years of research to obtain a MD. Though it is not necessary in order to become a specialist.' This was a long sentence despite her best efforts to condense it and she had to use a few words in English to carry it through. Her brief was pure Hindi as much as possible.

Pramod at this point wanted to ask about the salary of a specialist but thought better of it and kept quiet.

'That is similar to your MS degree, isn't it Avinash?' Harivansh turned to his son.

'Yes, the only slight difference being presumably that there the research is actually done while here it is only on paper,' he replied sheepishly.

His voice was certainly better than his looks, she concluded.

'So you got your MS without doing any research which you were supposed to have done?' father asks son.

'Where is the money? Where are the labs? But then you do learn a lot on the clinical aspects which you would not have otherwise.'

'As long as it makes you a better doctor clinically, it really does not matter,' Ramesh intervened on Avinash's side.

More mundane matters took over.

'Is *Beti* interested in the kitchen?' Radha asked.

'Oh yes definitely,' Savita replied instead. 'Both vegetarian and non-vegetarian. She spends hours in the kitchen if her father makes any special requests, not that frequently for her mother though.'

'Daughters are always more attached to their fathers.'

At this moment mummy, I hate you both equally.

An uncomfortable silence followed as everyone ran out of conversation. Puja welcomed it, everyone else, visibly embarrassed by the silence struggled to mouth some words.

'Sweetmeats anyone?' Savita had a bright idea.

'No.'

'No.'

'No.'

'In this no-no everyone will miss the train,' Pramod finally spoke after a long interval. 'Pass it on to me Bhabhi ji and I shall finish it on everyone's behalf.'

'Of course, of course, anyway you have not eaten much this evening.'

A burst of laughter, but he registered no impact and filled his mouth. Puja meanwhile was pinned down by an unwavering stare from Radha devi and somewhat wavering gazes from Avinash and Harivansh. So she kept her eyes down intently at the marble flooring and tried to work out different floor layouts. When she had done enough of that, she pinched Rama's hand hard enough to startle her in pain.

Rama jerked up in pain but quickly gained composure and invited everyone's attention. 'I can stand everything but the panic stricken expression on Avinash ji's face. With everyone's permission I would like to rescue him and Puja didi to the next room.'

Everyone nodded and smiled. Avinash blushed and blushed further in a vain attempt to cover up his discomfiture.

Once inside the hotel room an awkward silence followed again. It was Rama who broke the ice.

' Avinash ji, once after the marriage Puja didi will shut you up for good anyway. This may well be your last chance to open your mouth so please say something.'

Avinash gathered courage. 'I shall survive somehow but I pity the bloke who is going to fall in your lap.'

'Oh sweet Jija ji don't you worry about that. I am not going to marry after all. I am going to live with you and Puja in dull cloudy England for the rest of my life.'

'I better say my goodbyes now.'

'No need Jija ji. Stay where you are. I shall leave the room now and let you two to get along.'

'Rama stay,' Puja pleaded.

'No didi I can't. I am too beautiful. He may select me instead of you.'

'Shut up and stay.'

'It is your nervousness that is speaking didi. First time marrying, it is not uncommon.' Rama ran out and slammed the door behind her.

An awkward silence again. Lasting for seconds, feeling like hours.

'I really feel for the guy who is going to marry her,' Avinash said softly.

Puja tried a controlled smile but ended up laughing aloud. Avinash watched her in slow motion. The unfurling of the smile into an untamed laughter. The tilting back of her long neck and the upward roll of the black pearls. The *Dupatta* silk and the silken hair rising and falling like waves in the sea. All those days and weeks of agonising ended abruptly for him in that brief moment. She stopped laughing all of a sudden.

'What?' she said, catching his eyes. Her laugh contracted back into a smile.

'Nothing, nothing,' he replied.

They become more conscious of the occasion.

'Do you find this system of arranged marriages strange?' He asked.

'Weird in theory but it seems to work in practice.'

'Only for the pre-programmed. You see we have grown up all these years knowing the inevitability of an arranged marriage and have accepted it in our hearts. But I do not know if it is fair on you?'

Puja was confused and did not know how to respond. Was he for or against arranged marriages? Or was he just testing her?

An awkward silence again.

'How has your visit been so far?'

'Enjoyed it so far.'

'I bet not the weather though?'

'No not the weather.'

Silence again. A long one this time.

'Puja ji...?'

'Don't call me ji, please. It sounds very odd.'

'Very well then do call me by first name as well.'

'Sure. You were saying something?'

'Puja, I know our parents are at this moment sitting in the other room and deciding our future but I think ultimately it should be me and you who should have the final say. And this is the moment that will shape the rest of our lives. The whole thing may appear stupid and absurd but this is the only chance we might get to decide our destiny.'

Absurd but true, Puja thought.

'So if we have any doubts about the whole thing, now is the time to express them before it gets too late. Let us be frank and honest for there is too much at stake.'

'I know.'

Puja did not know what else to say. For the first time she raised her head and looked intently at him and tried to search for some answers. Were the looks enough to sweep her off her feet? No. Were they two people of the same wavelength? Most probably not. Did she want to marry a complete stranger? No. Was he a decent person in himself? Perhaps. Life had turned out to be a gamble and here she was shaking the dice vigorously in her hands in desperation for some luck.

'Puja?'

'Sorry I was miles away.'

'Is there anything you want to know about me?'

She smiled. 'Anything you would like to tell me?'

'Nothing out of the ordinary. Though I wish there was. I have led a relatively simple and uneventful life so far. Our family is a close knit one. One brother, two sisters both married and my parents. We get along fairly well. I would say democracy generally prevails with no one dominating in particular and we have enjoyed living together. Ma is fairly religious and a bit more rooted to convention than Babuji who is very easy going. Childhood was spent mainly cramming books and playing cricket, a sport I confess I am addicted to. By the way I played for my District but could not go far beyond because of career considerations.'

'Batsman or Bowler?'

'Batsman. Used to open for my side. Are you interested in cricket?'

'Papa is, and he has sort of roped me into it as well.'

'You may not find Sitapur up to your expectations especially when coming from abroad but it has got its plus points. Subtle but still there.'

He could have been a good friend though. Someone she could have relied upon.

'What about the future? Would you consider moving out of there?'

'Probably, I will need to. It is a small town with its own limitations. No proper schools, limited diagnostic facilities. Not much in way of shops. Yes, I think I would not like to narrow my options to Sitapur for the rest of my life.'

'What about living abroad?'

'I cannot say for sure about a place that I have never ever been to. I must admit though that the thought of living abroad for good frightens me. What about you Puja? Will you ever come back and live in India if it comes to that?'

This was the crunch point. She was well tutored by her mother for this question. No groom or his family with any pride would accept the precondition that their daughter-in-law would not come to live with them. The plot was to entice him to England and then when the charms set in, he would make his own decision not to go back. It had worked for the vast majority and it would for Puja, her parents had assured her.

'My preference would be England as I have lived there all my life but no I have not shut my options of living here.'

Half-truth, half lie, but Avinash's face lit up with this moral victory of male vanity.

Rama rapped on the door. 'Dinner is being served. Come down in a few minutes. Time for the closing statements.'

Another long silence. Uneasy shrugs and audible breaths. Time for the closing statements. Only the mind had gone blank.

'Can I suggest something?' asked Avinash.

'What?'

'When we go back tonight, we both will be asked for a decision. "Yes" or "no". Let us both give a common answer. That will at least avoid a public rejection of each other. Call it vanity or ego. I can live with a private one.'

'But do you think we have had enough time together to make that decision Avinash?'

'No Puja,' he looked into her eyes. 'But we never will.'

Puja looked outside the window. The night had turned darker with the clouds coming together rapidly to blanket the whole horizon.

'Have you made up your mind Avinash?' she asked without looking at him.

'Yes.'

She turned to face the jury.

'What is it?'

'A yes.'

A bullet from a silenced gun. Hit her just below her sternum in the abdomen. Hurt but did not quite kill her. She walked up to the windows.

There was a long silence again.

'Puja?'

The skies had finally given in. Giant tear drops lashing against the closed window panes. Seen but not felt, felt but not seen. She looked outside and searched carefully. Thunder but no silver lining.

She nodded simply when her voice refused to lie about the heart.

XIII

The heavens poured like never before. Silver arrows pounded the mighty earth with scant mercy, carving tiny wounds all over her body and then submerging her in its watery fold. The archaic drainage croaked under the onslaught and weakened, decided to join the enemy camp by overflowing its effluents into the stagnant rainwater.

But life carried on in this bustling capital city as normal. In ankle deep water, handkerchiefs firmly stuck on the nostrils. Shallow breaths in a fine balance between the need to survive and the stench to percolate within the lungs. The urchins were extracting the most out of the day jumping into the water from the walls and making futile attempts to swim in six inches of water besides the spewing gutters.

And so with nothing grossly amiss, Harivansh saw no reason to postpone the next stage of the talks till the water drained away and the roads resurfaced. He was thrilled to get an affirmative answer from Avinash and when Ramesh had phoned him with Puja's answer, he closed his eyes and thanked the good Lord. He therefore phoned early next morning warning Ramesh of his impending arrival at around mid-day.

Puja woke up late that morning, mentally and physically drained by last evening's events. When she glanced outside her window, she thought that there was a flash flood from an invisible river only to be told that it was only rainwater and a decrepit drainage system. Last evening Savita had crept into her bedroom and held her hands without saying anything. She searched her eyes and Puja had just nodded gently. She did not see the flash of happiness she had expected to see on her mother's face. For Savita, trapped between the knowledge of her daughter's unhappiness and the shackles of family traditions, could only manage a wry smile.

'We will always have each other,' Savita said to her, wiping her eyes from the corner of her sari.

Action plans were chalked out in a strategy meeting soon after the phone call. Premshanker and major Ranbir would do the dowry negotiation with Pramod while Ramesh and Bacchan would look after Harivansh and his ego as the groom's father. Savita and Premeshanker's wife, Kamla, would attend to Radha devi. A grand menu for lunch was planned to lessen their appetite for other material things. An upper ceiling for the dowry was then discussed. Ramesh proposed a figure of eight lakhs including goods and cash but Savita intervened to lower it to five lakhs. Bacchan advised that given the market conditions it would be difficult to achieve such a low figure for a medical graduate. Savita was unhappy with his suggestion and ultimately a figure of seven lakhs was agreed upon. The aim would be to negotiate as low a figure as possible. Ramesh emphasized that the groom's family should be happy with the dowry lest Puja could become a victim of their taunts after the marriage. At the end of the meeting Bacchan was despatched to buy new clothes as gifts for the guests and fetch a Brahmin priest to read the horoscopes and fix a marriage date.

The static of excitement rippled through everyone in the household except Puja. For her the inevitable descent to *fait accompli* had begun in earnest and she could only sit back and wish it bad luck. She felt emotionless almost to the brink of peace. There were no other coping mechanisms she could summon for help.

Harivansh, Radha devi and Pramod arrived right on time upsetting everyone's calculation who were banking on at least an hour delay. Avinash was left out as he was redundant to the present purpose and could even be a hindrance. Hush knocks were given on the bathroom doors requesting Kamla and Savita to hurry up while the guests were seated in the lounge and looked after by Bacchan.

The Brahmin priest was huddled in one corner feasting on a huge mound of beaten rice, curd and mangoes. As the guests entered the lounge he raised his smeared hands in acknowledgement and resumed eating instantly. Harivansh was effusive as usual but Pramod maintained a grave posture to preclude any friendliness creeping in to the hard bargaining that lay ahead. They talked about the weather and the corrupt politicians but largely remained silent and waited for the priest to finish eating while they sipped the tea.

The Brahmin belched at last to displace some air so that the last few sweetmeats could be accommodated within. Radha devi opened her purse and took out the neatly folded horoscope of her son and placed it on the table. Kamla and Savita meanwhile had also come in bringing with them the computerised horoscope of Puja which was only generated that morning.

The priest meanwhile settled on the floor and took out a few books which looked as ancient as the scriptures within from his shoulder bag and spread them out on the floor. A pall of nervousness descended upon the occupants of the room as he started to assemble the horoscopes side by side. If they did not match, then all their hopes and dreams would be dashed in one swift stroke. The Brahmin could sense that in the air. Hopes shimmering in those still eyes, all in his direction.

He began examining the charts and the figures intently, jotting occasionally on a piece of paper. Almost immediately he detected that the girl was a *Mangli* and the boy was not. He wiped his sweat and began comparing the *Gunas* from both sides. He would strike a line every time he had a match on his piece of paper. At the end he counted the number of lines on the paper. Only eighteen out of a possible thirty-six. He matched them again but could not improve that figure. He then checked the *Grahas* and found them divergent too.

This was no match at all.

The Brahmin continued to pretend reading as he thought fast. He was a poor man desperate for a good pay out on that day. Times had been hard and getting harder over the last few years. The advent of the modern age had meant less fear of and less emphasis on religion. Ten years ago he could demand a fee but today he had to beg for it. Earnings from priesthood were so low that he had to take up a part time job as a Night watchman. And what tip would he expect today if he conveyed to them the bad news. Perhaps they would get some greedy priest for a second opinion who would contradict him anyway.

Human conscience has won many a battle but seldom against the human stomach. He raised his head and in a voice barely audible said, 'the match is perfect. This union will bring good fortune to both the families.'

There was an audible combined sigh of relief. Ramesh took out a five hundred rupee note and circled it over the priest's head and let it drop in his lap. Harivansh followed suit. The Brahmin collected the money and prayed for forgiveness.

As they raised a sweetmeat to each other's mouths, tears rolled over the women's cheeks, Pramod got up and suggested it was time for some serious negotiations to hammer out the finer details. Premshanker took

Pramod along with Major Ranbir into his bedroom while Radha devi was whisked away by the women. Harivansh and Ramesh remained in the lounge.

Puja was inquisitive about the conspiratorial segregation of the adults in different rooms. She had vaguely heard about dowry in Indian marriages but when she expressed her suspicions to her confidante, Rama had dismissed those thoughts with a wave of her hand.

'This is how marriage negotiations go didi,' she told Puja. 'The women discuss the clothes and jewellery while the men finalise the dates and other arrangements.'

Puja did not disbelieve her cousin.

But there was a crisis emerging in Premshanker's bedroom. As soon as they had settled in the chairs, Pramod had put his hand in his pocket and produced a slip of paper which he passed over to Premshanker.

Pramod read the demand list. Maruti car (air-conditioned), twenty *tolas* of gold, silver dinner set, colour TV, sofa set, double bed, washing machine, VCR, video camera, refrigerator, fifty one silver coins.....his eyes tired rapidly as irritation took over and he passed over the slip to Ranbir.

'And five lakhs in cash,' said Pramod looking directly into the eyes of the two men and sipping his whiskey. There were red threads in his eyes. A few of greed but mostly of intoxication. From alcohol and power.

'This would come to a million rupees,' Ranbir pleaded.

'This is the market rate,' pleasure seeped in Pramod's voice. 'Besides Ramesh ji does not have any other children to wed.'

'This won't be acceptable Pramod ji,' said Premshanker. 'It is too large a sum.'

Pramod appeared to think for a moment. He took a few gulps down his throat and belched loudly before resuming his erstwhile thinking mode. The two men watched him intently as Pramod appeared to do some mental maths and counted on his fingers. He finished the whiskey and slid the glass across the table and Premshanker filled it up promptly.

'I will settle for nine lakhs,' said Pramod. The expression as if he was parting with his own money.

Premshanker was resolute. 'Pramod ji we won't be able to give more than eight lakhs under any circumstance.'

Pramod slumped on his couch further, put his hand on the forehead and began to hyperventilate. He could not part with another lakh. He shook his head and raised his hands in exasperation. 'You have tied my hands now. I cannot go down any further. The responsibility will be all yours now.'

Premshanker was unmoved by the threat.

'Why don't you have a quiet word with Harivansh ji while we confer with Ramesh and Savita. Let us meet again in a few minutes.' He got up from the chair before Pramod could object to his idea.

In the lounge Pramod signalled Harivansh for a quiet word. Till then Harivansh and Ramesh had pretended to be untouched with the lowly dowry business and had talked about general matters. But now with the talks stranded and their intervention needed, pretension was no longer plausible. Harivansh rose with a sheepish grin on his face and left the room with Pramod. Ramesh was dragged into the bedroom and Savita was summoned along with Kamla. Premshanker did the de-briefing of the talks so far.

Savita was furious.' They have the cheek to ask for such a large sum? The boy is so ordinary looking, the family is greedy. I am already having second thoughts.'

'Calm down Savita,' said Premshanker. 'These talks are never so easy.'

'The difference is narrowed to just one lakh anyway,' said Kamla.

'It is not the one lakh Bhabhi,' replied Savita. 'It is the principle. Do they deserve such a large sum? Shall we willingly get ripped off?'

Premshanker looked at Ramesh who was still trying to collect his thoughts and had not spoken so far. Ramesh felt humbled and humiliated by the whole process. Powerless to the extent that he felt physically weak in his muscles. He sat down on the bed and his face turned grey. The chain of events in England flashed before him again.

'Get whatever deal you can get but do not break off the talks.' He suddenly felt very dry in his throat and walked to the kitchen for a glass of cold water.

Pramod presently walked in and the ladies promptly dispersed from the room. He and Harivansh had not had any discussions on the balcony. Their strategy had paid off well. To bargain from a higher level and agree around a target sum of eight lakhs. Harivansh had patted him on the back.

'Harivansh ji says that a *Bahu* like Puja is priceless. What difference would one lakh make? Eight lakhs it is then and let us fix a marriage date if you are agreed.'

The ladies behind the doors with their ears trained to overhear shrieked in delight and ran to spread the news. Premshanker, Ranbir and Pramod exchanged hugs.

The whole household, except Puja, crammed into the lounge as the Brahmin began consulting his charts for an appropriate marriage date. This was not a difficult task for him this time. As the horoscopes had not matched, there would be no auspicious date anyway. Any date would do.

'Fourteenth of July,' he said raising his head. 'That seems to be an excellent date for the couple.'

Chintu and Pinku started to blow whistles and dance on the floor. Radha devi leaned forward and whispered something in Kamla's ears who nodded and then hastily went out of the room. A few minutes later she returned with Puja behind her. She looked confused and unprepared as all eyes converged in her direction. There was a complete silence as Kamla pointed her in Harivansh's direction. Puja bent forwards and touched both his feet. Harivansh took out a thick gold chain from his pocket and placed it in her hands. She then turned to Radha devi who stopped her mid-way and took out two gold bracelets studded with precious stones from her purse. She began to put them on Puja's hand and when she encountered some resistance manoeuvring them over the hands on to the wrists, she began to sob. The other women too stuffed their sarees between their teeth as their eyes overflowed freely. She then took Puja into an embrace. As Puja opened her eyes to look at her hands, her eyes too moistened and a single tear welled in one corner and dropped unnoticed onto the marble floor.

The cuffs were on, the sentence had begun.

Dear Carol,
Sorry for the delay in writing to you. Events have been moving at such a rapid pace that I have been finding it hard to keep up with it, let alone have some time to pause and write letters. I hope you got my message on your answer phone.

I was engaged yesterday. We briefly met once before that in a hotel and we were asked for our consent that same evening. Strange isn't it? A 'yes' answer was such a foregone conclusion among the family and friends here that I simply could not muster enough courage and strength to swim against the tide. And what would have been the consequence of that anyway? Seeing more boys, more misery?

I know you must be dying to know about Avinash. Yes that is his name. Rama, my cousin tells me that in Hindi it means 'Indestructible'. We both were very nervous at our first meeting. He tried to converse in broken English and me in broken Hindi. It was almost hilarious but since my Hindi was more broken than his English, we settled upon speaking in English. We were together for roughly an hour. He is quite gentle and soft spoken and came across as a nice man. He also showed some traits of male chauvinism but I am yet to come across an Indian male who is not afflicted with it. It was quite apparent that we were on different wavelengths. MW and FM. He was just another nice person who I would have barely noticed had we met under any other circumstances.

So at the end of the hour we decided that we should marry each other. Two people with little in common and a few seedlings of hope, honesty and optimism. Will it bloom or perish? I wish, I knew. Years with Lennie and I still did not know him. What chance did I have in an hour?

It is scary to depend on just luck as a float in face of a storm.

How do I feel on my engagement? You may laugh. But very business like. As if a deal has been clinched. Nothing? Neutral? It is hard to put it in words. I too had my dreams. Of a tall handsome man, humble on his knees, twilight in Paris, glint of gold reflecting in the crystal diamond, my heart in my mouth. Speechless.

But that was not to be. It hurts, it truly hurts to be deprived of that moment that you have cherished in your dreams right from being a little girl. Will love bloom without the seeds of romance? I am starting with no hopes just to avoid letting myself down again. Avinash came across as very frank and decent. Maybe time and effort will help to mould us in each other's directions.

Everyone else is so excited and ecstatic that it is hard to remain untouched by it. Yesterday evening my mother was in the kitchen, cooking, with some other women when they spontaneously burst into a marriage folk song. The cooking was soon abandoned and everyone gathered into the lounge and a full two-hour group singing session ensued. I myself could not resist participating in the clapping and thumping of the coffee table and momentarily forgot the reason for their singing. Seeing the happiness on my parent's faces makes me wonder that perhaps everything was worth it.

I often dream about England. It almost seems like a dream now. There are so many wonderful memories to cherish. Of us fighting over the popcorn in the darkness of the cinema hall. Remember the 999 par-

ties in Hammersmith? When four legs and locked arms were not enough to keep us upright. Now when I come to think of it, I have had a fabulous life so far and perhaps the good Lord decided that enough was enough.

Carol, you have been a true friend and without you the past few months would have been impossible to pass by. I can always draw strength from our friendship and it would be a shame if we let it wilt because of the distances or changes in our lives.

The marriage is fixed for the 14th of July. Make sure that you arrive here at least a week in advance. Confirm your reservation as soon as possible. Rama, my cousin, has told me to warn you against the boys from the groom's side in the marriage. It is traditional to flirt with the girls from the bride's side and seeing an English girl with blonde hair is sure to set them on fire. I have seen and met quite a few young men here including some doctors. They simply do not measure up to your class and so my dear do not bother with those precautionary condoms.

By the way, have I told you about Rama, my cousin? I wish she was my own sister and we could have grown up together. She has a cracking sense of humour and keeps me going in my darkest hours.

I must end this letter now. I cannot explain how much I need you at this hour by my side. You are my tower of strength. I love you, I miss you and can't bear the wait to see you again.

Give my love to Pete.

Hugs and Kisses,
Puja

XIV

With four weeks left before the actual marriage, Ramesh's camp was in complete disarray. They could not even decide where the wedding should take place – Bishanpur or Patna. Bacchan had argued fiercely in favour of Bishanpur citing that it was their ancestral place and it would be convenient for all the relatives who would have to otherwise make the journey to Patna. Premshanker had argued that with so little time left it would be logistically impossible to arrange a wedding in Bishanpur. Patna was the capital town. All the facilities were there. One could sub-contract the whole ceremony to the professionals and do away with the headache. Bishanpur was only a village. Every small thing had to be ferried from the nearby district town.

And so the endless discussions had continued over endless cups of tea till even God got fed up and intervened personally. The monsoons broke early bringing the usual floods and the only description of a road that connected Bishanpur to the rest of the world lay submerged peacefully under the muddy waters of the Kosi river. With the venue now decided for them, the enormity of the task hit the assembled advisors. They traded blame for the lost time and then realising the futility of it sat down to do some serious planning. Premshanker got a flip chart up on the wall and scribbled the major tasks that lay ahead to be solved in the next three weeks.

- Where would the hundred odd guests in the *Baraat* stay?
- What additional accommodation would be needed to house the guests from their own side?
- Venue for the marriage?
- Military band for the groom's procession.
- Catering.
- Preparation for the *Tilak* ceremony including shopping for the dowry.
- Lighting and music.
- Jewellery shopping. Clothes shopping for the groom and bride.
- Marquee, tables and chairs.

Everyone looked at the chart in complete silence. Numbed and dumbed by this objective breakdown of the tasks and the enormity behind it. The ladies took responsibility for the jewellery and the clothes and went out of the room. Once they left, the men began to concentrate on the remainder of the tasks and started coming up with the solutions.

The marquee would be set up in the Housing cooperative society park that lay adjacent to Premshanker's house. This was a barren plot of land that was left unbuilt on since the inception of the colony to be developed into a park at a future date. Over the next ten years the red brick boundary came up around it with a gap for the entrance gate. And then everyone lost interest and the funds ran out. Nature took charge. In the monsoon rainwater would stagnate and water hyacinths would bloom and carpet most of the ground. It would stay there throughout the winter till the hot sun intervened and dried the water and let the hyacinths shrivel in the dry spell. From mid-summer the bleached grass would reconquer some ground only to be smothered by the monsoon again. All it needed was a simple drainage plan but in the battle of the stench versus apathy, apathy somehow always managed to win.

Then a slow revolution began to make matters worse. Some of the neighbours began dumping their refuse covertly into the ground. There were loud protests from the residents initially but when no one took notice, more and more people availed themselves of the sheer convenience until everyone participated in the daily chore, unashamed and in the open. That attracted the pigs and the scavenging street dogs from far and wide in search of food as they ripped apart the polythene bags to release more stench into the air. Thus what was in the blueprint a children playground with Roses and Marigolds turned out to be a refuse dump and a haven for the street dogs and pigs.

Ramesh winced as he glanced outside from the window. 'You must be joking,' he said.

Premshanker smiled to dispel his doubts. 'Do not worry Bhai saheb. This park would be a different place in the next few days. We just have to bribe the municipality to remove the garbage and then we will burn the rest along with the uprooted hyacinths. We shall then dump some sand to dry the moist soil. We shall invite the neighbours for the wedding and at the same time ask them to desist from throwing garbage till the marriage date. Believe me, this is India. Everyone cooperates in a daughter's marriage.' There was a ring of conviction in his voice reinforced by the nodding of heads all around him. The neighbours would desist from dumping their refuse illegally to help his daughter's marriage. That is, if they are all invited. It seemed too good a deal to refuse. Ramesh nodded his head too.

The *Baraat* would be accommodated in two hotels, one a three star and the other with no such starry reputation. The village folk and the servants would stay in the less expensive one while the urbanites and the groom's friends would take the three star hotel with ensuite bathrooms. Catering, marquee, military band and the lighting were to be sub-contracted to a single firm. There would be a strict budget for the women to do the jewellery and clothes shopping in view of the inherent risks of them getting carried away.

The *Tilak* ceremony passed without any hiccups. Bacchan had led the delegation along with a few other relatives from Bishanpur. Harivansh had kept the number of guests to a bare minimum bearing in mind that the current District magistrate was a crusader against dowry and had in fact made quite a few arrests in the recent past under the anti-dowry legislation. The goods were quickly unloaded from the truck and locked inside the garage. The cash was counted and recounted by three different persons and then put away in three different places. Some was put in the safe for day to day expenses, a small sum in the bank and the rest was sown securely by Radha devi into the mattress they slept upon. Only she, Harivansh and Avinash were party to this secret. The reinforced, hardened mattress certainly cured her backache but gave her sleepless nights worrying about the Dacoits whose nocturnal visits were not that uncommon following a Tilak ceremony.

Back in Patna everyone assembled to watch the video of the Tilak. Once the lights were dimmed to enhance the glow of the television, Puja too slipped in and merged with the shadows of the children. They saw Avinash dressed in a cream coloured Prince suit squatting awkwardly alongside the priest. He looked more relaxed compared to their last encounter except when his eyes met the video camera. They looked at the house and commented at the fresh coat of paint. They decreed that the elder of the two sisters who constantly shadowed Avinash in the film looked sly and cunning while the younger sister was sweet. Someone noticed the large refrigerator at one corner of the hall and wondered why they had requested another one in the dowry. Though the camera rarely focussed upon Avinash's younger brother, Bharat, he barely escaped anyone's attention. He seemed to be the person in-charge and was always seen to be frantically running around. They laughed at the women singing traditional folklore cursing the bride's family and swore revenge on the arrival of the *Baraat*.

Puja also watched the video intently. In the multitude of the faces she tried to place herself. On the terrace by the parapet. In the kitchen, by the cement sink with the yellow brass tap. She was tapping the younger sister on her shoulders from behind unsure of how she would respond. She saw herself walking in the expanse of the big garden between the banana groves and the mango trees. She looked at the unknown faces and tried to connect with them. In the swirl of her thoughts she missed vital moments in the video which left her jigsaw incomplete and unsolved. When the lights were switched on all of a sudden, she blushed to acknowledge her presence in the room. Everyone complimented the house, the family, the groom himself and congratulated Puja on her good fortune.

Slowly but surely the relatives began to filter in from all corners of the state. The space within the house shrunk everyday with the new arrivals till there was barely room to move. They slept everywhere. Under the staircase, on the veranda, the floor of the lounge. Four to a double bed, twenty on the roof. However Puja and her parent's bedrooms were spared as their need for privacy, owing to their foreign status was deemed to be much greater than the native folk.

The atmosphere in the house was frantic and loud. Puja would shut herself away in her room and alternate between sleeping and reading novels. In late afternoon she would be dragged outside her room for the *Haldi* ritual where a paste of turmeric and sandalwood would be rubbed into her to make her skin more pale and fair. For those few hours, women from the neighbourhood would converge and the lounge would be packed. Males were prohibited. Her four limbs would be taken in four different pairs of hands as they painfully rubbed the paste over her. A fifth person would put a face mask and oil her hair. The rest would sing one song after another, irrespective of their individual merits, mostly in rhythm. On the third day a woman everyone addressed as Malkini broke the ice. She lived three doors down the street from their house. A huge woman, blessed with breasts and buttocks in equal proportions, she rose with assisted effort and began to dance. No finesse, no synchrony but everyone clapped and cheered. She dared the others to join her and a few emboldened souls shed their inhibitions and rose up to the challenge. Their hips gyrated to the claps and the beat on the *Dholak*. The lyrics turned lurid with the older women laughing unashamedly and the younger women and girls covering their red faces.

For the first time after a long period, Puja had laughed uncontrollably on witnessing that geriatric lap dancing. Malkini, on spotting that the bride was finally impressed, began to swing even more violently shaking the floor and the furniture around her. The old taunted the young for sitting at the sidelines. Babli, Sweety and Pinku deserted ranks and joined on the dance floor. The men were worried as it was getting past dinner-time and no one had even entered the kitchen to start the cooking.

Someone nudged Puja from behind. It was her mother. Panting and sweating from the dance, the loose end of the sari tucked into her waist, she urged Puja to join the dance. Puja shook her head and buried her face between her knees. She lifted her head only to see her last ally, Rama, desert her. Unknown hands tugged at her and someone from behind lifted her like a feather and deposited her in the middle of the dancing crowd. She tried her nightclub swing but it did not make sense and she abandoned it hastily. She saw Rama dancing wildly with her eyes closed and tried to copy her. Puja closed her eyes and then could feel the ripples of the music travel through her body in small currents making the toes tap gently on the floor. The current amplified and travelled upwards gently swaying her hips to the beat on the *Dholak*. Suddenly a loud thud on the Dholak, a cheer from the crowd and the soul leapt to freedom taking the body with it in its tide.

They danced late into the night, from song to song, catching breath and joining again. Sometime around midnight, the hungry men unable to bear the pangs any longer, broke the prohibition orders and stormed into the lounge demanding to be fed.

XV

It rained that day in the morning. The water seeped through the small crevices, entered the marquee and soiled the freshly cleaned carpets. But everyone said it was a good sign. The heavens were pouring their blessings. The clouds parted to reveal a densely colourful rainbow but it still drizzled. One of the older ladies commented that the drizzle in the sunshine meant good fortune for the couple.

Premshanker announced that the Chief-Minister had kindly agreed to come to the wedding. He and the present Chief-Minister were friends from the student revolution days in the seventies when they had both gone to jail together. The marriage was sure to be featured in the next day's newspapers. Ramesh was not sure if it was a good idea but seeing the glee on Premshanker' face did not complain. However he warned him that the spotlight should be on the wedding and not on the Chief-Minister.

Puja was more concerned about her friend's arrival. Carol had phoned from Delhi the night before and was due to arrive by the morning flight. Puja was desperate to go to the airport but the customs dictated that a bride never ventured out on her wedding day. Rama was despatched instead with a chauffeur. There was an unspoken excitement amongst the family members on receiving an English guest. For most of them it would be their first encounter with a white person. The subtle shift from *Aloo* to potato and from *Namaste* to 'Good-morning' had begun in earnest a few days in advance. Michael Jackson was in full volume from early morning.

As Carol alighted from the car, the women craned over the railings overhead to catch a glimpse of this petite, attractive blonde dressed in a short skirt and sleeveless top, shake hands with Ramesh and Premshanker. The children giggled and hid behind each other while the men casually criss-crossed her path appearing to be busy conducting the affairs of the day.

Puja cried with unconcealed delight, her nervousness and pain all blurring into a singular emotion, when she saw her friend. She dragged her into the bedroom and bolted the door shut. They both hugged and kissed and then lay side by side on the bed and began chatting.

'How has India been treating you?' Puja asked.

'It is an experience I tell you. Never been out of the first world before this.'

'How did you find Delhi?'

'Grim on first impressions. Its take getting used to at first, doesn't it? But after that I have enjoyed every moment of my trip. It's the splash of colour, bright and random, everywhere that enchanted me. Clothes, houses even the walls with its graffiti. People are so friendly and courteous.'

'Where have you been to so far?' Puja asked.

'Agra and Jaipur. Puja you should go and see the Taj-Mahal after your wedding. It is out of this world.'

Puja smiled at Carol and stroked her golden hair. She was relieved that Carol had enjoyed her trip so far. There was a brief silence when the servant entered with some tea. Carol took Puja's hands in hers.

'And how are you sweetheart?' She asked.

'Scared.' Her voice had a thin tremble.

'Of what?'

'Of bloody everything. I am in a country I hardly know, am marrying someone whom I have hardly met, going to live with people who are complete strangers and probably from a different planet. Don't I have enough reasons to be scared out of my wits.'

Carol gave her a light hug. 'I know it must feel scary. But Puja I have known you for a long time. You will come out of it smiling. Laughing with your head high. Just give it your best and the rest will follow. Believe me.

'You know what I mean Carol?' Puja desperately wanted to believe Carol.

'Of course I do darling,' Carol reached instinctively and hugged Puja again. 'You will be back in England in a few months time for good. We shall anglicise your hubby in no time and you shall live happily ever after.'

Puja laughed. 'You are an optimist.'

'No I am serious Puja. There must be something in it. You cannot simply deride the whole system without having even tried it. Look at your parents. They had an arranged marriage and is there a happier couple around you after all these years? My parents dated for seven years before marrying each other and divorced soon after I was born. Till this date even when they are not together, they hate each other and I am the one caught in between. There are no fixed rules Puja and I only ask you not have any fixed notions either. Just give it a fair chance.'

'Today is my wedding day and there is no spark inside me. No excitement only fear. How can it bode well for the future?'

'There is no spark because your will be starting today from scratch. You, together with Avinash will start laying the first bricks from today. In your way and in your time. Your system of arranged marriages presumes that if any two normal and decent human beings come together and make an honest effort to build a relationship then they will succeed. And that is a perfectly valid presumption. It is us out there who make a hash of it. Because we love ourselves more than we can ever love that other person. That is where we fall. That is where we are dishonest. Lennie loved himself more than he loved you. Otherwise he could not have brought himself to hurt you so badly. Don't do the same mistake yourself.'

Puja took a deep breath in. What would she do without Carol. Her words had not erased her doubts or apprehensions but blunted it to some extent. She had sowed a few seedlings of hope and left it to Puja to either nurture or destroy them.

'A week in India and you sound like a holy Hindu,' said Puja.

'And I have brought something else for you which you must have overlooked whilst doing your packing.'

'What?' Puja was genuinely surprised.

Carol opened her bag and took out of six packs of what appeared to contain some medication. Puja took one of the green and white packs to have a closer look. It read 'Microgynon 30'.

She had just been presented with a six month supply of oral contraceptive pills.

Puja burst out laughing and then Carol by induction. They perpetuated each other's laughter till their stomach began to ache and then they begged each other to stop. But then even a small hiss or a giggle would detonate another burst of laughter again and again until Puja physically got up and ran into the bathroom to break the chain reaction.

Rani and Laxmi, Harivansh's two married daughters, were up in arms. They insisted that they would go in the *Baraat* and attend their brother's marriage. The two brothers were backing them but Radha Devi had put her foot down. Women never went in a *Baraat* and she was not willing to break tradition for her insolent daughters. Arguments and counter-arguments were exchanged. Witnesses were brought to testify that in the modern age even the groom's mother went see her son's wedding. Radha Devi thumped her feet and jangled her bangles to emphasise that it was precisely the reason why the modern families were divorcing each other and splitting up joint families. Harivansh remained neutral, the sisters begged and the brothers pleaded but she remained unmoved. The video cameraman was then given the task of redeeming their misfortune and capture every moment of the wedding.

There were a few other complications yet to be sorted out. Including the dear old Ambassador, there were six cars and a bus to take the *Baraatis* from Sitapur to Patna. One car was to be exclusively for the groom and his nephew only. That left twenty-two VIPs to be accommodated in five cars. These were the urban, professional elite for whom it would be an anathema to sit in the bus with the commoner relatives hailing from the villages. Apart from the driver each car could take a maximum of four other passengers and that left two VIPs out in the lurch. The family pondered over the problem.

'Is every one of them coming? No one sick or pulling out at the last moment?' asked Harivansh.

'No these names are the confirmed ones,' said Bharat.

'Professor Verma can go in the bus. He is not the fussy type.'

'He will be if he finds out that he is the only one that has been dumped on to the bus.'

'I and Ashutosh babu can go on the bus,' the younger son-in-law proposed with a nodding assent from the older one.

Harivansh shook his head in complete disagreement. Tradition and protocol dictated that the son-in-laws be accorded the highest of privileges. 'I have made a decision. I and Pramod will go on the bus. This will make the relatives on the bus feel valued as well. Please let Pramod know of the change in plans.'

Happy with the arrangements, Harivansh shuffled his feet and got up to disperse the meeting. 'We shall be leaving in half an hour. Better tell Avinash to get ready in time.'

But Avinash was far from being ready. He paced restlessly in his room as the hot weather and the nervous mind made him sweat profusely. This evolution in his life had been so sudden and profound that any attempts to prepare for it was ending in despair. Twenty eight years of his life and he had barely known or spoken to a girl and from today he was to share his bed and life with one. Why did it provoke more anxiety than excitement?

He stopped in front of the mirror and inspected his virginal features carefully for the last time. He lifted the scissors and trimmed his moustache to align it over his upper lip. He stood sideways and twisted his back and neck to inspect his balding crown. He combed a few hairs away from the sides to cover it. He pulled his lips in different directions in front of the mirror and then chose a smile for the cameras and practised it a few more times.

There was a tap on the door and it opened ajar as Bharat poked his head through.

'Time to roll on Avi.'

' Yeah. I shall be down in a few moments.' He put on his white jacket, ensured his reflection on the shoes and set off for his final act of prophylactic urination before a long journey. He checked himself in the bathroom mirror again. He liked the bathroom mirror. Somehow he looked less fat in this than the dressing table one. As he shut the door of his bedroom behind him, he looked at the double bed one last time and chose the side nearer to the bathroom door for when he came back.

As he stepped into the lounge, the full volume of the folklore sung by different women in differing tones, pitch and rhythm struck his eardrums painfully. The video photographer swung his hand to clear the way for his own vision and that of the groom. The women at catching sight of him protested in unison.

'Why is he leaving in a simple white suit,' asked his mother's sister. 'Don't we get the chance to see the groom in his wedding dress? '

'Because *Mausi*, if I wear my *Sherwani* now and travel in the car, it will be crushed and of no good for the marriage itself.'

'But this is the only chance that we get to see the groom in his full attire. We have dreamt for years of this day,' said another relative.

Radha devi nodded in agreement and the protest gained pace at the doorway. His route was blocked. But Avinash was determined not to give in.

'I am sorry, I cannot agree to that. Those clothes are all ironed and folded neatly in my suitcase. You will all see the video anyway.'

The crowd was adamant. His sisters also sided against him. Someone suggested that he change into the *Sherwani*, get in to the car and then change again back to his suit at her house which was a few blocks away. Avinash flew off the handle at the suggestion and refused to even consider such an idea.

'Son, try to understand our emotions,' Mrs. Verma said. 'We want to see what our handsome groom would look like at the actual wedding. This is the least you can do for the unlucky women who cannot go to your wedding. Try to listen to your elders.'

Radha devi, who was crying partly because it was customary, began to sob even more loudly. The women looked at him blaming him for her plight. This could rapidly degenerate into a bad omen on an auspicious occasion inviting its own added complications. Avinash turned on his heels to go upstairs again.

He finally emerged dressed in his *Sherwani* and headgear. The women gasped and praised his looks. Their eyes were moist as they bid him farewell. His mother wept openly. The priest raised his voice to have his hymns heard over the wailing and singing. The band began to play, 'today is my friend's wedding'. The Video-photographer shot frantically and waved furiously, walking backwards, till he stumbled over a brick and took a clear shot of the clear sky. Rice and flowers were showered upon him as he walked to the car. Onlookers stopped to gaze at the spectacle and a traffic jam ensued. Finally the bus driver sounded his horn to signal departure. The women ran to the gates to get a last glimpse.

Slowly the convoy inched forwards, the traffic policeman making way for them by stopping all other traffic.

Radha devi sat on the bamboo chair on the veranda, wiped her tears and ordered that tea be served.

It was half past two in the afternoon when a large elephant marched up Premshanker's road. He uprooted the Banyan tree in the front garden and began to devour the unripe bananas. The trainer seated on the top poked his blunted spear around the elephant's neck to deter it but the animal was so hungry that he only stopped after having eaten the fruit and the leaves. There was pandemonium in the campus at this unexpected visitor. Finally

Premshanker solved the riddle.

'The groom will ride on him for the *Baraat* procession.'

'What?' exclaimed Ramesh. 'This is a town, not a village.'

'So what. This is quite fashionable nowadays with the urban elite especially within the *Rajput* community.'

Ramesh looked unsure and puzzled. The trainer made the elephant raise it front two legs in a salute to impress him and change his mind.

'Have you asked the groom's side?'

'No.'

'What? What if they are totally opposed to all this? What if the groom refuses to mount this beast?'

'Don't worry Ramesh,' reassured Premshanker. 'I have also asked for a Mercedes car from the Tourism department. Our groom will have a choice but I take a bet that he will choose the elephant.'

The children insisted on a ride before the elephant was bathed and decorated. So did an adult. Off they went, with Carol sandwiched in the middle even before they got the consent.

One corner of the park was bordered off by marquee cloth and flat sheets of corrugated tin to work as a temporary kitchen. Inside the cooks, tearful of the smoke, onions and low wages, were cutting the vegetables and washing the meat. The reflective tin made the heat even more unbearable inside the enclosure. The chief cook was furious because the coal stoves were not lighting up satisfactorily. Acrid smoke rose to colour the sky but the red glow from the stoves were still missing. He could not cook till the stoves were smokeless and the coal itself red with heat. He was fanning at the mouth of the stove with a folded newspaper without any luck. He shouted at one of his assistants to get a pedestal fan, hung it upside down at the mouth of the stove and handed it back to the assistant with firm orders not to move till the stove lit up properly.

Inside, the house was a riot of colour, cloth and jewellery. Every mirror however small, basked in its importance. Irrespective of age, respective of sex, the women jostled for space in front of the mirrors. Silk and gold and flesh flirted with each other till they synchronised in perfection. There were stylists and beauticians floating from room to room offering advice and giving the finer touches. A pair of them had worked on Puja since late morning. First the application all over of the sandalwood paste and then the finery of Henna on the hands. The fine green paste drying and then shedding its skin to reveal the livid red sculpted patterns set in perfect geometry. They rubbed special oil in the palms and the red blushed into crimson. Carol had the Henna too and afterwards could not take her eyes off her hands. Carol wore a *Lehanga* and *choli* but walked stiff as if still in a Black English dress. So she was made to walk across the bedroom again and again till she acquired the indigenous gait. Her carefully pleated hair was unfolded and left to rest, bare and defiant, on her shoulders. Her fake pearl necklace was dumped unceremoniously and replaced by Puja's own jewellery and matching golden bangles. Proud at the conversion, she paraded herself in front of the other women who looked at her with admiration and showered genuine praise.

Somehow in the festivities of the day they forgot about Puja. In a quest to finish the physical chores that the day demanded of them no one paused to peek into the blankness of her eyes. In that ocean of smiles the house was that day, no one noticed a missing smile. She wore a jeans and a shirt for most of the day. Even when they put the bridal make up on. Even when they painted her toes. She stayed impassive and immobile as they worked on her. Lifeless to let no emotions seep in. When they had finished she lay down elegantly on the bed in her bridal attire and closed her eyes.

The *Baraat* reached Patna two hours behind schedule. The procession for the bride's place would be delayed accordingly. The message was conveyed on wireless to the Chief-Minister's residence. The Chief-Minister was to catch a late evening flight to Delhi and a message was sent back to urge the groom's party to hurry up if they could. The priest was happy. The auspicious time extended right up to midnight. Ramesh was unhappy.

'We cannot be dictated by what the Chief-Minister's schedule is.'

'No we aren't,' said Premshanker. 'But there is no harm in pretending that we are.'

However when Harivansh heard that the Chief-Minister would be gracing the wedding, he exhorted everyone to get ready immediately. For the first time in many years he combed his hair in front of a mirror in anticipation of the waiting journalists. He applied gel to his moustache to keep it taut against the winds of fame and publicity.

'I told you,' he nudged Pramod. 'We are marrying into no ordinary family.'

Downstairs in the lobby a big debate was going on without any conclusions. Should the groom choose the car or the elephant? Avinash was confused but Bharat was convinced about the merits of leading the marriage procession on an elephant. Pramod was expressing his reservations. What if the creature ran amuck with the noise of the band and the gunshots? The trainer was insistent that the elephant had an outstanding record of attending previous marriages. He cited the elephant's pedigree as reference and said that his mother was a court elephant in one of the princely states. Finally Avinash relented and agreed to ride the elephant.

The news that the *Baraat* had left the hotel sent everyone in a frenzy of activity. Some rushed around with a sense of purpose while others were too ashamed to stand still. Rama ran inside and alerted the women and the bride. Final checks were made in the marquee. The Marigold garlands were handed out to welcome the *Baraatis*. The children congregated on the balcony early on to get the best view. Soon they could hear the sound of the military band interspersed with gunshots in the far distance. Everyone ran downstairs to catch a glimpse. Carol stayed behind with Puja. They sat silently in the dimly lit bedroom, holding hands, listening to the distant noise marching steadily towards them. Finally Puja signalled Carol to go down and witness the spectacle. Once alone in the room and the house, she lay on her bed and closed her eyes one more time to blank out the reality.

Carol eased her way to the front of the crowd downstairs. At a distance she could see the fluorescent lights hazed by the virgin evening fog being carried by the dark silhouettes on their shoulders in two parallel rows. There were gunshots and fireworks glittering the sky. As it came more into focus she could see the military band dressed in white leading the *Baraatis*. She could see the elephant draped in a blanket of flowers behind the band. The Baraatis dressed elegantly, marched towards them slowly. Some had swords hanging by their sides while a few were firing guns jubilantly into the air. The younger ones in that group, clearly inebriated were dancing wildly in the centre. The fireworks lit the moonless night under which this florescent column advanced on the beat of the military band, marching and dancing. Neighbours craned over their balconies to catch a glimpse of the groom. Carol saw the elephant, now transformed under the floral mesh of Marigolds, roses and Jasmine lumbering proudly towards them. She saw the groom riding straight on the elephant's back, his face covered by a floral veil of Jasmine dangling down from his headgear.

They were now yards from the bride's gates. They halted on a signal from Bharat. The youths asked everyone to move back to create a space in the centre of the road. The band played a racy tune which had recently topped the charts and the final dance began in front of the bride's family and their guests. They urged, challenged, and taunted the hosts to join them but they smiled back with dignified reserve and showered rose petals and perfumed rose water upon them. One of the lads, dressed in a white three-piece suit, took a chance and came up to Carol but only received a polite refusal. He seemed very content nevertheless.

The prospective in-laws hugged each other and then Harivansh was garlanded by so many from the bride's side that his neck and chin began to disappear under the girth of the garlands.

The trainer gently guided the elephant to sit down. The women and the girls rushed forward to catch a glimpse of the groom. As Bharat lifted his brother's floral veil to reveal his face, the women gave a customary gasp of admiration. Carol too had had a good glimpse of him. Blushing and nervous, he still looked handsome and much better than the photographs she had seen before. Maybe it was the dress and the occasion. She turned back and ran upstairs to tell Puja.

Inside hectic preparations were on for the *Jaimal* ceremony. Savita and Kamla were putting the final touches to the bride's dress and the facial make-up. Now finished, Savita straightened back and lifted her daughter's chin tenderly with her right middle finger.

'Tell me everyone. Have you ever seen a more beautiful bride?'

There were nods of approval.

Rama had her own agenda. 'Didi, whatever happens make sure that he bends down to get the garland around his neck from you. He who bends on the first day remains faithfully yours for the rest of the life. It is true.'

Bacchan poked his head in the bedroom and announced that everyone was waiting for the bride. Then she rose, under the weight of the clothes and the enormity of the occasion. Soft hands took her elbows and lead her down the aisle. Carol on her right and Rama on her left. A nervous mother walked behind her. The crowd froze to pay attention, only the silence of the whirring pedestal fans. Avinash rose as she climbed the steps on to the stage, her body lifted by a dozens pair of unknown hands. She was turned slowly around to face the guests. Rama gently lifted the veil to reveal the bride and whispered in Puja's ears to open her eyes. Her face shone radiant under the golden arc-lights as the pride of the Chauhans' drew gasps from the assembled guests and then a dignified applause.

Someone brought the garlands on a large silver plate and placed it on the small glass table. The crowd was cheering and clapping. Both were turned to face each other and then the slight adjustments for the benefit of the cameraman. The first garland was placed in Puja's hands. She lifted her head to look into a nervous but smiling face. Eager and waiting. She lifted her trembling hands to encircle his neck. The first touch of warm flushed fingers on the moist nape of the neck. The shuddering, fluttering of the eyes and then regaining poise.

The crackles on the wireless set warned everyone of the imminent arrival of the Chief-Minister. People rose from their seats in anticipation and huddled around the gate. The pressmen polished their camera lenses and the khaki policemen lining the road, shed their lazy acquired scoliosis and bored looks and put on a mask of alertness. A row of six white Ambassador cars screeched to a halt. The security personnel scurried around first to secure the area and then opened the door of the car for the Chief-Minister.

At forty-seven, his looks were a bit of a contradiction. A boyish face bolted on a body that had aged. It had expanded beyond it means and the protuberant abdomen curved the spine forward with it. That made him walk with a precarious lurching gait which continuously adjusted its centre of gravity to maintain the balance. He had sparse grey hair which was trimmed to a short crop but there was generous compensation of hair on his earlobes which were never trimmed because of a superstition that its length had a direct bearing on the longevity of his political career.

Puja was unsure as to how to respond to this phenomenon hurtling towards her, when she saw Avinash almost take a dive for the Chief-Minister's feet. She also leant forward and gently brushed his knees. Absurdly the crowd clapped. She herself was smothered by a fine spray of betel-juice when the Chief-Minister opened his mouth to give his blessings to the couple.

The Chief-Minister was a bit bewildered as to why the bride had left in a huff but put it down to shyness of the bride. Inside the beauticians were interrupted in their dinner to redo her makeup after she had scrubbed her face sore.

Outside too a crisis had erupted without warning. Dinner was being served and the guests were feasting and praising the sumptuous culinary delights. But no one from the host side had taken into account the six car-loads of hungry, low paid security staff who primed themselves for such occasions when accompanying their master. In their grim day to day life of sustained poverty and hard work, this was their only perk. A full feast till their stomachs burst and then the tales of the food to their wives and neighbours.

They ate as if the earth was coming to an end. They concentrated on the chicken and the fish, as they could seldom afford to eat non-vegetarian food in their homes. Piles of freshly stripped bones stacked on their plates. They pushed and jostled in the buffet queues irritating the more graceful *Baraatis*. They would take two spoons of rice with five helpings of chicken and would reappear in the queues in a matter of a few minutes. A few had polythene bags into which they stuffed the food from their plates to take it back home for their children and wives. Some with a hint of shame were chucking the bones beneath the table.

It was soon apparent to the chief cook that a food shortage was in the offing. He sent one of his underlings to summon Ramesh and Premshanker. Ramesh was livid, Premshanker was thoughtful.

'Will it be possible to cook some more?' Premshanker asked.

'No way sir. Even if I start cooking now it will be well past midnight before anything will be ready. Besides where will you get chicken and fish to cook at this hour of the night?'

'You should not have called the Chief-Minister,' said Ramesh.

'Well I never knew he would come with this pack of hungry wolves.'

'We cannot turn the guests back without serving them dinner.'

'That is out of question anyway.'

There was silence as everyone racked their brains. Even the cook contracted his forehead muscles whilst keeping his mind blank. It was not his problem and he did not give a damn. Premshanker finally broke the silence.

'Okay here is the plan. The *Baraatis* who are the guests have nearly eaten and there is enough to see them through. The only people left would be the ones from our side, a hundred odd. I will order some food from the restaurants for them and it should be here in no time.'

‘Don’t you think that they will notice that?’

‘Of course they will. But it does not matter. They are the home-side, not guests but hosts, in a daughter’s marriage. No one will raise a finger. They will all understand.’

‘Nevertheless we have invited them as our guests. They will probably comment that I was not able to even feed everyone properly in my only daughter’s marriage.’

‘There is no better alternative Ramesh ji. And do not worry, the food they will be eating would be far more expensive if not better than the one the *Baraatis* had.’

Ramesh shrugged his shoulder in resignation and walked away from the crisis leaving it in his brother-in law’s hands.

The priest started the marriage after much delay at twenty minutes to midnight. The *Baraatis* were not allowed to witness the ceremony after consultation with Harivansh as most of them were too inebriated for such a pious occasion. Instead they were packed off to the hotel to consume even more alcohol.

The whole ceremony lasted for a little over three hours. Misty smoked eyes in a foggy summer night; they watched it on the roof in a specially erected *Marwa*. The priest was ranting off the *mantras* in Sanskrit that no one understood but yet they watched and listened with rapt attention. Around the sandalwood fire in which the offerings to the Gods went, they watched silently with watering eyes from the smoke and the emotions. Their daughter slipping away, *mantra* after *mantra*, into an alien’s shadow. So when the priest placed Puja’s hands into Avinash’s and asked them to walk around the fire seven times to take the seven vows, the women wept openly. Joy and sorrow indistinguishable in those tears.

Puja felt that she had crossed a line and it felt numbingly painless at that moment of time.

The less involved gave a sigh of relief at the conclusion of the ceremony. The couple were led into the bridal bedroom to rest for the night which was already being threatened at the edge of the horizon. Avinash was dragged out instantaneously by a posse of sister-in-laws who demanded money, gifts and various other favours before being let in with their sister. He in turn pleaded and bargained, but it fell on deaf ears of the adamant ladies. Half an hour later, robbed of a few thousand rupees, he was rescued by his mother-in-law and ushered into the bedroom.

In the dimmed lights, behind the Jasmine laces hanging from the four-poster bed, he saw a heap of silk and gold and glistening skin lying still on the bed. He tiptoed through the silent air to have a closer look at the tangled mass. He stared at the glow in her face despite the closed eyes. A few pearls of sweat lined on her forehead. A few strands of hair fallen carelessly across the face. A half smile of a sweet dream. He lifted those few strands with precision and care and put them back to their rightful place. He wanted to touch her skin but instead opened the window and let the breeze wipe those beads off her face. Now content, he took off his shoes and crept into the far end of the bed taking the minimum of space.

Before long exhaustion won over euphoria, the only shade left the half smile on his face.

Singing, sizzling, lashing and bashing, the heavy raindrops fell in synchrony with the storm within. Lakelets on the surface, a torrential flood within. A day in a parent's life, which they both aspire for and dread. They had come to take their daughter away. Into a new world, away from them. A new wound etched with every footstep she took towards the door, smudging the present into a nostalgic past. Puja hugged her cousins and aunts. She clung to Carol and did not want to let her go. She lifted her pall to search for her mother. Someone pointed her towards the bedroom.

There was her mother hunched like an orphan on the edge of the bed. The pillow in her mouth failing to muffle the wailing. Puja hugged her mother and squeezed her tight to stem the tide flowing through her eyes. Savita clutched at her daughter, desperate not to let her go but then Kamla Mami poked her head and said that it was getting late.

'Ma,' Puja whispered in her ear almost kissing it. 'Nothing has changed. I am still your daughter and I am coming back to you in just a few months.'

On the veranda facing the lounge, the males congregated waiting for her to emerge. The Baraatis stood outside solemnly by the row of cars waiting for the bride.

Ramesh had sought refuge on the veranda, wearing dark glasses and hiding behind Premshanker and his brother. As Puja began to walk towards him he began to shake and crumble. She steadied the tall gaunt figure now crying shamelessly like a child with a tight embrace and hid her face within him just like before. When mummy told her off for not finishing her dinner. Or when she had smashed the portable TV by accident. It felt nice and warm in there and for a moment as before she stopped crying. Then she felt the strength return in his arms as he detached her from himself and wiped her face dry with his handkerchief.

'I love you beti,' he said. 'Remember this is a beginning not an end. This old man desires nothing more than happiness for you.'

'I love you papa,' she had never said that before. 'With your blessings behind me, it cannot elude me for long. Look after yourself and Ma.'

She turned to walk down the small flight of stairs onto the garden. At the last step she paused and looked back to see her mother peeping through the bedroom window and her father slumped in Premshanker's arms. She undid the knot in her sari, which held a few rice grains. She took them in her palm and without looking back threw it back over her head.

Symbolically wiping out all the debt she owed to her parents and the household.

So the Brahmin said.

XVI

As the longer, longing days rolled into months, the mighty summer continued to wreak its elements with scant mercy. It parched the earth, then crumbled it and swirled it with mighty gusts into a dust bowl which coated everything from the mind, morale, skin, plants, houses and the landscape. As if a shade of grey had descended from the heavens. It hung menacingly over the drooping leaves, refusing to be shaken off by the wind. The roads were black-grey, lined by green-grey trees and white-grey houses. The winds howled all day, teasing and whipping, till long after the sun had set. Then as the moon climbed from the other side, as if under a spell of the starlit sky, it would transform itself into a wispy cool breeze and embalm the baked, burnt earth and its living souls.

In a new climate, in a new home, Puja wilted while desperately trying to keep up appearances. A surreal train of events made the first few days pass in a flash and then life stuttered, stopped, and restarted again in an agonizing slow motion.

For the first few days she mostly stayed in her bedroom. Sitting on the bed in full bridal attire from late morning to early evening. A model sitting still watched by the crowd on the catwalk. It felt like the whole town of Sitapur was taking turns to see the new bride. The women would pause in front of her, lift her chin and drop a compliment. The males would only politely fold their hands and drop an envelope with cash in her hands or a small wrapped gift on the bedside. Puja kept silent for most of the duration but her face ached from the continuous smiling. The queue was kept on the move continuously by her two sister-in-laws. Occasionally, Rani, her younger sister-in-law would drop a covert nod on arrival of an important personality and Puja mechanically would stoop from her bed to touch their feet. Few of the guests dared to speak to Puja, unsure of their own English and her Hindi speaking abilities. She was entitled to lunch and tea breaks and then the programme resumed. Once Radha Devi was satisfied that enough compliments and presents had fallen in her lap, she ordered a halt to it. For the odd relative or friend who had missed the show and turned up at the house, Puja would get a two-minute notice to put on her sari and jewellery and come downstairs into the lounge. A ritual that could happen up to three or four times a day.

Rani had become a close friend in those first few days and her saviour. The ordeal could have been much worse without her help. She zealously guarded her from the elements as best as she could. Rani was like a shadow in the first few days of her arrival. She would help her get ready, fetch her dinners, iron her saris and tutored her about the ways of the household.

She told her for instance to touch her in-law's feet every morning when she came downstairs from her bedroom. That gesture of touch was so touching indeed that Radha devi cried as she told her neighbour about it. Harivansh swelled with pride. The word spread about a *foreign* daughter-in-law more conventional than a conventional daughter-in-law. Rani advised Puja to spend a few minutes downstairs in the *Pooja* room every morning after having her bath. As Puja closed her eyes with folded hands in front of the deities and thought about the night club in Hammersmith, Radha devi would gaze at her in amazement and taunt her own daughters. When Puja confessed her ineptitude at cookery to Rani, she took upon herself to teach her the art and smuggled in recipes from the magazines to be hidden under the mattresses. These would spring up as specially cooked dishes from time to time under fascinating western names.

Her rising acceptance and popularity in the household spread general delight but also sowed a few seeds of envy. Her elder sister-in-law, Laxmi, was clearly upset at the attention a newcomer was attracting. She herself had had a very tumultuous experience in her *Sasural* after marriage and thought that so much affection so soon for Puja was grossly undeserved. Puja too had disliked her from the beginning. On the very first day of her arrival, Laxmi had raided Puja's suitcases on the pretext of arranging her clothes and other items. Laxmi would dig out a bottle of perfume or a cream from the cases and stare at it in a frozen state of dilated pupils and a gaping mouth, till it would be a violation of human rights not to part with it. During those two hours of emotional auction Puja was deprived of her favourite perfume, creams and moisturizers of various descriptions, cakes of soap and one piece of lacy, black, worn underwear.

Laxmi would often try to trap Puja with sarcasm disguised in praise which was apparent to no one but Puja. She would talk about the decadence in the western society with the implied message that Puja too was a part of it. She would praise her food for instance, but add that it would have tasted even better had Puja put in some extra chilli. She would harp on how close she was to Avinash and that how blood relation was above all other bonds. Puja at first was puzzled and irritated with this behaviour but later she adopted indifference as defence and that worked well for her.

But it was her relationship with her mother-in-law that stood undefined and blurred for a long time. Both of them were cautious, apprehensive and waited for the other to take the initiative. For Puja it was like gauging the depth of a pond through opaque waters, one foot at a time, wary of taking the wrong step. Radha devi spoke little and gave little away. In the first few days they seldom spoke to each other though Radha devi sent a lot of messages through her daughters. Puja felt awkward with her broken Hindi to start a conversation with her but feared that her silence might be construed as coldness or arrogance. So she would rehearse some preconceived dialogues before coming downstairs and try to jump-start a conversation. When Radha devi would initiate some conversation, Puja would try her best to engage with words ably supported by gestures and even an occasional English word. Slowly but surely the communication evolved from its embryonic state into a viable, sustainable life form. Once the bridges of language were built, both were excited and keen to nurture the relationship further.

The seedling grew with the feeding of the mother-in-law's ego and total subservience. Then motherly love seeped in when the tests were over, for the heart unshackled of apprehension was aching to embrace her daughter-in-law anyway. When Rani and Laxmi left with their husbands there was a void that needed to be filled. Puja was sometimes though annoyed with Radha devi's attempts to equate herself with Savita. How often would she dwell upon the fact that there was no difference between Puja and Rani or Laxmi. How often she would remind Puja of the lesser relevance of biological parents in a Hindu woman's life. It was not expected of Puja to be convinced of it but to accept it as gospel truth.

Yet through all this Puja saw a woman who was plain and simple at heart. With her baggage of biases and beliefs, but also naive and innocent. A traditional, illiterate village woman who had created her own multiplex of hurdles over her lifetime and was now breaking them one by one in order to reach out to her foreign daughter-in-law. For that Puja respected her and responded in kind. She too reached out for her mother-in-law; a bit of pity and duty, but largely out of a budding genuine affection.

Soon after her arrival, the relatives started to leave steadily to their respective abodes. Rani and Laxmi left after two weeks. The home contracted further when Bharat left for his college with the promise to come back in the *Dussehra* holidays. Puja and Bharat had got off to a good start after an initial period of shyness and hesitation. In the evenings they would gossip idly for hours on the terrace. About Bharat's college life of freedom away from his parents and Puja's England. He spoke fluent English, much better than Avinash and had an excellent sense of humour. It was an easy and informal chemistry between them and when he left to rejoin his studies both were saddened to suspend a relationship that was just beginning to bloom.

Avinash got somewhat blurred at first in the melee of inquisitive relatives and prying sister-in-laws but then gradually he crept back into the focus of her thoughts. The union with him had yet not firmly crystallised in her mind and she tried subconsciously to deceive truth with a detached approach. But that worked only till the house was packed with relatives and she could melt into them. Now in the emptiness of the large house she could no longer avoid facing him or his thoughts.

It was plain to her that Avinash was trying his desperate best to build bridges between them. Desperation camouflaged in a male's ego. Moves made within chauvinistic limits. Like coming early from the clinic and going late in the mornings or lingering in the bedroom in the mornings on one pretext or other. At first their conversations were very formal, centred on the needs and the occasional gossip. It felt odd and awkward but it was also a protective wall for Puja who had yet not reconciled to Avinash being her husband. But it also generated some guilt inside her which chipped at that wall from within while Avinash knocked it down from the outside.

The inevitability of sex was known to her, and was more apparent after Avinash started to make his first hesitant overtures. In a non defiant way she sought to postpone it for as long as she could. In the evenings she would curl up before he crept up into the bedroom and pretend to be fast asleep in seconds. She could feel his stare burning her back as both of them lay awake, eyes closed and open. Sometimes he would gather courage and slide his hand over her thighs and she pretending to be asleep would leave it for a few minutes and then turn over to dislodge it gently. Once she had felt sorry for him when he had got up and disappeared into the bathroom and emerged a few minutes later slightly short of breath.

At first it was effortless. But then the weight of the hand increased each day. It jangled some odd nerves, aroused some old sensations. Banal, carnal desires long suppressed in a quiescent volcano. So one day she turned and faced Avinash with her eyes closed, his hand still on her thighs. Encouraged he slid it upwards. As he touched her nipples under the thin cotton fabric, she drew a deep breath in, still asleep. He began to unbutton her gown and she accidentally rested her hands on his bare chest. He unhooked her bra and cupped the unstrapped expanding bulge in his hands and then between his wet and thirsty lips. Though the pretence was over, shyness conspired to keep her eyes closed and her body from responding. As he worked his way down, she kept still because she was asleep and felt the static burn her from inside. A maze of nerves firing impulses down taut muscles heaving the whole body in unrevealing waves. As he entered her, she constricted her pelvic muscles to feign virginity and let him in with a grimace of pain.

It finished as soon as it had started. A few rapid movements, shuddering and then the stillness. Both panting, one still in anticipation and the other at the finish line. She stroked his back in solidarity and understanding but his ignorance of her plight was quite obvious to her. He lay snoring by her side while she was still panting, sweating and staring at the invisible ceiling.

Their first encounter galvanised their relationship though in many other ways. Avinash transformed overnight from a shy withdrawn husband into an extrovert. He shed all pretence and buzzed around her like a moth around a flame. At last, the floodgates had opened for him before the dam burst through its walls. His adulation for Puja hatched out of its secrecy and grew into a giant. She was both flattered and embarrassed initially by his overt expressions of affection but later got used to the indigenous ways of venting emotions. Many an evening on the moonlit terrace, he would talk to her for hours from love to nonsense.

Their sex life peaked immediately in quantity then gradually some quality began to seep in. Avinash, with years of unearthed passions and no real experience, poured out like lava, as if in a rush to make up for lost time. At first she was just a receptacle for his body fluids but slowly as married sex took its slow journey from the exotic to the mundane, he began to last longer to her relief. Without appearing to be an expert, she coached him in the many ways of making love. Like a blacksmith to molten metal, she moulded him around her tastes and needs.

Within six weeks she had her first orgasm. A final bolt to the coffin of Lennie Riviera. No more closing her eyes and imagining someone else on top of her.

First sex then love, western or eastern spirit, their relationship blossomed nevertheless.

Slowly, in subtle impalpable ways, Avinash began to happen to her. Not as a big flood but in small tiny rivulets across a parched riverbed that ached for some moisture. Still largely dry but with ribbons of liquid coalescing into an enlarging glistening sheet somewhere downstream. The first signs of a mossy life taking roots on erstwhile dead rocks. She tried to analyse why, but could not put it down to lack of choice or an escape from boredom. Perhaps it was the man himself. She found herself waiting on him in the evenings, even dragging herself to the gates to look on the road. She found herself laughing at his jokes when she had presumed his humour to be non-existent. She found the same eyes deeper than before, the same smile more enticing than ever.

Sitapur though, emaciated her spirits like a slow deadly virus. The town was like a stillborn child; a form but no life. She wanted to break out of the house but there was nowhere to go out to. She wandered in her open jail from room to room, garden to terrace. Life had become an unshakable routine of waking up, cooking, staring into the vacant space and then sleeping again. She sometimes tried to beat it by oversleeping. The town held no attraction for her. She had ventured out on a few occasions but gradually gave up on it. There was this one main road with motley of shops dotted incongruously on both sides. They sold nothing that interested her. Further along there were two banks and a government office and then without warning the town ended with the bus stand on one side and a large garbage dump on the other. The countryside began thereafter with semi-constructed houses strewn randomly in the paddy fields. There was a sweet shop that served some vegetarian fast food but no restaurants. The only magazine shop was in the railway station called

'Wheeler and Co', named after some Englishman during the Raj who had started a chain of magazine stalls across the railway stations in India.

Yet it was a bustling town propelled by some secret source of energy unseen by her. People went about with their daily chores from early dawn, smiling and uncomplaining, as if charged with some divine energy that desperately eluded her. Oblivious of the dead town, the dust bowls, the prickly heat. Her own life ran parallel to them in slow motion, no slip roads to jump tracks.

There was no company, either, apart from Avinash who ran a busy life as a medical practitioner. Since the marriage a new phone had been installed and but for that Puja could have contemplated running away. Her mother rang her twice a week on Wednesdays and Sundays and Carol rang her every fortnight on a Sunday. Those phone calls helped her to preserve her sanity and were something to look forward to everyday. On the phone she plotted her departure back to England along with Avinash. She coaxed Ramesh to tell Harivansh that the job situation was getting tight and Avinash should try to come to England as soon as possible. Soon a consensus began to emerge that the couple should leave for England sometime in November. It was still only August and Puja gritted herself to tide over the remaining few months.

Meanwhile her medical prowess was being put to test with increasing frequency. At first it was just a few close friends and relatives of the family who came for consultations but as the word spread, the trickle enlarged into a regular stream of patients. And that is when the hard life began. Owing to her female gender, everyone assumed that she was a gynaecologist and despite her best efforts to counter that belief, they presented in droves with problems which she did not have much clue about. Pregnant women, bleeding women and some even requesting terminations. She borrowed some of Avinash's books to brush up her knowledge and often rang Avinash in the middle of her consultations to get advice.

'Whatever you do, do not forget to give them multivitamins and antihelminthics,' he would say. 'Also always do a chest x-ray.'

'Even if they present with a vaginal discharge?'

'Oh yes! Otherwise they think that you have ignored them and did not carry out the proper investigations. A normal chest x-ray is the greatest placebo in rural India.'

It did not matter that she was not a gynaecologist and it did not matter she was not even locally registered in India. Word began to spread about this foreign trained specialist who saw patients for free. Sitapur had one doctor with a FRCS degree but the town had never been privileged with a MRCP qualified Practitioner. Harivansh was filled with pride with his daughter-in-law's popularity. In the daily evening congregations of the elite in the town when anyone flocked to anyone's house without prior notice, he would boast in detail about the individual cases that were miraculously cured by her daughter-in-law. Fellow caste men and women took upon themselves to propagate her name in the surrounding villages.

Puja though was wading in troubled waters with her gynaecological status. She conveyed her concerns to Avinash who brushed them aside with a laugh. She discussed it with Harivansh who promptly took upon himself to redress the situation. The outer room adjacent to the veranda was formalised into a consultation chamber and a huge notice in Hindi hung on the wall by the side of the door.

Dr.(Mrs.) P. Singh MRCP (London)
Physician and Cardiologist

Note: WOMENS' DISEASES NOT SEEN HERE

A prescription pad was printed promptly and a *Compounder* from Avinash's clinic was transferred to work at the new clinic with the task of rigorously screening patients without any concerns for their confidentiality to ensure none of the problems were of a gynaecological nature. Harivansh himself held regular inspections throughout the day to make sure that everything was in order.

Restored to her original self as a physician, Puja however still found herself on a learning curve. Thus quite a few gallstones diagnoses turned out to be Intestinal worms. Firm diagnoses of incurable cancer turned out to be Tuberculosis and treatable and when she thought it was TB this time, it would turn out to be Typhoid. All her mis-diagnoses were always corrected by her surgeon husband. A gradual tropicalisation of attitude and thinking started to make matters better for her.

Her new engagement filled a major void where boredom had taken roots. It kept her out of the kitchen as well. She began to enjoy the warmth and gratitude she received from her patients. Folded hands, expectant eyes, almost begging for a miracle from her. It was impossible to let them down. In some contrast to her patients back home who enjoyed free treatment and yet threatened to sue and complain at the slightest of errors. People trekked for hours or came in bullock-carts from distant villages to be seen and patiently waited for hours without grumbling. She would get gifts in kind of anything from fresh vegetables, beaten rice to freshly caught fish.

A fee system had to be introduced to stem the deluge of patients that were beginning to arrive. Puja was hesitant initially but the logic stared in her face. On the first day of the fee system, her total earning was twenty-four hundred rupees. She carefully folded the smeared notes and went inside the house to look for her in-laws. They were both watching a religious serial on the television. She touched both their feet and neatly placed the money in Radha devi's lap.

Radha Devi hugged her daughter-in-law with pride as Harivansh got up to switch off the television. She counted the money and told Harivansh the amount Puja had earned in one day.

'You have already overtaken your husband,' said Radha devi.

'That is because she is more talented than your son,' replied Harivansh with pride.

Radha Devi closed the crumpled notes between her hands and closed her eyes to soak some pride herself. Then she let her hands part and placed the money back in Puja's hands.

Puja protested. 'You keep it Ma. I do not even know where to spend it and besides I can always ask for some money from you should I need it.'

'No Puja it is your hard earned money and you should keep it.'

'But I do not need it. In a few months we shall be going back to England and all this money won't be of any use anyway.'

'No Puja it is a sin to take money from one's children.'

'I have a suggestion,' said Harivansh. 'This is noble money so why not put it to a noble cause. Puja should keep half the money for her expenses and donate half the money to the orphanage by the municipality office. Children there get only one meal a day and hardly have any clothes to wear. They could do with this money.'

'They eat one meal a day because the wicked Principal swindles all the grants from the government. He won't hesitate to swallow our money as well.'

'That is only partly true Radha. There is little money coming from the government to be swindled at all. Besides they have been in dire straits since the Rotary club withdrew theirs sponsorship.'

'It sounds like a good idea Babuji,' said Puja.

'Then it's done. I shall take you to the orphanage tomorrow and you can see for yourself, how desperate their needs are.'

When Avinash came back from work in the evening he protested jocularly. 'All my dreams of living off my wife's earnings seem to be coming to an end. But first I have to speak to that principal, Ram Babu Singh, and threaten to cut his balls off if he misappropriates any of our money.'

Next morning Puja, Avinash and Harivansh set off in their Ambassador for the orphanage. It was a short bumpy ride on a dirt track that led them to the outskirts of the town. The orphanage constituted of a row of thatched huts arranged in a rectangle at the centre of which was a dusty courtyard. There was a well in the centre of the courtyard and a hand-pump on one side. An open drain with its black effluents and sickening odour ran parallel to the front of the huts before disappearing in a bigger open drain by the side of the municipality office.

Ram Babu Singh had advance notice of the VIP arrival and had attired himself in a spotless *Dhoti-kurta*. He was a tall and chubby person with thick black moustache and near absent eyebrows. His hairline had receded posteriorly in a uniform fashion and somewhere around the midline it started abruptly and densely almost curling from want of space. That combined with his ununiformly carious, betel stained teeth and dark eyeball sockets made his overall appearance from ugly to even menacing.

Presently he rushed forward to open the gates as the car screeched to a halt emitting a bolus of black smoke and dust around it. With folded hands he bent repeatedly to acknowledge every guest individually. Behind him the children stood in neat rows and columns wearing Khaki shorts and soiled white shirts. As if in a parade ready for the ceremonial welcome. They looked no older than ten years or younger than four.

Ram Babu cleared his throat as a signal to one of the girls who hesitantly inched forward and presented a bouquet of flowers to Puja. The girl could not be have been more than eight. Thin and of dark complexion, slightly lightened by the dust powder. Hair browned and knotted by malnutrition and dust. A shine in her big white eyes that defied her poverty and stamped her beauty. A sprinkle of a smile, of awe and anticipation.

'What is your name?' asked Puja.

'Shruti, *Memsahib*,' answered Ram Babu instead. 'She is not even a complete orphan but we accommodated her here. Her mother died giving birth to a still-born. Her father is a drunk who used to beat her regularly till the villagers took pity and brought her down here. Her father knows that she is here but has never bothered to come and see her. Today happens to be her birthday as well.'

'What did you get for your birthday Shruti?' Puja asked.

Ram Babu laughed. 'They feel lucky if they get one full meal *Memsahib*. Presents are a distant dream.'

Puja was beginning to get a bit irritated with his voice but kept her cool. 'What would you like for your birthday?'

She did not answer. No one had asked her such questions before.

'Say something you rascal,' intervened Ram Babu. 'You do not get anything from not opening your mouth.'

Shruti hesitated. Compelled by her Principal to say something and unsure of what to say. She started digging the loose soil with her right big toe and mumbled inaudibly, 'A frock.'

'What?'

'A frock,' she raised the decibels slightly.

'I shall get you a frock.'

Shruti became bolder. 'With flower pattern?'

'With flower pattern.'

A shriek of a delight swept across her face which she then covered with her hands and ran inside to conceal it from her friends.

Ram Babu took them on a tour of the orphanage. To the communal kitchen with the coal stoves, blackened walls and the stench of rotten food. Through the sleeping quarters where dirty rags strewn in a random fashion on the floor outlined the individual sleeping domains. Into the office, neat and tidy, with a proper bed, table, chair and a large portrait of Lord Shiva. Ram Babu was sensible enough not to take them to the latrines and bathrooms and when Puja insisted, Avinash gently squeezed her hand in an indication to back off.

The children still stood to attention, in rows and columns, their necks craned to follow the guests. As they sat down after the walkabout, Ram Babu cleared his throat again in another signal and the rows and columns erupted in a welcome song. Ignoring the rhythm, ignoring the tune, each one of them at their highest pitch, begging for help and mercy.

As a thin film rose in her eyes and a smile spread over her lips, a new resolve began to take birth inside Puja. She clapped and clapped after the children had finished their song. The children, who had been quite tense until then under the watchful eyes of Ram Babu relaxed, smiled and then joined in the laughter with their honoured guests.

Puja came back the next day with the flower-pattern frock for Shruti and five thousand rupees for the orphanage. Over the next few weeks she began to take an active interest in the workings of the orphanage. She bought food in kind instead of giving cash to Ram Babu. He objected initially but downgraded to a grumble after a berating from Avinash. She hired a contractor to cover the open drains and fit proper toilet seats in the latrines over the gaping holes in the womb of the earth laden with months of faeces and generations of flies. She made a two-meal day mandatory and made surprise inspections to ensure that the children were being fed and the repair work was going as planned. Books were collected through donations and purchases and an additional teacher was employed to share the burden with the sole teacher cum principal cum warden.

Shruti became her personal assistant and spy. She would cling to her like a shadow from the moment she would arrive and report to her about the wrongdoings that occurred behind her back. She told her about the missing potatoes which she was certain that Ram Babu had taken home, the leaking ceiling which dripped upon the sleeping children in the rains and the homosexual relationship between two boys in class VI. After a few days Shruti started to come to the house after school and helped her in the clinic. She would bring tea and coffee for Puja and occasionally shout at a noisy patient asking them to shut up. Radha devi banned her initially from entering the house because she belonged to the untouchable caste but after mild protestations from Puja the ban was restricted to the kitchen and the private rooms of her in-laws.

In one of her letters to Carol, Puja wrote:

> ....*Life has certainly picked up a bit after getting involved in the practice and the orphanage. Less time to get bored I guess. I am even beginning to enjoy my work in the clinic. The respect from the patients is very humbling. The changes in the orphanages are beginning to show on the children's faces. As if these kids had not had enough already in their short lives. It almost felt when I first met them that they had for-*

gotten to smile. It is difficult to be left untouched. But above all the most intoxicating part of all this is the newfound power which I never enjoyed before. The power to affect other people lives so dramatically and profoundly. These eighty orphans with their welcome songs and a new shine in their eyes. The hundreds of patients who pay you both in cash and in gratitude for even the most trivial things you do for them. There revere you as if the art of healing was not an act of science but the hand of God himself.

Don't worry. I am aware of this subtle Indianisation of the self and I am letting it happen on the premise that it is temporary and in a few months time will just be a chapter to reflect upon. The gap year which I never took. I read an article in the papers the other day which stated that a 'Happiness poll' done worldwide has suggested that the Americans and the Indians were amongst the happiest while the Chinese and Russians amongst the most miserable. From my perspective I somehow cannot see that. Day to day life is a constant struggle and even the basic amenities like water, electricity and roads are not to be taken granted for. People talk about foreign land as if it were a fairyland and when I close my eyes and bring forward the dust free lush-green English countryside, I know exactly what they mean...........

PS: The same poll also suggested that the British and the Indians were among the most satisfied with their sex lives. I think we can safely disregard the whole thing.

XVII

As life in Sitapur rolled out each day in the same mundane and dusty fashion, there were some subtle changes taking place in the firmament. The floating white clumps of wool were becoming larger and greyer. From aberrant to permanent. Threatening the mighty sun, but still playing hide and seek in a carefully conjured plot of deceit.

It fooled no one. The winds picked up in gusts in anticipation. The heat bowed down in submission. The moths, the frogs and the snakes crept out from nowhere. Human eyes charted their movements with clasped hands in prayers.

Till one day when the clouds closed ranks and poured down onto the earth below. To the drums of the tribals and the shrills of the cricket. To the sprightly dance of the livened up twigs and the gentle sway of the washed green leaves. To the parched earth which soaked every drop within itself in silent ecstasy. The dust mask, peeled and dissolved, exposed the unrivalled beauty of the body and the mind.

When Avinash dragged Puja forcibly on to the terrace, she trembled initially with the tickling of the heavy raindrops that lashed at her. But then she relaxed her tensed body, closed her eyes and let the prying drops seek every pore of her skin that had suffered under the oppressive heat of the last few months. She almost forgot how much she had hated the clouds and the rain when she was in England. Every morning waking up, drawing the curtains and peeking out in the hope that they might have gone.

From the terrace she saw the postman in his Khaki dress and his sieve umbrella open the gates. Their airline tickets had arrived from London. Departure date, the fifteenth of November. Avinash must have read his own name on the ticket at least five times. He would be boarding a plane for the first time in his life.

Long after the euphoria had settled and the welcome signs had gone, it had continued to rain. For days on end with patchy breaks in between.

The mighty earth soaked all at first and then saturated, spilled over in tiny puddles, coalescing into larger lakes. They began to appear everywhere. On the playing fields, the craters on the roads, by the burst pipes of the elementary drainage system. They joined hands and trickled inconspicuously into the womb of the Bagmati river, which pregnant with new life, began to threaten the unprotected half of the town. That half, which did not have the government offices and the official's residences and hence did not have the raised dykes to protect it from flooding. That half, which did not have the shops and the shopkeepers who had bribed the officials not to swallow the funds allocated to build dykes for their section of the town.

The heavens oblivious to such inequalities on the ground continued to pour relentlessly. One such night when the town slept in absolute darkness of the dark clouds and the usual power cut of the electricity board, the river crept into that half of the town. In a noiseless gush it ran over the streets and entered people's homes. The first few, sleeping on the floor, felt the flood rather than seeing it and ran outside to raise the alarm. Their sound competing with the lashing rain and the cracking thunder. There was pandemonium as the water levels rose with alarming speed. It dissolved most of the mud walls of the huts and swept it occupants in its swirling waves. People ran in the darkness often in the wrong direction of the advancing water. Shrieks and calls for help rent the fearsome skies but there was none forthcoming. There were no roads to run onto, no shores to swim to. Those who had roofs climbed onto rooftops while others clustered atop the few unfelled trees. A few roofs collapsed under the sheer weight of its occupants and on the others, its first few conquerors repelled and pushed back others from climbing onto the rooftops for fear of them giving way as well. There were mothers swimming with their infants on their shoulders begging for a rooftop or a treetop.

The death toll would have been much lower, had it happened in daylight or there had been more cement constructed houses with flat strong roofs.

That morning when Puja tried to open her eyes to wake up, they burnt and felt heavy. She first thought it was lack of sleep but then she recollected she had gone to bed earlier than usual. It took her a few more seconds to realise that she had a temperature. Avinash unusually was up before her and was combing his hair in front of the dressing table with a bath towel wrapped around his waist after having had a shower. She stared at his semi-nude contours for a few minutes and when it stirred no waves in her, she softly asked for the time.

'It is ten 'o' clock,' he turned towards her.' Last night part of the town got flooded. There were a few dozens deaths from drowning. It came without warning in the night.'

'In England no one drowns in a flood.'

'In England there are no true rivers. Most of them are ten feet wide and one foot deep. Heavy rainfalls can double their size overnight.'

'Another factor might just be good early warning systems and efficient rescue services. Which part was flooded?'

'The Dharamtala area,' he paused. 'Where the orphanage is.'

She began to wake up.

'Is everyone safe?'

' Most of them. I have sent Ramdin to get the exact details. The cook from the orphanage brought us the news this morning.'

'Shruti?'

'She could not be found this morning. They are still looking for her all over. They are confident....'

Her eyes were wide open despite the burning.

'You don't mean she could be....?'

'No Puja,' Avinash gently put his hand on her shoulder. 'It's just that she could not be found. A lot of people were swept away in the dark. No one knows how many are alive. That boy did tell me that Shruti was a good swimmer. My God Puja you are burning?'

'We have to find her.'

'We cannot do anything more Puja. They all are looking for the few missing children.'

'Are the police involved?'

'The Police are unlikely to get involved in search operations in these times.'

She began to tire. From the temperature. From the unbridged gap between her and Avinash. She raised her hand. 'You do not understand. We have to go to find her. Let us go Avinash.'

'Where?'

'I do not know where but out of this house. Take me to the Police.'

'Puja you are not well. You just rest at home. I shall go out and see what can be done.'

'I have to go with you.'

There was something defining in her tone that arrested his speech. He just nodded in acceptance. Puja rushed to the bathroom to get ready.

Outside the rain had halted and a few brave rays of sun were trying to wedge through the thick clouds. The ground was moist and the air thick, but there were no signs of flooding as they set out in the car. Puja told Avinash to take her to the Police station.

It was an old building painted in the familiar government-yellow with pockmarks of grey from the denuded plaster and works of nature. There were two police jeeps in the courtyard, one active and the other inactive. It was easy to distinguish between them. The inactive jeep was rooted firmly into the earth blending with the wild plantation that grew underneath and around it. There were no tyres on its wheels and no foam or leather on the rusty golden spring coils which once formed the seats. The number plate was still on.

They found the Sub-Inspector sipping tea in his chamber. He would pour the tea from the cup on to the saucer and let it cool before sipping it with a loud spluttering noise. There was a photograph of Mahatma Gandhi on the wall and a poster, which said, in large black print- POLICE ALWAYS AT YOUR SERVICE.

The Sub-Inspector immediately rose to his feet on seeing the couple and asked them to take a seat. A trinket of the tea that hung by his moustache shook off and fell on his lap as he let out a broad smile and asked how he could help.

'We have come to report a missing person,' said Puja.

His expression changed. A spectrum of surprise, sympathy and disbelief. Feigned exclusively for the VIPs. 'What are you saying madam. Is everyone well at home? Is Harivansh ji all right?'

'Everyone is okay at home,' Avinash intervened, 'It is a girl from the orphanage. She was swept away in the floods last night. Her name is Shruti.'

The tension lines relaxed on his unshaven face. 'Oh a girl from the orphanage,' he murmured. The fear of responsibility and a busy day receded in his mind. His thoughts converged on an exit strategy. 'Last night was bad,' he gestured to the guard for two more cups of tea. 'It was so sudden. Hundreds have been swept away. Traceless. So many people have come today to file a report. I wish I could help them. The police are helpless.'

Avinash knew that he was lying. The police station would be the last place families would come to in such a crisis. He nodded in agreement.

Puja's temper and temperature was rising again. 'Are the police not capable of doing anything?' she tried to keep her voice as plain as possible.

The Sub-Inspector sensed the irritation in her voice. This must be one important orphan, he thought. He lowered his eyes in thought and rested them on the bulge of her breasts, above the blouse line, behind the transparent chiffon sari. Something to fantasize about tonight, he decided. He lifted his eyebrows to look at her concerned face. He had this urge to hold and comfort her. He remembered his own ugly, arthritic, pale wife and swallowed a sour spit from the corner of his mouth.

'I can assure you madam that we shall try our level best. I am going to head this hunt personally.' Such fluency in lying can only come after a long experience in the police service.

'Shall we file a written FIR?' asked Avinash.

'There is no need for any paperwork, Doctor saheb. Your request is my command. How often do we get the chance to serve you important people?'

Avinash rose but Puja remained seated. Both men looked at her with questioning gazes. She hesitated and then opened her purse, took out a wad of notes and placed it on the table. This was her first attempt at bribing and she felt very nervous.

The Sub-Inspector recoiled back and pushed the money back towards her. 'What are you doing madam? There is no need for this at all.'

'Yes there is. You will need money to hire boats and swimmers. If you do not find Shruti I will take it back.' She caught Avinash's arm and dragged him out before either of the men could utter a word.

'Why did you do that?' asked Avinash, shrugging his arm free.

'Because that bastard would not have set his foot out of the room without the bribe that I just gave him.'

The police found Shruti later that afternoon, cold and hungry, clinging to a branch of a Peepal tree that was half uprooted in the gushing torrent.

Puja felt progressively unwell over the next day. Her body ached and her temperature kept rising despite the cold showers and the Paracetamols. She and Avinash differed on the diagnosis. She was certain it was a viral infection while Avinash floated the malaria theory. There was even a heated debate till Puja reminded him that she was a physician and he was a surgeon and medical diagnoses were best left to her. Surgeons are not allowed to prefix their names with the doctor title in England, he was informed.

Though the rainfall had abated in Sitapur there was more rain in the Terai region of Nepal and the river levels continued to rise as a consequence. That evening Avinash came in quite concerned about the turn of events.

'There are rumours that the villagers might dig the dykes to divert the water to this part of the town. They are angry with the Administration's tardy relief effort and water is already reaching the first floors in most houses.'

And surely they did. Right under the eyes of the sleeping duty policemen stationed to protect the dykes, they dug ferociously in the night to breach the dyke. Just a small breach which widened itself under the impact of the gushing river. A more equitable distribution of misery for the better half of the town. Socialism at its highpoint.

The first clues of an impending flood often comes from the toilet. It overflows and refuses to flush. The backflow from the creaky drainage overwhelms the olfactory senses and one knows that there is more trouble to come. So when Avinash emerged from the downstairs toilet with a dejected look on his face and announced to his tea sipping family that the floods were on their way, Puja was very surprised.

'How do you know?'

'Believe me, I can smell it.'

Everyone but her nodded, understanding what he meant. The servants were ordered to seal the downstairs toilets with sandbags. Radha Devi went inside to check her food stores and ensured it would outlast the coming floods. The television was shifted upstairs just in case the water entered the house.

The floodwater first emerged from below the earth. From the cavernous, antiquated drainpipes in a darker, viscous form which carpeted the land and awaited the advance from the banks. Then all in unison –

rainwater, effluent and melted snow from the Himalayas, covered the lowland areas and then submerged the roads. By midday it had swept over most of the town and was threatening to enter through the gates of the *Haveli*. It rose further in level but could not breach the sandbagged gates.

There was an eerie sense of calm and acceptance in the colony. Adults were seen shifting the household goods on to rooftops or the first floor. They waved at each other and shouted invitations to each other from their balconies to come across should their rations run out. The children were an excited bunch floating freshly made paper boats in their newly acquired water-world. Some even ventured for the occasional swim.

As anticipated the water entered the ground floor next morning. The whole family and the kitchen moved upstairs. Puja's temperature continued to rise and she spent most of her day lying in her bed watching her family members stream in and out through the room to get to her bathroom. There was a great debate at one stage about the servants using the same toilet, as all the other toilets downstairs were unusable. Radha devi almost choked at the thought of sharing her ablutions with the lower caste servants and ordered them to swim every morning to an unsubmerged ridge to defecate. The servants incensed by this blatant discrimination only swam to the boundary wall, sat on it, and lobbed their excretions into the flowing water.

From her bed, glancing out of the window, Puja saw a carcass of a cow floating towards the colony. It drifted slowly along with a few twigs and an earthen pot. It almost seemed to be coming towards their house but the currents changed direction and it headed towards Mr. Patwari's, the newspaper editor, house. It hovered uncertain of its intentions and then gently wedged itself against the rear wall of the house.

There was a huge commotion at her neighbour's house. A dead cow against a Hindu house. Mrs Patwari was raging like a mad woman. Why had the Gods sent this dead cow to her house. Could there be a worse omen? Mr. Patwari was aghast with his mouth wide open as he leaned over the terrace to confirm what he had been told. The children were animated and seemed relatively less distressed. Eventually the servant got hold of a bamboo pole that must be at least twelve feet long. Abetted by Mr. Patwari, they pushed the cow away from the wall and into the main current. The dead cow then resumed her heaven bound journey. Mr and

Mrs Patwari, her sari covering her head, folded their hands and bowed in the direction of the floating cow. They noted but did not raise a hue when the cow abutted against the rear of their neighbour's house.

Her temperature continued unabated over the next few days. Her appetite disappeared and the weakness now confined her to the bed. She was plagued by a body ache and she felt as if her muscles were being ripped off her bones. Radha devi was worried and Avinash pleaded with her to abandon her viral theory and take some pills for malaria.

But the chloroquine tablets did not have any effect. As the illness crept into the second week, Puja developed diarrhoea with persistent abdominal pains. She barely had the strength to stand up and walk to the bathroom. She had persistent nausea and stopped eating all together. The flood was still around and all day long she would stare at Mr Patwari's wall to read the watermarks and decipher whether the levels were going up or down.

There was a palpable concern in the house over her continued deterioration. There was a constant vigil by her bedside, day and night. Avinash and Radha devi would take turns in the night to stay awake and watch her sleep. In the absence of maids, Radha devi even massaged her daughter-in-law's legs when she complained of bad cramps. Avinash too gave her massages when everyone else was sleeping. Imprisoned by the rising floods they tried with some desperation all the available in-house remedies. Avinash kept giving her as many different antibiotics as he could get hold of. Harivansh tried his own homeopathy failing with some herbal treatment. Radha devi forced her to drink a weird tasting soup of Tulsi leaves. When that failed she was asked to gulp a spoonful of a paste made from raw egg, garlic, ginger and turmeric. It tasted so foul that her nausea transformed into copious vomiting. Undeterred Radha devi added honey to the concoction to make it more palatable and Puja had to take a few more doses.

On day ten when the first broad strip watermark emerged on Mr. Patwari's wall from the receding flood, her abdomen began to swell. She became delirious and called out her friend's names from England. Radha devi went into the adjacent room and began to weep softly. Harivansh emerged from his room wearing only a pair of shorts and vest.

'I am going to fetch a boat,' he said.

'Why?' asked Radha.

'Because I want to get another doctor to see her.'

'Babuji, you sit by her side. I and one of the servants will go out to find a boat. I will get Dr. Manibhusan from his house. He is only half a kilometre away.'

'No son,' Harivansh was firm, 'You will be the best person to be around Puja if something went wrong. I shall take one of the servants.'

So they set about in the murky, muddy water. The servant in front, measuring the depths with his body as a scale and Harivansh in tow was keeping a close eye on him. There was a stench in the air. From the vegetation first killed by the floods and now decaying in the intense heat of the sun. One hand on the nose retarded their wading speed through the slow current. They went to the Muslim colony and enquired about a boat. When people heard about the illness of his daughter-in-law, they let him hire a boat at a reduced black market rate.

When Harivansh reached the semi-submerged gates of Dr. Manibhusan, he found the leading physician playing Carom with his eight year old son on the balcony. Reluctant to step in the water again he explained on the top of his voice the reason of his arrival. Manibhusan, in order to be able to decide what medicines and injections to take with him, took a detailed history from his first floor balcony. Friendly necks craned from neighbouring balconies in total disrespect for patient's confidentiality. Some even suggested a few diagnoses and treatments and Harivansh gracefully acknowledged them without revealing his irritation.

Finally Manibhusan emerged and dangled his medicine bag by the end of a roped bed sheet for the servant to grab. Next he climbed over the parapet and pinching his nose by one hand jumped into the water by the side of the boat. He was quickly hauled into the boat and they set sail again.

By the time they moored back at home each one of them was dry and smelly. Unsmelling to each other, they barely noticed the wrinkles of disapproval as they entered the house.

Inside the bedroom Manibhusan checked Puja's pulse, asked to protrude her tongue and without further ado simply said, 'Typhoid.'

Puja nodded her head slowly. A grim surrender of the foreign physician to the local one. She did not protest that he had not even examined her properly. She did not question the lack of any investigations to prove the diagnosis. A voice from the corner of her medical brain told her that despite the incompleteness of everything he was most probably right.

Manibhusan took a step back to a respectful distance from a prostrate lady. 'Bhabhi ji, there are some signs of ileus with septicaemia. We will need to put up a drip for hydration and give some intravenous Ciproxin.'

Puja nodded again, this time with a wry smile in acceptance, hiding her phobia of needles.

A drip was set up next hanging from the poles for the mosquito net and the antibiotic was commenced. Despite their persuasions, Manibhusan declined to leave for his house that night till his patient got better. He, Harivansh and Avinash camped on the terrace and chatted late into the evening. When Harivansh got up and retired for bed, the whisky bottles were surreptitiously whisked out and they settled to drink the night out. Every hour they would go in and check on Puja. Her abdomen was beginning to settle down and so was her pulse rate though the temperature remained high. Somewhere around four am Avinash abruptly stopped in the middle of describing his love for music and went to sleep immediately. Manibhusan rightly resolving that it would be improper to enter Puja's room without Avinash, put his legs up and slumped on the sofa too.

They were awakened by a smiling Puja standing by the doorway, one hand dangling the drip bottle unhooked from the mosquito net pole.

'I feel much better,' she announced. 'Even my temperature is down.'

There was joy and relief on both men's faces.

'I am sure we can take down the drip now and switch you to oral Ciproxin,' Manibhusan said lifting his bag.

'You are going nowhere without having breakfast first. So put down your bag,' said Avinash.

More things positive happened that night. The water levels receded dramatically retreating from the ground floors of most houses and exposing the surface of the metalled road. A more puckered, cratered surface but nevertheless allowing road transport to resume. Once the water receded from the ground floor rooms, the spoils of the flood were revealed. A carpet of thick mud with an underlay of debris. Debris of the items that could not be shifted upstairs. Of the foreign articles which had just floated in from distant corners and deposited themselves in the safety of the four walls. Of the dead rats that perished in their hiding holes, now bloated and floated out by the persuasive waters.

The servants descended with brooms, buckets and disinfectants. Handkerchiefs tied so tightly across their noses that they almost suffocated. Periodically they would come upstairs to take off the handkerchiefs and breathe some stench free air.

It was not misery for all human souls in Sitapur. Certainly not for Munawwar Ali, the local MLA who was elected from Sitapur to the state legislative assembly. His heart was filled with joy when the river waters entered the town. His happiness soared with the rising water levels. For more floods meant more money pouring in for relief and reconstruction. More money to be grabbed and swindled away. The day was not far when he would join the ranks of his peers and have his own Swiss bank account.

He had wept with the families of the deceased. He had lobbied hard with his ruling party to allocate more funds to his affected constituency. He had sworn before the television cameras to fast unto death if relief was not forthcoming.

And when it came he made sure that he had a tight grip on how relief was distributed. Thus the grain meant to feed the destitute was diverted and sold at exorbitant prices on the black-market. The blankets and the tents were sold to the affected victims instead of being distributed for free. The dykes were rebuilt with more sand and less cement to stave off the allocated funds and ensure that it gave way again in the following year.

In those two months he amassed no less than ten million rupees from the prolonged misery of the people who had voted him into power. It did not go unnoticed. There were protests and even small rallies against him but he silenced them through his musclemen.

Despite the odds of nature and mankind, life in the poor suburbs, regenerated itself gradually to its former state. The passion to climb back to the edge of survival, the genetic building blocks of hay and bamboo and some well photographed aid from the local charities helped them rebuild their lives again.

Until the arrival of the next monsoon.

XVIII

Time and nature gradually healed the wounds of the mighty floods. Nature, donning the new robes of autumn, erased the stains with a brush-leaf. The sun, cooler than before, nevertheless contracted the Bagmati river into its old self of a crumpled muddy ribbon. The sodden banks shrivelled, dried and then powdered into dark grey sand. The washer-women returned to install the slates and rocks on which they resumed their chores of beating the dirt out of the clothes. The barren fields bristled with new green offshoots of the paddy crops. The birds and the poor collected hay to make new homes and reconstruct their lives piece by piece. The human spirit, endowed with survival, resurrected its physical form to its former glory while time healed the painful memories. Soon it would be Dussehra, the festival of joy and celebration and the past would be forgotten.

Puja too limped back to health though it took a surprisingly long time. The typhoid had drawn out from her body the last of her reserves and in the first few days she had felt like the trunk of a tree whose roots had been scorched. Lifeless but standing. She felt dizzy on walking a few steps and got exhausted even in taking a bath. Avinash nursed her and cancelled his evening clinics. She was fed like a premium racehorse round the clock. Radha devi was forceful by nature and did not take 'no' for an answer. She was in a race against time to get Puja back to her normal girth or even a few inches more before she left for England lest her parents accused her of neglecting their daughter. She created history in cooking non-vegetarian food after twenty-five years. She begged Puja to take more morsels at each meal despite the belching protests from the amateur glutton.

The autumn evenings were pleasantly cooler with a clear-lit sky of sparkling stars and an evolving moon. Puja and Avinash would sit on the terrace and talk for hours. It was in those evenings that Avinash introduced her to Indian music. To the *Ragas* and *Suras*. To the lyrical dictionary of the Hindi language not used in common conversation. To the hidden subtleties of the lines wrapped in the culture of the subcontinent, which was otherwise meaningless to a foreigner. He would explain the songs line by line, stopping and rewinding the tape till he saw the appreciation in her face. How true love brought joy in pain, ecstasy in suffering, reward in sacrifice.

Till a time came when she could lie down in her rest-chair, alone, switch on the music and swing her head like her father and his friends back in England.

She restarted her clinic downstairs. The word had spread that she would be leaving for England soon and there was a mad rush to have all ailments cured before she left. Without her knowledge and in view of her recent illness, Harivansh had put a cap on the number of patients she was to see.

The orphanage had been greatly affected by the floods. The west wing that included the classrooms and the kitchen had collapsed and then been washed away by the surging water in bits and pieces. The children had slept and fed on the rooftop for ten days and when they had come down, they witnessed a devastation which shook their tiny hearts. For they saw nothing they could recognise from before. Their tiny cots or the wooden benches. Even the Gods in their fading frames had deserted them. Nothing but the thick slimy mud and the stench. They had quickly climbed back onto the roof.

When Puja came to witness the scene, tears welled up in her eyes. There were no physical signs left of the enormous effort she had put in over the past few months. She wiped her tears with the corner of her sari. Without speaking a word to the rooftop orphans she climbed back into the car. She went straight to the post-office and sent a telegram to her father:

> *The orphanage has been badly damaged by the floods. Needs a lot of reconstruction. Please send by wire two thousand pounds. If you are lucky then one day you might even get it back. Love, Puja.*

Next she went to Avinash's clinic and dragged him out of there and drove back to the orphanage.

'Do something,' she asked of him under the watching gazes of the children on the edge of the roof.

'You want me to start cleaning the rooms?'

Puja burst out laughing. The children joined in a laughter chorus not knowing why they were laughing.

'That might be an idea but first I want you to hire a contractor to rebuild the demolished wing.'

'That will need a lot of money.'

'I have just asked papa to send two thousand Pounds.'

'You...what? Are you crazy.'

'Avi, we do not have this sum of money and you know that.'

'And where did you get this two thousand Pound figure.'

'The driver told me that it would need that much money.'

'What? He told you the figure in Pounds?'

'No he told me in rupees and I converted it into Pounds.'

There was this tight tug of war between laughter and irritation.

'This bugger, who lives in a hut, has never constructed anything in his life, gave you a figure on the basis of which you robbed your father?'

'At least he had more idea than me.' The driver, standing behind her, nodded vigorously to claim his architectural credentials.

Work began in earnest the very next day. The first thing that Puja ordered was a ban on drinking tap water. Only cooled boiled water was allowed. Only three children developed cholera and were quickly isolated to Avinash's clinic where they were treated intensively. None of them died. The kitchen remained on the rooftop where strict hygiene was observed during the cooking. The orphans themselves under the supervision of Ram Babu Singh undertook the scrubbing and cleaning of the undemolished section. For the children it was like a picnic. No classes, communal work and a hearty meal after that. They cleaned with zeal and burst into a smile on receiving a compliment from their doctor didi. They chose the colour of their walls after full campaigning and mass voting. The repaired furniture went to the younger children and the new ones were kept by the seniors. They demanded larger windows in the west wing and insisted on toilets with flushing capabilities.

For only that would break the idiosyncratic tradition of going in with a bucket of water to flush the wastes of the previous person and leaving ones own behind in revenge.

Bharat arrived one Sunday morning from college. The sun was still a pale golden and the household was still stirring when he knocked at the door. He had lost considerable weight eating the mess food, ready for the ritual fattening at the hands of his mother. Radha devi exclaimed with shock at his concave abdomen and prominent cheekbones and rushed into the kitchen to cook his favourite foods. Bharat slipped upstairs and rapped on his brother's door. It was Avinash who opened the door still half-asleep, rubbing his eyes. Bharat leapt to touch his feet and both brothers exchanged hugs. Puja was still in bed observing the brotherly affections.

'*Bhaiyya,* I suggest you go downstairs now as you would not like to see someone else hugging your beloved wife,' Bharat said.

Avinash laughed. 'You are getting desperate now. We ought to marry you off.' He wrapped his gown and made an exit for the morning tea.

Bharat rushed at the still bemused prostrate Puja, touched her feet and jumped on to the bed beside her.

'*Bhabhi*, I have got a girlfriend.'

Puja clasped his hands. 'You are joking?'

'No I am not. I am in love. Can't you see? I have lost weight, my beard is growing, my vacant looks.'

'Congratulations my darling. Is she blind?'

'Oh! Come on *Bhabhi*. This is serious stuff.'

Puja put on her serious mask. 'How did it come about?'

'I have been courting her for the past six months. She is in my class. I had been dropping hints on many occasions without a response till finally I dropped a letter to her explaining my emotions.'

'So you cringed for six months and then dropped a letter. Why did not you ask her out on the first day itself?'

'*Bhabhi* this is India. You do not approach a girl on the first day. You let her know that you like her. Then you give her time to mould her emotions. To think about you. To let her feelings ferment like good wine.'

'Or a pickle.'

'And then you drink it after it has matured.'

'So you put your lips to it.'

Bharat blushed. 'No she met me in the canteen after getting the letter and said she understood and respected my feelings towards her.'

'So?'

'So translated into Hindi it meant that she liked me as well.'

'Bharat, translated into any language it does not mean anything.'

'Oh *Bhabhi*, in India it does. That is officially falling in love.'

'You Indians are a strange tribe. What happened after that?'

'We have met a couple of times since.'

'Have you had sex?'

'Bhabhi !'A bridal flush swept his face.

'Have you kissed her? Have you even touched her?'

'Bhabhi you are mad. It has been only a few weeks and you want me to get dumped? It is their hearts and souls that we are supposedly after. You touch the skin and the fuse blows out.'

Puja laughed aloud. 'Love is a tragedy here. Do you have a photograph? What is her name?'

Bharat let go a big sigh and held his hands to his chest. 'Why should I keep her photograph. I just have to peep inside my heart to look at her. I pen her name with dewdrops on green leaves unseen by a stranger's eyes.'

Puja raised her closed fist in the air and Bharat ran out of the door laughing aloud.

The festival of *Dussehra* was making subtle changes to the landscape of the small town. It is one of the most important festivals of the Hindus. It takes weeks of preparation and then ten days of pure celebration.

With only a week to go, preparations had taken a sense of urgency. Volunteers joined the municipal workers in sweeping the roads and painting the city walls to erase the political slogans, betel stains and the urine marks. Bamboo poles slung parallel to the roads from which would hang the ropes of electric bulbs. Loudspeakers hung at strategic places blared a mix of devotional songs and the latest hit numbers. The annual fair was taking roots at the college grounds. The rusted rides were being painted and pasted with colour paper while at the far end a mobile circus was putting its tents under the watchful gaze of a caged lion.

The Goddess *Durga*, herself was bracing herself up for the grand occasion. From a mould of hay and clay a few days ago, she was now emerging into her famed beauty and glory. The artisans sculpting the finer contours before the clay dried. The finishing touches with the jewellery, silk and her weaponry took place behind the walls till the final unveiling on the first day of the festival. A brazenly beautiful Goddess, draped in red silk and full jewellery, with a spear embedded into the chest of the evil demon prostrate at her feet. Hindu hearts swelling with pride at their mother's conquest and the victory of good over evil.

Festivity, a fusion of religion and celebration, hung in the air like scent from the Jasmine sweeping away the hearts and the minds alike. As the mighty sun retracted its golden arrows back into its quiver every evening, the homes would be deserted. Rich and poor, attired in their best clothes, would spill onto the fluorescent streets of Sitapur. A river of colours under a cacophony of loudspeakers. From one pier to another. They would stop in front of each of them, close their eyes for a few moments and pray with folded hands. Then they would lift their eyelids over their glazed eyes and adore the idols, their hearts brimming with devotion. The priest would pour some holy water in their hands. They drank some and ran the rest over their hair. Their feet rooted their hearts reluctant, they would succumb to the push from behind and the rainbow lava would make its slow progress up the bazaar road.

They were also speeded up by the hounding from the *noveau* roadside merchants who had surfaced from nowhere during the festival season. They would tug at their shirts and saris and beckon them to buy whatever was being sold. Bangles, small idols of the Gods, dresses of cheap cotton with reflective mirrors. Sweetmeats sellers with their uncovered, dust smeared sweetmeats and the swarm of wasps that never stung anyone.

For Puja it was a totally new experience. Flanked by Bharat and Avinash to protect her from the touch sensitive yobs, she had joined the crowds each day from the seventh day onwards. She had never seen so much colour in her life. Unaccustomed, it almost hurt the eyes. A religious carnival of sober devotees, inebriated with happiness and unconcealed delight. She had initially only admired the Goddess's idols for its sculpture and beauty but a subtle change took place over the next few days. An incipient awe knocked at the atheist's doors. She had never taken religion seriously in her life. But in that sea of folded hands and closed eyes, she had found herself raising her hands and humming a short prayer. It was almost a relief to be a part of that mass and not something apart. She let the doors open wide and wilfully closed her eyes for longer. She was now part of that happiness queue inching slowly forwards.

People stopped to greet her in the crowds and she would smile back without even recognising them. She was surprised at the number of people who knew her in that small town. One old woman had dragged her son from the crowd to meet her. She thanked her for saving her life. Puja vaguely remembered that woman presenting to her clinic a few weeks ago with acute heart failure. The old woman was telling her son that Puja was no less than a Goddess to her. Embarrassed and flushing red Puja hastened away from her.

Avinash was laughing. 'You must not have only saved her life but also reduced her fees.'

XIX

Rajaram Sahni twisted his moustache tight to match the tension in his mind. He stared at his distorted image in the glass paperweight on his table and reflected upon the problems facing him. He loved the power but hated the responsibilities of his job. He had never dreamt in his wildest imaginations that some day he would become a District magistrate. He had started as a humble Block developmental Officer and but for the idiosyncrasies of the government reservation system which propelled officers from the backward castes upwards in the promotion ladder, would have remained one.

He had just concluded a meeting with Munawwar Ali, the local MLA. From across the table he had watched that ugly pockmarked betel-stained face spout insults and threats at him. He had listened quietly for Munawwar was a powerful person. A MLA from the ruling party. He was hearing but not listening as rage swept inside him. An uncontrollable urge to lift his boot and ram into the politician's face. To drag him through the streets with the crowd watching.

To mask his inner thoughts he put on a smile and forgot to withdraw it. Even when the MLA was threatening of dire outcomes if the Hindus were allowed to march with their idols through the Begumpura road which was predominantly inhabited by Muslims.

Munawwar Ali was irritated. 'Why the hell are you smiling at the prospect of communal killings in the town.'

Rajaram hastily broke through the shell of his thoughts. 'Er...no problems sir! No problems.'

'What no problems? The Muslims are very agitated and apprehensive. I am asking you to ban the march.'

'It is not that simple sir. The march has been going through the same route for the last twenty-five years. What will it do to Hindu passions if a sudden ban was imposed?'

Munawwar got up from the chair and stared directly into his eyes. 'Either way you are in trouble if anything untoward happens. And don't say that you were not warned.' Parting with his punch line, he had stormed out of his office leaving him alone, shrunken and small.

Rajaram buzzed the bell to summon the doorman. No slave eyes peeked through the green curtain. He buzzed it angrily again but there was no response again. He stormed out to see if the doorman had again dozed off but there was no one outside. As he re-entered the room, he spotted the doorman from the window behind his leather chair. He was urinating on the compound wall right behind his office.

Rajaram watched him carefully. He was clearly enjoying his pissing. He first drew a mountain with a steep slope on the yellow walls and then beside it a circle. After the borders he carefully filled them up with exact precision.

Sunset or sunrise depending on the way you interpreted this modern art.

'Shambhu!' Rajaram barked at the top of his voice.

From behind Rajaram saw his body convulse as if electrocuted by a live wire. In one quick movement Shambu tried to put his floppy penis back, run his zip up and break into a sprint. Alas it was beyond human capabilities. The mid-flow interrupted suddenly, resumed its flow inside his pants and the zip caught the skin of his manhood freezing him in his tracks with agonising pain.

Rajaram turned his head away to save him the embarrassment and then collapsed on the floor laughing, holding his stomach. His mood improved and an inner voice told him that the Dussehra march would pass without incident.

Munnawar Ali told himself that he was a decent and caring man. He too did not want any killings or riots. Just a little bit of trouble to polarise the Muslim votes back into his fold. The floods had earned him a lot of money but his reputation had suffered enormously. It was no secret that he had swindled the relief money and most of the victims were poor Muslims. They were seething with anger and were swearing to bring him down at the next Assembly elections that were only six months away. He simply could not afford to alienate them.

His constituency of Sitapur had thirty percent Muslims while the rest were Hindus. In the last election he had that thirty percent vote firmly behind him to scrape through a victory with the narrowest of margins. A mild trouble with the Hindus will unite them once again under his banner whilst still leaving the Hindus divided. A riot may solidify the Hindus strongly against him. It was a delicate balancing act.

Besides he was a decent man.

So after he spat the betel juice in the Spittoon, he warned his assembled henchmen not to be overzealous. To stockpile the country-made guns and grenades but not to use them unless there was an overwhelming necessity. He had spoken to the District Magistrate and had been assured of a heavy police presence. The aim he told them was to erect a dam of tension but not to let it burst. Make the general Muslim feel unhappy and fearful about the march but do no more. Make the hate against the Hindu strong enough to prevent the Muslims from voting for any Hindu candidate and yet not strong enough to result in an act of hatred.

'Unleash but rein in and victory should be ours,' he said and took out a wad of rupee notes to distribute amongst his henchmen. He could not hold himself any longer. 'Besides I am a decent man.'

The sky's conscience was clear that morning with not a tiny fleck of cloud across its vast expanse. The golden rays emerging from the sun rendered a shimmering hue to the Ghats readying themselves for the immersion of the idols. Back in town the priests were chanting the final mantras in undue frenzy to conclude the whole ceremony. For them this would be the day of deliverance. Not from the Gods but from the organisers who would pay them for fasting and worshiping for the past ten days. Bonus time for the whole year. The devotees had been filtering out from their houses at the crack of dawn to offer their last respects to the departing Gods.

By ten am most of the worships were concluded. The idol at the Bazaar road by the Laxmi-Niwas college gate was by far the largest and was designated to lead the procession. The various stands across the towns were thronged by hundreds of volunteers clad in saffron who would carry the idols, perched on their shoulders by bamboo poles and wooden planks, to the river banks. Some of the zealots had consumed *Bhang* and Cannabis in good proportions. Their religious fervour thus pumped up, they rent the air with cries of '*Jai Ma Durga*'.

The police had seeped in inconspicuously throughout the whole morning in a careful coordinated operation and on closer inspection looked omnipresent throughout the town. This was an annual trouble day for them and they were well rehearsed for the occasion.

The idols finally began to be raised amidst the beating of drums, celebratory cries and frenzied dancing. Twenty to thirty pairs of shoulders groaning under the weights of the mighty Goddesses. The air was coloured from the smoke of the fireworks and the coloured powder, *Abeer*, which they smeared on each others' faces. Tiny processions snaked through the small streets and merged together on the Bazaar road. There the pallbearers had a rest as they put down the idols and waited for the other processions to join in.

By mid-noon the main road was a brimming river of saffron with Khaki shores keeping a careful eye. Finally the college gate Durga idol was lifted with a huge cry. It was too big to be carried on the shoulders and so it was put on the back of a tractor. The crowd which by now was a couple of thousand strong, lurched forward led by an Inspector of police and two naked *sadhus* who kept coming to the front despite being dragged away repeatedly. The bands and the drums played incoherently in no rhythm but with a deafening noise. Locked shoulders kept the staggering legs in place as alcohol was passed around in earthen pitchers. The line between festivity and frenzy was blurred for once.

The Bazaar road technically ended on the west side of the river bridge though the shops continued on the other side of the bridge as well.

The road on which the procession stepped after crossing the bridge was known as the Begumpura road. It was completely deserted. Two stray dogs and an off limits pig. The shutters were down and the shops were shut. Above them were the flats where most of the inhabitants and the shop owners lived. The green wooden windows were shut, not tightly but slightly ajar with a sliver of darkness, from behind which anxious eyes looked down at the procession.

Dozens of pairs of eyes. One above another. Unseen but felt by everyone on the road. A strange tension gripped the procession. Nervousness, fear, defiance and bravado. They coagulated in a more compact column and inched cautiously forwards. The police cordon around them tightened and two more police jeeps joined in.

The sticks hit the drums a bit harder to allay the fears. The shouts of 'Jai ma Durga', changed to 'Jai shree Ram' as a mark of provocation. Two thousand devotees and fifty Goddesses, there was nothing to fear. They began to dance again, laughing and cheering in a taunting way. Despite warnings from the police their swords and spears pierced through the air in a show of strength and defiance. Most of those green windows shut tightly but some opened a bit more widely.

Suddenly there was a loud bang. The crowd thought that it was a shot fired from within the ranks and looked at each other. Then they searched the police who had equally puzzled faces. They were still solving the puzzle when one of the green windows parted and a Molotov cocktail was lobbed in the general direction of the crowd. It landed on one of the idols being carried on the shoulders and instantly set it alight.

There was pandemonium in an instant. Idols crashed from shoulder tops and lay strewn, broken and dismembered, all over the road. People ran for cover to avoid being sitting ducks. The police was caught in utter surprise and stood frozen in its tracks. For the briefest of moments there was complete stillness. Like the flash of an explosion that almost looks beautiful. People pressed against the walls and behind anything solid. A burning *Durga* and several broken in the middle of the road. The police frozen in anticipation.

They watched their mighty *Durga* dismembered and humbled first with disbelief and then with rage.

And then someone shouted, 'Jai shree Ram!'

As if everyone was just waiting for that holy commandment. Nothing could stop them after that. The police charge, the raining glass bottles and the bombs from the rooftops, the tear gas shells.

The holy carnage that followed numbed even the bravest of senses. Shops were set alight. Men and women were dragged from their houses and slaughtered begging for mercy. Children were shot deliberately in the crossfire. Hatred splashed on the walls in bright red blood. Men shouted 'Ram' and 'Allah' as they plunged the daggers into someone they did not even know. They would wait and watch the shiny eyes turn to glass before retracting their vile weapons. They would pause to snatch the gold rings and the chains from the dead victims and then search for the next one who looked slightly different. Victory, somehow absurdly, was defined by numbers and hence the momentum to go for anyone in sight.

The Muslim youths hiding in the mosque were much better armed and prepared than their Hindu counterparts. Hundreds of them streamed out with the battle cry of '*Allah-o-Akbar*'. But the Police force, predominantly Hindus, didn't fire into the air this time. When after an hour, the policy of batons for the Hindus and bullets for the Muslims did not control the rioting, Superintendent Yuvraj Singh asked his men to fire directly at the Hindus. It had the desired effect. The crowd retreated and ran back with their blood dripping swords over the river bridge.

There was stillness on the Begumpura road again. Just the spluttering of the wood in the fire. Forty Muslims and fifteen Hindus lay dead in the gutters and on the road. Difficult to tell from the back or the blood whether they were Hindus or Muslims. The street, a funeral pyre for all of them burnt with billowing smoke upwards to the sky. The two stray dogs and the pig were still there, somewhat bewildered at the human race.

The Goddesses got their final immersion. In the blood of her own subjects.

The anatomy of a religious riot is simple. It is instigated by the most secular of minds purely for reasons of self-interest.

Usually by politicians, usually for votes. To consolidate the hatred of the masses into solid vote banks. Divide and rule, a continuation of the tradition from the old British Raj that still plagues modern India.

Jhumri Yadav, the Chief-Minister of Bihar, was an artful exponent of such politics. He had won two successive elections in the state under the banner of 'MY' people. Muslims and Yadavs. Together they constituted nearly thirty percent of the State's electorate. Add to it the misuse of the state administrative machinery, vote rigging and his musclemen, it was a winning combination. He had veered out of his way to woo these two sections. Job reservations, promotions and above all security for the minority community. In his ten years of rule there had not been a single caste or religious riot in which these two sections had taken the brunt. Though they might have inflicted misery on other sections of the population.

And now this riot in Sitapur, just a few months before the elections.

He ground the tobacco in his palm with the other thumb and paused to add some lime to the potion. He looked at his bespectacled Chief

Secretary who was looking back at him with a tense but puzzled expression. Only a few minutes ago they had received an agitated call from his party MLA in Sitapur, Munawwar Ali. He had sounded both furious and desperate on the phone.

'Sir, the Muslim community is in absolute fury today,' he had said. 'Women have been raped, men and children slaughtered on the streets. The police were just bystanders and even fired at our men. There is Muslim blood spilled all over Sitapur and the whole community is feeling totally let down.'

Now that the texture was right, Jhumri Yadav pinched the ground tobacco from his palm and placed it carefully between his lower lips and gums. He spoke in a soft muffled tone so as to not dislodge the tobacco.

'What shall we do Mr. Prasad?'

'Sir, we have received urgent communication from the District Magistrate that the situation is highly tense tonight. Retaliatory attacks are a distinct possibility according to Intelligence. We have three battalions of the CRP force awaiting your orders for immediate despatch. They would reach Sitapur in less than four hours. The Police force there is too few and too stretched anyway. The Army is willing to do a flag march tomorrow morning if necessary.'

Jhumri Yadav rotated the glass paperweight on the table thoughtfully. He tried to look into the crystal ball to predict the final outcome. He weighed the pros and cons, conscience and realpolitik and slowly made up his mind.

'Send the CRP battalions tomorrow morning,' he said. 'And contact the TV stations for an evening broadcast by myself.'

'But Sir the troops are ready to go in this evening? Tonight will be the most crucial period.'

'Tomorrow morning Mr. Prasad.' There was a frost of finality in his voice that was not to be questioned again. The Chief Secretary rose to leave the chamber when his master's voice arrested him again. 'Also prepare the transfer orders for the District Magistrate to be posted to the Animal Husbandry department. Its time he fed some chickens.'

From the terrace of their house they had heard and felt the unfolding communal riot in the town centre. They saw the plumes of black smoke rise behind the mosque. Now and then a burst of fireball would leap upwards into the sky to remind that all was not over yet. They heard the shrieks, the cries and the piercing sound of death. They saw no victims or villains but did not need much imagination to conjure up the scenes. And when they did that, it numbed and froze them. Disbelief and truth in total conflict with each other. Long after the noises subsided and the smoke kept rising, no one spoke or moved. Then Harivansh broke the trance and walked away downstairs. Then Radha devi and Bharat.

Puja still was not sure what exactly was happening and why. She turned to Avinash for some more clues. He looked tense and shaken, perspiring in the cool breeze.

'Let us go downstairs,' he simply said.

Downstairs, tea was being served by the servants. Harivansh and Radha devi sat on the sofa with pensive looks. Avinash slipped to the adjacent room to make a telephone call. Puja began pouring the tea.

'The last riot here was during the partition,' Harivansh broke the silence. 'Never since then had we had any trouble here.'

'Do you think people might have got killed today?' Puja asked.

'I pray not, but my mind says otherwise.'

'These Muslims neither live in peace nor will they let anyone else live in peace.'

'Shut up Bharat's mother,' Harivansh interjected. 'The flames are being fanned from both sides. Just look at the hatred in your heart.'

'It is not without reason. I do not eat cows.'

Harivansh raised his hands in despair. Avinash entered the room and sank on the sofa. Raised eyebrows waited for him to speak.

'More than fifty people have been butchered. The whole of Begumpura road is on fire. I have just been speaking to the Police Inspector in charge of Begumpura. The situation is extremely tense.'

Till then the gravity of the situation had escaped Puja. Now it hit her with full impact. She had heard about these things in news and television but this was unfolding right in front of her. She was in Begumpura yesterday. She could feel the spilling blood flowing over her footprints on that dusty track. Even now she stood just half a mile away from the butchered bodies of innocent human beings. She began to shake uncontrollably. Avinash rushed to her side and tried to comfort her.

She sat down on the divan and tried to steady her nerves. She attempted to gulp some tea but the trembling was so bad that she gave up in frustration. Bharat entered the lounge. He had a rifle in his hand. He looked calm and composed.

'I have oiled the rifle.' Everyone looked up at him. 'Just in case.'

Puja's violent trembling began again. 'Are we at any risk?'

There was silence. Everyone sort of knew the answer but was grappling to phrase it rightly. Avinash finally spoke.

'Very unlikely Puja but the risk is not zero. There is no rhyme or reason to such happenings. It can turn ugly in any instant. Besides we do live at the edge of a Muslim locality.'

'Why do not we leave this house immediately then?' asked Puja.

'And leave the property unoccupied? Looters will have a party in this house.'

'No Ma,' Avinash replied. 'We should think about this in all seriousness. Property can be bought again but life cannot. It might just be an idea to move away just for a few days till the situation calms down. Maybe just across the town in the safer sections or even go to Patna to the sisters.'

'Bhaiyya, do you really think that they will dare to attack this house fully knowing the reprisals that will follow ?' Bharat asked.

'A mob has no brains, a fanatic has no brains. If they only had brains do you think a riot would have even happened? Do you understand how low one has to stoop to plunge a dagger into someone you do not even know? So my brother a headless mob can take any direction. And what better revenge and publicity than to attack a respected Hindu household in a Muslim neighbourhood.'

'I agree, we should leave for few days,' said Harivansh.

'We cannot cross the bridge without going through Begumpura road. The only option might be to escape the other way to Patna.' Bharat was right.

'That might not be an option either. There are Muslim and Hindu Villages on both sides of the highway. Any mob can stop us along the entire route and attack us.'

'We are trapped?' Puja was appalled

'No Puja,' replied Avinash, 'I am just thinking of the best option. I think I will give a friend in the police a call and see if he can escort us across the town.'

There was a tense silence in the room as Avinash left. Suddenly Bharat burst out laughing to everyone's annoyance. 'Why is everyone so tense?

No one is going to attack us. We are just taking normal precautions because we have ladies in the house.'

Avinash walked back into the room. 'I phoned DSP Choubey at the police station. He cannot come tonight as he is absolutely stretched with the patrolling and the curfew. But he has promised to pick us up, first thing in the morning. He has also assured me that the situation is totally under control. They have arrested all the known miscreants and there is a heavy police presence everywhere. I know him well. He is a very close friend. If there was any risk tonight he would have come to take us out even without me having to phone him.'

Harivansh rose and dusted his shawl unnecessarily. 'I feel much better now. It was right to be cautious but we might be just over worrying a bit. Let's prepare dinner and wait for the morning.'

The afternoon melted into evening, which dissolved painfully into the night. The moon which was just a curved stripe and the stars were unable to shed any light on the happenings in that small town from their rooftop terrace. There was an eerie silence as indiscernible as the night fog. The curfew was in place and the only creatures on the streets were the police and the stray animals. Anyone else was likely to be shot down by the government forces.

At around 9.00 p.m there was a sharp rap on the door that startled everyone as they sat to have dinner. It was Sufeduddin, their Muslim gardener, alone, with a muffler wrapped around his face. He came inside and touched Harivansh's feet.

'Just came to see that the Masters are all well.'

'How are you Sufeduddin and how are things in the town?' There was a newfound respect in Harivansh's voice that was never there before for his servants.

'It is better that you do not ask Master. What happened this morning is beyond description. Both Allah and Durga must be weeping in the heavens. It seems much quieter now.'

'Do not just stand there and stare at us,' Harivansh chided one of the servants. 'Bring some food for Sufeduddin.' Radha devi blanched but refrained from saying anything.

'No Master, I have had my dinner. I have just come to tell you that the villains would have to tread over the dead bodies of the Muslims of this colony before they could even lay a finger on the boundary of this house. We shall keep an all night vigil. Now please give me permission to leave. I shall see you tomorrow.'

Harivansh did not feel it necessary to tell him that they would be leaving in the morning. 'I have full faith in you Sufeduddin,' he said thrusting a hundred rupee note in his hands. Sufeduddin departed with his head bowed.

The mood lifted slightly after his departure and they retired to their rooms soon after. The servants would keep vigil all night and wake up everyone at the slightest hint of trouble.

At midnight everyone was woken up, not by the servants but a phone call from Ramesh who had just heard the news on the BBC. He had to be reassured by everyone including Harivansh, Avinash and Puja before he put the phone down.

Puja had a bizarre dream. It was so bizarre that she concluded in her sleep that she must be dreaming. She saw that the man who had visited them earlier in the evening was mowing her lawn in England. A large garden but an Indian style house. Flat roof and veranda. But it was definitely England as Ramesh had just left for the Surgery. And there were signs to Oxford just outside her house. Savita was having tea on the patio and at the far end there was a cowshed that housed a white cow with patches of brown on her skin. She could not hear the noise of the lawnmower as she was inside the house and the windows were shut.

Suddenly she saw the big cow break off the chain and run towards the patio. The man saw the cow but continued to mow the grass. Puja was shouting to get his attention but he was not listening. Perhaps because the windows were shut. She started banging on the glass windows.

The man was not turning his back. The enraged cow was yards away from Savita. She banged on the window harder.

Her eyes opened as someone was banging on the door.

Avinash leapt out of the bed and opened the door in a flash. It was Bharat shaking like an autumn leaf.

'Bhaiyya, they are coming towards this house.'

Without uttering a word, Avinash rushed to the bed and dragged Puja out of the bed. She had a fleeting glance out of the window where she saw dawn just melting out of the night but nothing else. Downstairs,

Harivansh and Radha devi were standing in a corner, trembling with their hands folded in a prayer. The servants had fled the house after waking them up. No one had put the lights on. Avinash ran to the front window.

In the few filtering sunrays of the dawn, he could just see a large mob. Dark silhouettes with flaming torches, swords and spears rushing towards the house with cries of 'Allah-o-Akbar'. They were approximately five hundred yards away from the front gate. Eight to ten minutes away. He turned back swiftly.

Bharat had blood in his eyes and the rifle in his hands.

'We have to defend the house,' he said.

'Have you gone mad,' Avinash shrieked. 'How many will you kill before they wipe us all out. Five, ten...fifteen? They are more than a hundred and they want blood.'

'I will end my life before those bastards can even lay their hands on me.' Bharat was now shouting incoherently. Trembling and twitching with anger and fear.

Avinash too was panting for breath. Trying to outrun time, death and this futile rambling from his brother. There was only one way out and that too was not foolproof. He scanned the faces in front of him and saw the shadows of death upon them. That indefinable expression of 'about to die'. He suddenly felt very tired and sick but there was no time for that. He snatched the rifle from Bharat's hands and steadied his voice.

'Bharat listen to me very carefully. In twenty seconds you will leave this house with Ma, Babuji and Puja. You will climb over the rear fence and run as fast as you can to the river bank. There are always empty boats on the bank. Row as swiftly as you can. The mob will be here in roughly four to five minutes and it will take you ten minutes to reach the bank with Ma and Babuji. I shall start firing at them as soon as they reach the gates and try to hold them as long as I can. Once I see that you all are in the boat, I will run for the riverbank myself. The mob at the gates would not know that the family have already fled as long as I am firing at them.'

Harivansh finally spoke, his voice quivering under his rapid breathing. 'Son, hand me the rifle and you all escape. I have lived my life to the full but you all have plenty to live for. Look after your mother.'

'Why don't you come with us Bhaiyya?' Bharat asked.

'Because then they will chase us all and then kill us all. We have to hold them here and not let them know that the rest have escaped. They are all coming from the front.'

'Then I shall stay. You have Bhabhi to take care of but I have no such responsibility.'

Avinash slapped him hard across the face. He was exasperated at losing any more time. 'Do you want us all killed by just continuing this discussion?' He pointed the rifle at his brother and shouted. 'No one is going to die! I will join you on the other side. Now go!' The lie paradoxically raising the pitch.

There was a stunned silence in the hallway. Just the sound of death in the background growing louder. Puja stood still frozen in shock. She had not spoken a single word but had listened to the whole conversation in total disbelief. Bharat stepped forward, touched his brother's feet and turned towards the rest.

'Let us go Ma.'

No one spoke to each other as they moved apart. Avinash touched his parent's feet. Bharat was dragging Puja towards the backdoor. Suddenly Avinash did something he would not have even imagined doing in front of his parents. He ran forwards and hugged Puja. He pulled his head back and looked straight into her eyes. Black pearls, glistening in a thin film of tears. He took her hands in his.

'You were the most beautiful thing to happen to me ever. And I love you beyond human endurance.'

Time stood still. On its toes, heels raised upwards, suspended between those eyes. Even the noise outside died momentarily.

'You will meet me on the other side?' she asked.

'On the other side, my sweetheart,' he nodded gently. 'Heart and soul, I shall never leave your side.' He released her soft tender hands. Bharat resumed dragging her out of the house.

The dark mass of humanity was now just a hundred yards away when it suddenly stopped for a mid-road conference. Even Avinash could make out that heated discussions were taking place but the words were indiscernible. A flicker of hope lighted within as he carefully loaded the rifle. He glanced backwards and saw Bharat lift his mother over the wall. He kept the lights off to keep his pupils dilated. The discussions on the road ended and a small mass detached itself to attack his neighbour, Mr. Patwari.

His mind was split into halves and racing parallel of each other. One half trying to concentrate on the present and the other rewinding his whole life in front of him. Or was it doing both, alternating in a rapid sequence? The childhood, Medical College, fights with Bharat, his marriage.

Puja.

The crowds had reached the gate which was locked by a strong iron chain. Some tried to climb over the walls but there were glass shards embedded on the top. Avinash glanced backwards. They had barely covered fifty yards beyond the fence. Bharat was carrying Ma on his back as they raced against time. Someone was hammering away on the iron chain. He lifted his rifle and fired in the air then ran quickly to the other window and fired straight into the iron gates to give the impression of two armed persons in the house. The crowd hushed and retreated a few steps.

He remembered the first time he had met Puja in the hotel before the marriage. The first touch as they both reached for the door knob. That tiny jolt of an electric current under the whiff of the perfume. The casual unnoticed brush of his fingers against his lips.

A smile spread under his watchful eyes.

The iron chain was finally snapped and the gates flung open. The mob was in full view now. There were shots being fired at the house from the mob. They had indeed come fully prepared. Should he kill someone to instill the fear more securely? To kill someone to gain some time was tempting but not a choice he was willing to take. He looked over his shoulders. His family were just two hundred yards from the bank. He fired twice from the two widows of his living room. The mob cleared from the open gates and huddled behind the walls for cover. He had three bullets left. There was no sound of a police siren.

Strangest of the thoughts come at the strangest of times. No sense of timing or occasion, these thoughts. The first time he had made love to Puja. How hard he was concentrating his medical skills to discover whether his foreigner wife was a virgin or not. Almost twice he had lost his own erection in that quest. Five years of medical training and still he was no wiser at the end.

He laughed softly.

A small section entered the garden and took cover behind a tree under a volley of fire from behind the wall. He took a shot in their direction but they were protected behind the trees. They were closing in, running behind the trees and the dense vegetation. He fired again into the bushes and it stopped their advance. No one moved for a long time as proximity raised the stakes.

'Avi when we are making love, try kissing on the lips instead of the cheeks. See whether you like it more.'

He glanced back again. They had almost reached the river bank. Bharat had run ahead and was untying a boat. They would be safe now.

And one last thing. Very quickly. Lying on the terrace, she in his arms. Under a carpet of stars and a full orange moon. A sprinkle of diamonds on dark velvet. Her lips to his ears. Her whispers flowing like honey into his ears. Those three words he had longed to hear from her. And then the bite on his ear lobe. Okay, Okay it is time now.

The heavens had lifted the shutters to let the golden sunshine pour in. Everything was much clearer now. No cloak of darkness. The mob approached cautiously forward in absence of any fire.

Avinash felt surprisingly calm within. He had known what would befall the moment Bharat had banged on his door. He knelt on his knee and placed the barrel carefully under his chin. The mob was only twenty yards away staring at him from behind the grill windows. He spotted Sufeduddin amongst them. He blanked them all out and brought those luminescent black pearls, floating in the welled up teardrops, before his own eyes. He was so close that he could almost drink from them.

I love you too Puja.........

XX

What is the heaviest weight that can ever come to bear on a man's shoulders?

It is the weight of one's own dead child lying in a coffin. No inner strength can be called upon to bear that burden.

There was him, shrouded in a spotless white sheet from head to toe. A gentle breeze made the cotton sheet flutter to mimic life but when that brought even more tears, it retreated quietly shutting the window in the room behind it. The Brahmin priest leaned forward and gently rolled back the white sheet to reveal the face. There was a collective loud gasp which gave way to muffled sobs as someone hushed them to let the priest carry on. Some who could not bear went out of the room and wept openly in the kitchen.

The priest continued undeterred, laying the wreaths and chanting the mantras.

Puja stood by the pillar in the hall. Her heart relentlessly pounding at her fragile physical self. She searched his face carefully for any left messages. The thick eyebrows placidly apart. The smooth face with no lines. Eyes closed, as about to open. Lips sealed with so many unsaid things. The whole stillness unaware of the storm around him.

The Priest sprinkled the holy water on the body and asked everyone to stand as a mark of respect.

Radha Devi was still unconscious. Or rather under heavy sedation. Every time she had come around, she would stare at everyone carefully and then shriek at the top of her voice before falling unconscious again. The doctors decided to keep her sedated for a few days. Harivansh had transformed into a stone. A moving stone. His face had hardened and the lines did not shift. His lips never moved, his eyes never blinked.

Puja had had some help. Rani had come to her bedroom early in the morning. She had taken her hands into hers and led Puja to the bathroom. She made her sit on the floor and gave her a bath. She also washed her hair and then snipped a few hairs from the bottom with a pair of scissors.

After the shower she helped her put on a white sari. Puja had always struggled with a sari. A plain white sari; no colour or embroidery. Rani had then wiped the vermilion from her forehead. Whatever traces that were left behind despite a shower. She had taken the bangles off Puja's wrists and smashed them against the wall. Then Rani had hugged her and wept on her shoulders.

She was now officially a widow.

Her eyes met Bharat's who was sitting on the floor with the Priest doing the last rites. There was nothing to exchange. She had seen him rage like a lion and sob like a four year old. There was pain and choking in his cry. As if someone was pressing on his windpipe to prevent the cry from escaping.

'*Ram naam satya hai.*'

The cracking voices in chorus. Louder, to drown the emotions.

When they lifted Avinash for his final journey to the funeral pyre, Harivansh buckled and fell on the floor, fainting for a few minutes. Everyone insisted that he should not bear the weight but he did not want to let go his last hope. The body was sacred and carrying it would secure his place in heaven. Where his son was destined to. He got up, wiped his tears and took his place just behind Bharat.

'*Ram naam satya hai.*'

Rani and Laxmi started to wail loudly. For the women it was time for the final farewell. The pallbearers inched forward lead by the Brahmin and the male mourners just behind them.

The rusty iron gates swung open and Avinash went out of her life once and for all.

Ramesh and Savita came the very next day from England. They were to stay for the next two weeks till the *shradh* ceremonies were over. Little was exchanged in form of words but Puja drew immense strength from their presence. Savita would sleep with her and hold her just like when she was a child till she closed her eyes. Avinash never came in her dreams even once. Savita told her that when the soul is happy it takes care not to trouble the loved ones left behind.

Harivansh and Bharat were to go to Patna to immerse the ashes in the river Ganges. They were having breakfast when Puja came downstairs after a bath.

'Babu ji, I wanted to request something from you,' She said to Harivansh.

'Yes *Beti.*'

'Can I keep some of the ash back with me?'

There was a stunned silence for a long time. Everyone stopped eating. Ramesh searched her face. Radha devi stood up from her chair. Savita rushed to her side. Bharat kept his head lowered.

'*Beti* I shall need to speak to the priest. It might be deemed inauspicious to keep the remains back,' said Harivansh.

Radha devi spoke. For the first time since her son's death.

'No one needs to ask the priest. Puja's right to my son is more than that of the God's. He has already taken his life and soul, what more does he need? There is nothing inauspicious in what Puja is asking for even if a Brahmin says otherwise.'

'Thank you Ma.' She turned around and ran upstairs to her bedroom.

She was still sobbing with her face in the pillows when Bharat came in with a brass pot covered by a red cloth. He placed it gently on the dressing table and quietly left the room.

After a brief pause, time resumed its relentless journey at least outwardly. The shradh was over and the guests had left, back to resume their normal lives. It was only there that time hung with its emptiness in suspended animation. The days passed, unregistered, in their lives. They seldom spoke, for grief was infectious and they chose to quarantine it. His absence was omnipresent and no one could avoid bumping into it, day in and day out, but they hid their bruises from one another. Hoping that time eventually would nurse them to health and until then they chose to cover it. Simple gestures like cooking the food or making the bed were the pillars of emotional support that conveyed solidarity in that hour of darkness. Unspoken, they clung to each other searching for that ray of light.

Ramesh and Savita had left for England a week ago. A day before their departure, Ramesh had come upstairs to Puja's room along with Savita. Ramesh took her hand and sat on the edge of the bed. Everyone was searching for words but nothing that could make sense was coming to mind. Finally Ramesh broke the silence.

'We shall be returning tomorrow'.

Puja nodded her head. Ramesh scanned her face carefully for any emotions but did not find any. His life had centred on the happiness of his only child and here he was, writhing in his own impotency.

'Beta, we have had long discussions with Harivansh and your mother-in-law. They are the most decent of human beings. Both of us strongly feel that your life should not stop because of this tragedy. Harivansh himself proposed that you return to England and try to reconstruct your life once again.'

Puja stared hard at the tiled floor. There was this brown mark from the stub of a cigarette. Avinash use to smoke very occasionally and always tried to hide it from her.

Savita was speaking, 'Puja we will have each other there. Now than ever before, we need each other. Life is harsh and unforgiving for a widow in this country.'

She tried to rub the mark off with the ball of her big toe. But some imprints are hard to erase.

'Say something Puja?'

She raised her head, frustrated and angry at that brown stain. There were tears in her eyes and she made no effort to stem them. She hugged her father and sobbed unstoppably.

'Yes Papa! I want to come back. Please take me to England.'

'Yes Beta, and when you come over there we will go on a long vacation to wherever you want. Just the three of us, in peace somewhere.'

'Canada?'

'Canada.'

A faint smile shone in her tears. Enough to elate Ramesh and Savita.

'And I have decided to take early retirement now. You too are going to take a career break. We will stay at home, wake up late and let this old woman feed and fatten us.'

Puja laughed while the tears still streamed through. After a long, long time. She pulled her mother towards her and embraced both of them in a threesome hug.

There was just a week left before her departure. From tomorrow only six days. She felt that she was at the bend in a dark tunnel. From where she could feel the light but could not see it yet. She had begun her packing quietly, strangely sensitive of detection though there was no reason to be.

The news of her departure had spread and the gentries were streaming in to bid her farewell. The top officials, fellow doctors, businessmen. Little had she realised, the respect she had earned in that short duration. Some begged her not to leave, others wished her all the best. With just two days to go she went to the orphanage.

Bharat accompanied her. The children knew in advance that Didi would be coming.

The children were standing at attention in the Assembly area. Feet apart with their hands behind them. It took her a few seconds to realise that they were standing in a formation of 'DIDI'. Rambabu signalled Shruti to move forward and garland the visitor. Puja smiled to suppress her emotions. The children began to sing a farewell song as she stood in the courtyard feigning dust in her eyes. Once they had finished she distributed the sweets amongst the children which she had bought for them. That brought the smiles on their faces and they forgot momentarily that it might be the last chocolate of their childhood.

Despite her efforts she could not talk much. She promised Rambabu that she will be sending money on a regular basis and told the children that she would visit them every year.

As the Ambassador sped away raising a mini dust storm behind it, she did not turn to look back. For she would have seen the children running through the dust behind the car, waving their hands. As fast as they could, as far as they could.

Something unusual happened the next day. There was a knock on her bedroom and when she opened it, she saw Harivansh with Radha devi standing at the door. Never since her marriage, had he ever come upstairs to her bedroom except during the floods. She touched their feet and moved away to let them in. He sat down on the chair but Radha devi kept standing. Then an uncomfortable silence ensued for a few seconds.

'Is the packing nearly done?' he asked.

Puja nodded her head.

'Bharat will go as far as Delhi. He has made all the reservations.'

'Ji.'

There was a long pause again. Puja took her mother-in-law's hand and guided her to the bed. Harivansh kept looking at the rings on his fingers. He did not raise his eyes when he spoke to her again.

'Beti, when you came to this house initially you were Avinash's wife and that's how we related with you. But then some bridges formed directly between you and us. Did not quite realise when the 'in-law' suffix got detached and fell away. It feels like another of my blood is being taken away.'

He paused for he had forgotten to breathe while he was talking. His chest heaved and sagged with the breathing effort. The strain of expressing and hiding his emotions was telling on his face.

'But you have to go and you should go. You are young and your whole life is before you. Never give up in your pursuit of happiness. We have just one request to make Beta. Let us not end this relationship just because Avinash is no more. It will be such a great waste. Just keep in touch wherever you are. That shall be the biggest favour you could do to us.'

Puja looked out of the window at the green fields and the Bagmati river. She was determined not to cry, as she was tired of doing so lately.

'You are not like my parents,' she said, 'You are my parents. Another set of parents. I am so lucky. I have never felt like a daughter-in-law in this house but always like a daughter. Even more precious than Rani and Laxmi. How can I let it go? I am too selfish.'

Harivansh lifted his face up. 'Beti, with those words you have nearly made up for our loss. Our blessings will always be with you.'

Radha devi wiped her eyes and spoke for the first time. 'Beti, there is one other thing that we wanted to say.'

'Yes Ma.'

'Try to find another partner. Life can be lonely without one. I know Avinash would have wanted that and we too want the same. You being happy again will mean so much to us.' She thrust forward a red muslin cloth, which felt heavy with the contents it wrapped within.

'What is this Ma?'

'Some jewellery which I had set aside for our grand-daughter's marriage. Whoever her father is, she will still be my grand-daughter.'

'But Ma?'

'Keep it Beti, one should not turn down an old person's request.'

Harivansh got up from the chair. 'Try to get some sleep Beti. Tomorrow you have to start early for the journey. Do not forget to take the pickles for Ramesh from downstairs.'

Without further ado they walked out of her door. Harivansh paused turned once to see his daughter-in-law standing in his son's room. Long enough to have a picture with a frame. Then slowly together, they made their way downstairs to resume their lives which fate had now changed into a countdown.

Just best wishes for everyone else.

XXI

My dearest Papa,

My hands are trembling as I sit down to write this letter. The ink still lacks the dye of conviction. But the truth lies condensed on my mind, despite my fervent attempts to wipe it away. One can run away from it but then exhaustion sets in and it catches up with you anyway. So there is not much point in running away.

Papa, I am not coming back to England.

You must think that I am crazy and strangely I am with you on that. I laughed at myself today looking into the mirror. It sounds like choosing hell when given the choice. My innate hatred for this place could only be reinforced by the chain of events which has overtaken my life. I still see Avi draped in that white cloth, lying on the floor. The stench of the murder still fills my lungs. The pain still numbs me beyond pain itself.

But Pain germinates emotions and emotions provoke thoughts. New unrealised thoughts, with that brush of introspection, on your own canvas of life. In my undulating, predictable life until now, these forces had never come into play. Never saw beneath the surface of career, fun and Sterling Pounds. Strangely enough, if my tragedy and this country had not opened the gates to this new world, I would have carried on that way till the very end. And what a waste it would have been.

Avi outdid me by a mile and it is hard to forget and forgive him. While I was still grappling with my building blocks he had reached the outermost frontiers of love that a human being is capable of. And when the test came, he did not even flinch for a second. Now when I am in love with him more than ever before, he is nowhere around me. Lost moments come back to haunt me again and again. That morning is still vivid in my memories. His eyes bursting with love for me as he had held my hands. Yet shouting at everyone to clear the place as fast as possible. In that one moment I had seen love in its total entirety. It was a vision of God. How selfless can one be? How high can one rise?

Strangely though his absence has not yet translated into a sense of loss. For I feel him even more intensely around me than ever before. With all my senses and even in those long dreams that remain fresh in my memory each morning. I am sane and I tell you that the glow and the warmth that wraps my heart and body are for real and not an illusion.

Is this some miracle or just love which I had not experienced before?

And here I was packing my suitcases. Running away for the second time.

I am jealous of him. Of everybody around me in this place. Why can't I be like him who gave his life away without second thoughts to save his family and me? Why did he not run away, suffer from the guilt and trauma for a few years and then start all over again. I would have done that. At least he would have lived. Why can't I be like Babuji and Ma who want this widow to go back, be happy and remarry again? Happiness was to be showered upon but at the slightest hint of sorrow, they shield me with all their powers? Or even like that doctor who was just a family friend but stayed all night at the house when I was dying with Typhoid.

It is tempting to accept smallness and take an easy exit.

Avi introduced me to Indian music. He told me that to appreciate the full depth of the lyrics, I had to not only understand the meaning of the words but also the culture that wrapped it. And then it becomes the sap of the Opium. Indian life is similar to Indian music. Crass and ugly to an ignorant eye but give time and patience and it grows around you. I look at the women working in the fields from my window. Walking on the raised mud pathways in their colourful, cheap cotton saris, like a flock of exotic birds laughing their heads off. I feel like running up to them and ask why they were laughing? They don't have a proper house, no stock holdings, no pension plan or social security. But I fear that they will laugh at me. Make no mistake, Indians are perhaps more materialistic than us in the west but somehow the lack of it does not seem to have the expected effect. In this country of abject poverty, corruption, riots and natural disasters why is everyone much happier than the people I lived with in England?

Is it their superficiality or just the reverse? Though I do not understand it but will it affect me in the same way? For Papa, I am desperate for some happiness.

Avi showed me how there is more joy in giving than taking. He died in that pursuit of joy. If you wanted a suit and I a dress, we can both feel happy if we went to the shop and bought it for ourselves. But we can simply double that happiness at no extra cost if I bought you that suit and you bought me that dress.

Simple trickery, isn't it.

I have experienced it first hand here. With my patients and the

Orphanage. With Ma and Babuji. This kind of happiness is different from the one I got on buying my sports car or some designer dress. More level and sustained, rather than the crescendo and the rapid fade away. I cannot forget the expression in the eyes of the children when I visited them for the last time. How do you combine betrayal and 'Thank you' in one? It will take even Satan some effort to walk away from them.

Human beings and animals alike, we all look after our families and us. There is nothing special about that. But it is the ecstasy and power of affecting other people's lives that fills the heart to the brim. I have not done anything more gratifying in my life than to pursue the cause of this Orphanage. I am moulding the life-stories of these innocent young children with my own bare hands. And more importantly, they look up to me to do so. How can I just turn my back and walk away from this eternal source of joy and power being the selfish human being I am. Each smile or laughter can smother your day with pure delight. A hundred of them can leave you delirious.

Being a Doctor here is also different. In England it has degenerated into just another job that needs to be done well. No longer are you revered as the healer. Abuse and complaints are commonplace there but almost unheard of here. There you live under the dread of making that one major mistake that could finish your career. Here it is still a vocation if you choose to make it one and the idealism, which had long died since qualifying, is beginning to sprout again.

England has got embedded in me some of the best memories of my life. Even now when I close my eyes and bring forth the lush green countryside, a painful pleasure sweeps me over. I can often laugh on my own, recalling some of the craziest moments of my life. I feel lucky and privileged to have grown up and been educated there. But there comes a time when one has to move on. I have found my identity and purpose of life. I'd better not let it slip away.

Nevertheless I shall be coming to England at least once a year to meet you all and also perhaps to detoxify myself.

By now you must be gravely concerned about my sanity. I must be sounding like a different person. But when one experiences such extremes of pain and love as I have, it does leave its indelible marks on the soul and mind. But have faith, I am still sane. In this dustbowl of turmoil and grief, my peace and future lies hidden somewhere. I cannot find it yet but I know it is here and not anywhere else. Just have to wait for the fine weather.

Papa, this has not been an easy decision. I have spent the last few nights awake in my bed, trying to pierce the darkness around me. The scales have oscillated constantly between the pros and cons. I desper-

ately hope that I have made the right decision and I need all your support and blessings to see me through. This was a purely selfish decision taken in the best interests of only me. I am too weak for sacrifices. Avi would have liked me to go, you would have liked me to come but look, I have defied my loved ones all over again.

It is a strange twist of irony that you who always ached for this country could never make it back whilst I, who did not even bother to hate this country once, have ended up here. God plays his games in strange ways and constantly reminds us of our smallness.

I must go down now and tell Babuji and Ma of my decision. I have discarded the white Sari and am wearing a coloured one too. It will be interesting to see their reaction.

Give my love to Mummy. I hope she understands. You two mean more to me than anything else in this world. I shall see you when the summer sun breaks over my little England.

Love, hugs and kisses,
Puja

GLOSSARY

Aarti	A traditional way of welcoming an important guest or worshipping the gods with earthen lamps and flowers
Ashram	The residence of holy men
Almirah	A steel wardrobe
Aangan	An open area within the house
Baraat	The congregation from the Groom's side.
Bhang	A paste made from special leaves with hallucinogenic effects
Bhabhi	The wife of a brother
Bhaiyya	Elder brother
Bahu	Daughter-in-law
Bitiya	Daughter
Bhoodan	A gift of land
Beti	Daughter
Beta	Son
Baraatis	Guests from the Groom's side
Chachi	Auntie
Chacha	Uncle
Compounder	Male nurse
Darwaaza	The front of the house usually for the male members of the family
Dhatura	A plant whose seeds have hallucinogenic potential
Dhoti & Kurta	A traditional Indian dress
Dom	A member of the lower caste of Hindus traditionally involved in cremation of Hindus.
Diwan	Finance minister to the king
Dalal	Pimp
Dupatta	A kind of scarf for females to drape over the shoulders
Didi	Elder sister
Dacoits	Robbers
Dholak	Indian percussion instrument
Dussehra	Holy Hindu festival
Gulli-danda	A game mainly played in the villages
Ghunghat	Clothing that serves as a head veil.
Ghazals	Sad romantic songs mainly versed in the Urdu language
Ghat	River bank
Ghee	Butter
Grahas	Different stars in Hindu astrology

Hukka	Traditional Pipe
Haldi	Turmeric
Jija	Sister's husband
Jaimala	the custom of placing garlands on each other in the marriage ceremony
Karma	deeds
Lakhs	A hundred thousand
Mundan	Ceremony of the shaving of the head
Mama	Mother's brother
Mami	Mama's wife
Mausi	Mother's sister
Marwa	A temporary structure made with bamboos and hay where the priest conducts the marriage
MLA	A politician who has been elected as a member of the legislative assembly of the state
Naxalites	A guerrilla group with Maoists affiliations
Namaste	Traditional greeting with folded hands
Panchayat	An elected body of the village
Pranam	A custom of greeting
Pooja	Worship
Rajput	An upper warrior caste of the Hindus
Ragas	Tunes
Sherwani	A traditional male dress
Sasural	Home of the in-laws
Samaaz	Community or society
Shehnai	A type of flute
Sadhus	Holy men
Shradh	Funeral rites
Tantrik	A holy man with magical powers
Tamasha	Scene
Thali	Steel plate
Tilak	A pre-marriage ceremony where the dowry is exchanged along with some religious rites
Tolas	ten grams
Terai	Plains at the foothill of the mountains
Tulsi	A plant whose leaves have herbal properties and religious significance
Yaar	Friend
Zamindar	A rural landlord with considerable agriculture land